BREAKING
THE SURFACE

B.P. Thompson

Published by

MELROSE BOOKS

An Imprint of Melrose Press Limited
St Thomas Place, Ely
Cambridgeshire
CB7 4GG, UK
www.melrosebooks.com

FIRST EDITION

Cover designed by Jeremy Kay

ISBN 978 1 906561 73 4

FSC
Mixed Sources
Product group from well-managed
forests and other controlled sources

Cert no. SGS-COC-2953
www.fsc.org
© 1996 Forest Stewardship Council

Printed and bound in Great Britain by:
CPI Antony Rowe. Chippenham, Wiltshire

PART ONE

Chapter One

A SERIES OF PUDDLES SEPARATED BY MUD did not deserve to be called a towpath but Frank was prepared to forgive this particular stretch of canal; even in December it was a corner of England he loved. He'd been this way many times and was still impressed by its moments of beauty, places where the view was an idyllic landscape; but his thoughts were a long way from sentimental fantasy. Frank wanted his own existence and all human life obliterated from the scene; he pictured a distant past, a time before people. He'd read somewhere that England had once been entirely covered in forest. He pictured rivers winding through the trees and lakes encircled by lush woodland. His mind's ear listened to the ancient birdsong.

Along this canal you could still find landscapes that had no roads, no buildings, no electricity pylons, no mobile phone transmitters, no commercial forests, no beer cans or carrier bags trapped in the hedge. Frank was at one of those places now. He stood still and tried to memorise every detail. The fields and hedges were a temporary sculpture, like the canal itself, no more significant than a bird's nest in a two-hundred-year-old oak tree. His eyes soaked up the winter scene and his soul tingled at the potential of the land to retake its own territory. If mankind vanished overnight this chunk of England would soon return to wilderness. As long as that could happen, it was alive and full of ancient beauty.

He squelched on along the towpath for another half-mile until he came to the tree stump that assisted his climb over the hedge. The bushes gave him a soaking as he scrambled over. He pinpointed two distant beech trees to get a bearing and headed on across the field. He was heading for the old railway. The tracks had been removed decades ago and it was a wild overgrown mess untouched by ramblers' associations. Old railways had old buildings alongside them and he'd seen quite a few rescued for modern use as pubs or garages or dwellings, but this stretch was too remote for any of that. His building was hidden and safe.

He had no idea what it was once used for. It was about the size of a large garden shed but it was brick built with a tiled roof. He'd found plenty of similar ones but if they were easy to get to they were always smashed up and full of junk. When he found this one there was not a single used condom in sight. There were no windows so broken glass was not a problem, and apart from the roof needing a few tiles pushing back into place it was fine. On this visit, he was planning to stay for two or three nights.

Darkness was coming as Frank pushed open the door of his building. He shone his torch left and right; everything was just as he had left it. Not that there was anything in there except a few old lengths of timber, but it was reassuring that no one else seemed to have discovered his little den. He dropped his rucksack on the floor and unzipped the side pocket, where a box of six candles nestled in the waterproof liner. As soon as he had one lit he unfurled his sleeping bag and got into it. He wanted a couple of other things from his rucksack before he put it behind his head for a pillow: a pre-packed ham sandwich he'd stolen that morning, and his radio. He didn't switch the radio on straight away.

After two hours of silence he ate the ham sandwich and turned on the radio. A football match was just about to start: Everton versus Blackburn Rovers. He settled into his sleeping bag a bit more snugly and snuffed out the candle. It was an exciting game and the time passed quickly; Blackburn won three-two. He left the radio on for the post-match discussion but the only bits he found interesting were the Everton fans phoning in with their comments. Not for what they said but for their accent. Ever since the Beatles made the Liverpool accent a shared experience for most of the world, mainly by cracking jokes with their interviewers, Frank associated it with fun and humour and he couldn't listen to a Mersey voice without smiling. He had been to a Beatles concert in 1965; he couldn't believe it was thirty-five years ago.

The news came on at ten o'clock:

> *"John Fitzgerald Kennedy has died peacefully at the age of eighty-three. JFK served two terms as President in the 1960s and is widely regarded as America's greatest ever president. He survived three assassination attempts early in his presidency and went on to broker historic peace agreements in Vietnam and Israel. He passed away during his sleep at the family home in Massachusetts and tributes have been broadcast throughout the day on all the world's media. Special programmes will be broadcast on BBC radio and television tomorrow."*

The second news story was the assassination of an Italian billionaire and his Saudi Arabian wife. Her brother was on the boat with them and also died when it was blown up. Initial assumptions that it was accidental had now been refuted by forensic evidence from the wreckage. Frank had heard of this man before: Marco Columbari? ...Of course, it was big news three years ago when he married the Saudi woman: outrage all round from both families. His older brother was something big in European finance and her father was furious that she might convert to Catholicism. There were several days of sensationalist news stories. Marco was already well known to the Italian public as a wacky eccentric and the British media had an easy time regurgitating a few of his exploits. Frank couldn't remember any of them but he did recall his impression that Columbari was clearly another overgrown child with more money than sense. Their wedding had taken place in Pakistan for reasons no one seemed to understand, with not a single member of either family in attendance.

The rest of the news was a depressing catalogue of pain and chaos and information from it drifted to its natural home in Frank's mental filing cabinet – an overstuffed folder labelled 'People are a Big Worry'.

After the news a science programme began with a discussion between a woman named Hennessy and a man named Testerby. She was a distinguished physicist and he was a respected artist. The theme was creativity in science and after the introductions the presenter set things going by asking Hennessy what prompted her to write her recent book *Imagination and Physics*.

> "I was looking back at some research material from the seventies and something struck me about the tone of it. It was as if we were almost there, a quiet confidence that we had discovered most of the main features of the universe, the structure of matter and so on, and we just needed to press on to the final Theory of Everything… There was a feeling it would inevitably reveal itself. It was such a contrast with the way things are now and it reminded me that science does not actually progress in the way most non-scientists think it does. And a book seemed the best way to explore that idea more deeply."

Testerby leapt in with startling enthusiasm. "I love your book. Your insight into the creative process is remarkable and that link you make between the imagination and aspects of the autistic savant is very daring."

The presenter tried to rein it back a touch. "Resounding praise there, Gail, but can we unpack your theme a little before we get into the detail; are you revealing how creativity has always been involved in everyday science, or making a case that it's been a bit lacking and should be encouraged more in the future?"

"I certainly want to encourage it but really the book tries to focus on key moments when the imagination rescued us. It's hard to be creative in the everyday rigour of painstaking and detailed research. Once you've set off down a route that needs all the loose ends ticked off, that sort of work can take weeks or months before you get a chance to take stock and see where it's pointing you. No, what I really wanted to get across is the story of situations where everyone is stuck and someone's inspired imagination propels the problem into an entirely new area of thought. Einstein is the classic example."

Testerby was in again the moment she stopped speaking. "Oh yes, Einstein; I read a biography many years ago but you have finally made me understand what all the fuss is about. 'Inspired imagination' barely begins to do him justice."

"Indeed," said the presenter, "but….as an artist, John, perhaps you can give us your take on the artistic merit of an elegant equation…where does the creative genius stride boldly into artistic territory? Is there a moment when the artistic soul is enriched by mathematical beauty?"

Testerby gave a cautious chuckle. "Well, it's certainly possible but art is so much the sphere of the personal, isn't it? When I look at a painting it's about a great deal more than elegance and beauty; sometimes those things are not there at all and I am pulled in by the pain and drama; sometimes I can't identify the effect a work is having on me but…well, the soul is touched. What I will say is that for those who understand the mathematical language, I can certainly believe there is poetry woven within it; it can speak of mysterious realms only hinted at by the numbers and symbols."

Frank was tired and feeling the chill on his face. He needed to get his head scarfed up and zipped in. He turned off the radio and wrapped his scarf tightly around his head and face. He topped it off with his woolly hat and wriggled down into the bag, pulling up the zip until his face was almost covered. He was asleep within ten minutes.

CHAPTER TWO

THE HITCH-HIKER SPOKE FIRST. "I'M TRYING to get to the motorway."

"Yeah, no problem," said Kim. "My route crosses over it near junction six."

The hitch-hiker pulled open the rear door and threw in her bag, then got in the front next to Kim. "Thanks." She looked exhausted and very cold.

Kim drove off and turned the stereo up a bit.

After a couple of minutes the hitch-hiker said, "This is that Tara Pentire." She seemed to be asking Kim why she would be listening to it.

"Yeah, I was at school with her…and we were in a band together." Kim hadn't said this to anyone for many years. She was surprised at herself for coming out with it.

The hitch-hiker didn't believe her. "Yeah!"

Fair enough, thought Kim. "D'you not like her stuff then?"

"I wouldn't buy anything by her but there are a couple of good tracks on this CD."

Kim was intrigued that she had heard the whole CD even though she wasn't particularly interested; it had only been out a week for one thing and, for another, the girl only looked about nineteen and could be forgiven for never having heard of Pentire at all. "Is your mum a big fan of hers? Or – "

"God, no! ...No, I listen to all kinds of stuff. I kind of grew up in a narrow musical way...Irish Folk...and I've been checking out all sorts of other stuff lately."

She didn't sound Irish but Kim resisted the urge to blurt that out. "Did you grow up in Ireland?"

"No. All my family are Irish but I was born in Cornwall; they'd only just come over while Mum was pregnant with me."

"You heading down there now?"

"Yep, home for Christmas."

The ice was broken and the chat dried up for a few miles. They came to a standstill in a queue of traffic. The hitch-hiker pulled a banana out of her coat pocket. "D'you mind if I eat this?"

"No, carry on...I don't know what the problem is here. Don't usually get a queue like this."

A new track started on the CD and the hitch-hiker waved her banana at the stereo. "This is the best tune on the CD. She lets it rip a bit."

"Yeah, breaking away from her usual style."

"D'you really know her?"

Kim hadn't seen Tara Pentire for a couple of years but it didn't alter their shared history. "Yeah sure, we really did meet at school." Kim glanced over at the girl's face. She was believing it this time. "And we were in a band together; my band actually, I already had it running when she moved to my school."

"So that was her first ever band; cool. What were you called?"

"Same as I'm still called now...open that glove box and have a look at the CD in there."

The hitch-hiker bit off the last bit of banana and folded the skin neatly on her lap. She took out the CD and read the cover. "You're in the KB Blues Band? I nearly went to see these last year... In Leeds, but there was flooding and we couldn't get there."

Kim remembered that gig. "Shame, you missed a good one there; my guitarist was brilliant that night."

She turned over the CD box and saw the photograph of Kim; she looked at Kim and then the photo again. "Cool! So your band's been going since you were at school. That's fantastic."

"That's one word for it... No, I won't go all cynical on you; I'm still doing it the way I want to after all this time, and blues fans are a loyal lot, so sometimes it's fantastic. But don't be fooled – it's hard work being constantly on the road."

She was still reading the back of the box. "Vocals – Kim Barnes. So that's you?"

"Yep, at your service." Kim immediately thought that sounded a bit naff.

"My name's Teresa."

"Good to meet you...you warm enough now? You looked frozen solid when you got in so I gave the heater a boost."

The car was now like a sauna. "Oh sure, yes, thanks...you can ease it off if you like. Shall I just throw this out the window? We're by a ditch." She held up the banana skin.

"Yeah, it's biodegradable or whatever, isn't it?"

A welcome blast of cold air entered as Teresa threw out the skin. The queue of traffic crawled forward and temporary traffic lights could now be seen in the distance. Tara Pentire's CD came to an end and Teresa found its box but she couldn't find the eject button on Kim's stereo.

Kim ejected it and said, "There's a bunch of CD's in a box behind your seat if you want to find something you like."

"I want yours on...if that's okay? I've never actually heard you. It was a friend who was taking me to Leeds...she's a massive blues fan, but I...well I don't hang around with her that much..."

"Yeah, bung it in; it's our latest one."

After the first two tracks Teresa said, "Your voice is

tremendous. It's not like anyone else's I've ever heard. It's got...I mean...the tone of it and everything is completely individual."

"You remind me of my mum...in a good way...she used to encourage me, saying stuff like that."

The third track was a few bars in. "Oh, I know this song. Didn't Eric Clapton do it years ago?"

"Yes, and a few others. It's an old blues classic from the thirties. Carla does a brilliant gut-wrenching solo in a minute... she's lead guitar."

Teresa listened to the rest of the album with polite attention, or genuine warmth – it was hard for Kim to tell – and when the last track ended she said a solitary "Cool". She ejected it, put it back in its box and held it steadily on her lap, apparently reading all the track titles again.

"Keep it if you want," said Kim.

"Brilliant! Will you sign it?"

"Course... I don't get asked that very often...finding a pen in this car might be a challenge, mind."

"Oh I've got loads in my bag." Teresa undid her seatbelt and twisted onto her knees all in one movement. She tried to rummage in her bag while it was still on the back seat but couldn't quite reach and the headrest was in the way. Back in a seated position, the bag and several items from inside it were soon piled on her lap. "Got one."

Kim noticed a large red book on Teresa's knees with an incomprehensible title in small white lettering. "That looks heavy going... university textbook, is it?"

"Yep. Bit of homework over the holiday." She stuffed the book and everything else back into the bag.

"The title of it was over my head; seemed like something scientific? Am I anywhere near?"

"Yeah, sort of... Mathematics."

"Oooh, very heavy going; rather you than me."

"People often say that... I'm still a bit surprised, even

though, well…it's like second nature to me… It's sort of always been there in my mind."

The connections in Kim's mind ran through their sequence in a microsecond. The memory from her schooldays when she first knew Tara was musically gifted. The mixed feelings that she still felt about that. The intuition flashing neon-bright about Teresa. "Second nature…that sounds like you might be gifted…a mathematical prodigy?"

"Wow, how did you pick it up so quick? Anyway, it's just that I get things other people can't…but don't go all mystical about it. It's the way my brain's wired, that's all… How did you know?"

"Sorry, I didn't mean to put you on the spot… It was weird. You suddenly reminded me of Tara when we were at school. She's gifted in a different way."

"Oh, right, it's okay, only some people freak me out when they get to know. You're not going to ask loads of questions about it, are you?"

"No, I wouldn't know where to start. Anyway, we're not far from the motorway island, I think there's a lay-by just up there where we can have our signing ceremony… Maybe you should sign something for me as well," Kim smiled playfully.

Teresa was relaxed again. "I don't think so. Mind you, this is a very strange universe, I might make a small footnote in history if I can figure it out."

CHAPTER THREE

THE CROWD SHUFFLED FORWARD, WAFTING ITS quirky range of smells out into the street. A low-octane cocktail of wet overcoats, leather jackets, nylon umbrellas, cigarettes, perfumes and people smelling like their homes – wherever they lived you knew it had evolved its own aroma from which its occupants could not escape. But there was a whiff of something else in the city air that Greg was trying and failing to identify.

He'd taken shelter from the rain in the doorway of a large department store and, leaning on the marble cornerstone, he casually watched people flowing by. He was less than one step away from the pavement and the crowd bulged out at him, shedding the odd individual who cut past him into the store. Some of them nudged against him and some let their umbrellas skim a bit too near his face. He looked beyond them, at the shop windows full of Christmas paraphernalia; at the one streetlamp that had just come on; at his watch. It was 3.30 p.m. and not dark yet but it wouldn't be long – less than an hour.

A woman was getting closer from his left. She had a red umbrella and perfect make-up, and he had an idea she was someone famous, but he couldn't think where from. She came past and lifted her umbrella so that it would pass safely above his head. Her perfume reminded him of a girlfriend he had when he was fourteen, and his mind went on a ramble of adolescent embarrassment. He couldn't stand that for very long and swiftly escaped back to adult crustiness: surely they weren't still knocking out the same perfume thirty years on?

The wishy-washy jingle of stereo headphones came past his face and distracted him, rescuing him from a painful attempt to drag the name of the perfume from his memory. The headphones were attached to a very wet youth in a tee shirt and jeans. A drop of rain dribbled down the curve of his ear and dripped onto his neck, and he loped off, apparently unmoved by his cold winter soaking.

The rain eventually began to ease off a bit and Greg walked on in no particular direction. He was in the middle of a miracle at the moment: it was only December the 10th and he had done all the Christmas shopping. There was no hurry to get home; he had told his son, Roy, that he would be home well after teatime so there would be no cooked meal tonight. Money had been left on the kitchen table and Roy would soon be arriving home from school to find it, reading the note left to remind him of the arrangement, and relishing his freedom to order any kind of pizza. The other part of the miracle was that he had some money left over.

He strained to remember all the things he would get for himself when he had the time and the money. He knew there was a long list of music; the difficulty was remembering which music he had decided to let himself buy. Their titles had been entrusted to memory weeks or months ago and he couldn't recall any of them; he would have to browse at great length and trust that he would stumble across something eventually.

The same with books; well, almost the same. He had come to an agreement with himself over books. He had conceded that he couldn't possibly read all of the ones he might let himself buy, so the decision to buy a book had slipped into a unique rigmarole. He would browse in the bookshop and always there were too many he thought he wanted – usually about fifteen. Probably about half of them would be too expensive so a shortlist of seven or eight was left. In the past, before he had the rigmarole, these would have tortured him with agonising comparisons until the titles began to lose all meaning. He might have bought one out of sheer frustration which would inevitably turn out to be wrong when he got it home, or he might have bought three or four which turned out to be wrong, or he might have bought none and knew, as soon as he got home, which one would have been right. So now, the system was entirely unconscious. The shortlist would be forced into his unconscious mind and Greg would wait while a form of instinctive reflection took place. He would try not to let any verbalised thoughts run through his mind. He viewed it as the same sort of process that happens when you're asleep: you go to bed with a problem and when you wake up your brain seems to have sifted all the options and sent the best one back up to the top floor; somehow you know it's the right answer without having to go over it all again.

The only hazard with this method was a certain risk of being observed standing in the bookshop in a trance. While the unconscious mind did its work it was hard to carry on browsing as if normal thoughts were grinding away. The practicalities of it insisted that he ceased all activity so his consciousness could receive the decision when it came. Sometimes he would become aware of someone looking at him, but more worrying was the strong likelihood that he didn't become aware of it. People probably noticed it all the time. They probably mentioned it to the sales staff and had lengthy discussions over which emergency service to call.

So, which was it to be? A browse in the bookshop or a browse in the record shop? The record shop was slightly disfavoured because it contained a contribution to the irreversible decline of civilisation, or the IDC as Greg sometimes called it. He only sometimes called it that because occasionally he felt that abbreviations were part of it. The IDC was a phenomenon made up of many parts: to Greg's way of thinking there were huge parts, mighty forces propelling humanity towards dystopian languor; but there were also tiny parts, a thousand nudges and prods keeping up the steady decay. CD boxes were a prod – they were a part of the IDC. How simple and cheap it would have been to house CDs in cardboard sleeves just like the old LPs. They would slip out effortlessly, and slip in again afterwards with never a hint of damage against the soft welcoming card. But no, a designer had observed the light playfully making rainbows on the pale gold surface of an early CD and felt a protective instinct towards this newborn marvel. It was clearly not safe to let this infant snuggle into a cardboard sleeve – we must protect it against every known natural force and encase it in a plastic box. Not only that, we must design the box so it is sometimes really tight and hard to open, and even when the customer has penetrated the sacred interior we must hold the CD in the cunning grip of a central plastic thingy that really does not want to let it go. Then, when the kids don't bother to put it back properly and Dad opens the stiff box the next time, the CD will go flying out of the box, bang against the top of the stereo, bounce down the back, and embed itself in the dust on that bit of carpet where Tiddles did a poo when she was a kitten, and from which you have never quite managed to eradicate the smell.

Even though you didn't open CD boxes in the shop the thought of their silly design still tortured Greg. Sometimes someone would stand next to him, flicking through a rackful at high speed, producing a clacking noise, which forced him to consider sickening violence. He was not a violent person and the thought of attacking CD box flickers filled him with fear of their retaliation, but equally, the indulgence of imagining a scenario where he came out on top was quite satisfying. His memory drifted back to the peaceful days of cardboard LP sleeves silently being flicked on a Saturday afternoon. No matter how fast they were flicked it would have been impossible to make a noise. Their size was also so much more pleasing – they were nearly as wide as the average person's body so someone looking at the rack next door wasn't leaning into your personal space; and you could admire the artwork on an LP sleeve without the aid of an electron microscope. It was a pity the sound quality of the vinyl wasn't as good as the sleeves they came in. The agony and frustration of putting a brand new LP on the turntable and hoping the inevitable scratch would not be during a good bit, but knowing deep within your soul that it would be. If there was only one tiny scratch – one little pop noise – during one good bit, you almost felt you were up on the deal. An LP with only one pop, *and* during a boring bit would be somewhere up there with the Holy Grail. A totally popless LP would have been seized and sent to the Vatican.

Books or music? He looked up at where he was. The bookshop was nearest, so that decided it. He made his way there and prepared his unconscious for action. He emerged from the shop after forty-five minutes, with a book called *The New Media Generation*, about the effects of the last thirty years of television, magazines, and lately computers on the young people who have grown up through it. It was written by an ex-TV newsreader named Fiona Voden, whom he remembered quite well, even though it was fifteen years since she had appeared on TV. The blurb on the inside cover said she had three children now: ten, twelve and fifteen.

Greg was not entirely happy with television and often wondered how it was affecting Roy. At twelve years old his bed time was now fairly late and he often caught some of the more explicit programmes. Sometimes Greg would try a fatherly comment that the drama was a bit overdone and he mustn't take it too seriously, or something equally vague to perhaps get a reaction from Roy revealing what a twelve-year-old boy really thought. Nothing conclusive had resulted from this as yet.

He hadn't made up his mind whether television was part

of the IDC. A lot had to be balanced out: Jeremy Paxman versus Des O'Connor, *NYPD Blue* versus *Baywatch*, *Blue Peter* versus *Grange Hill*, *Last Night at the Proms* versus *Top of the Pops*.

His job connected him to bits of TV he wouldn't normally watch. He was the manager of a TV service depot for a national rental company. The customers rang in their jobs and he made sure there was enough of everything to get the hardware fixed: enough engineers to do the jobs, vehicles to get them there, spare parts to put in, stationery to write about it all. He had started out seven years ago as one of the engineers and, after a management training course, he had been promoted two years ago. He still had to do service visits sometimes, usually in the summer, when he'd already got five off on holiday, two on a training course, one at a funeral, one at the dentist, one off long-term sick with something mysterious nobody liked to mention, and then another two go sick. It was astounding: out of the twenty-seven he had on paper there were probably about ten days a year when all of them were actually at work. While working on a TV set he occasionally watched people on the screen in programmes he would normally avoid. He often found himself in a state of disbelief. The willingness of non-showbiz people to rush into TV studios in order to humiliate themselves was no longer funny.

He went for something to eat in a department store restaurant and had another look at *The New Media Generation*. He knew the IDC would be in there somewhere. Perhaps the IDC was the smell he had been noticing all day; not a smell at all but maybe an intuition masquerading as one. For something to be irreversible was taking pessimism to its upper limit, but a mere decline leaves room for something to rescue the situation. Greg had read a lot of history over the last few years and his feeling was that the opportunity for rescue had come and gone centuries ago.

CHAPTER FOUR

A FTER THREE DAYS IN THE RAILWAY building Frank was getting low on food and his radio batteries were failing. He packed up all his stuff and headed off back towards the canal.

Two hours later he was outside a village shop in steady drizzle, pretending to read the cards and home-made posters in the window. Two customers had come and gone in their cars and he was the only person on foot for as far as he could see both ways. The shop was now empty and he had already seen through the window that only one person was running it at the moment – a different person from the last time he'd visited. He already knew from that previous visit they had no CCTV.

As soon as the next customer's car stopped, he slipped off his rucksack and left it outside. He undid his coat as he entered the door and said good morning to the girl behind the counter. The car customer followed him in and made straight for the newspapers and magazines. Frank headed for the food shelves and paused, working out the position of least visibility from the counter. This fine tuning brought him opposite the fruit selection. The other customer had taken a newspaper to the counter and was nicely shielding him from the girl. He deftly slipped three bananas and an apple into his large inside pocket. The man was asking for cigarettes. A pace to the left enabled Frank to get a packet of biscuits into the large inside pocket on the other side. The man was making conversation about Christmas. Frank sauntered to the far end of the shop hoping for batteries and got lucky again, sliding a four-pack into his coat just as the man was bidding her goodbye with hopes she would have a good new year.

Frank was near the pet food by now and he studied the tins of cat meat intensely. He looked up and turned towards the counter, where the girl was standing expectantly for his custom. "You haven't got any Premier Cuts, have you? It's the only one she'll eat."

"Only what we've got there, I'm afraid. Don't think we ever stock that one."

"Not to worry, I'll try somewhere else." He did up a section of velcro on his coat just in case anything might become visible as he walked past her, and made his way slowly past, trying not to let the biscuit packet make any noises.

A mile outside the village the lane began winding up a hill and Frank needed to eat before trudging any further upwards. The drizzle had stopped so there was no need for shelter. He found a field gate to lean on and broke into the biscuit packet. Looking out over the field he remembered this view and worked out that he'd left the village by this route a few years ago, maybe after the first time he found the old railway building. He looked to his right and saw the hedge curve upwards and to the left, hiding the lane on the other side. He heard squeaking brakes and saw that a van had stopped some distance up the hill. He could see the top of it above the hedge. After a short pause, a black plastic dustbin bag came flying over the hedge and seconds later the van was heading down the hill towards him. It passed behind him and he didn't look at it.

A couple of cars went past the other way and when silence returned Frank could hear noises coming from the black plastic bag. It was too far away to be certain but it seemed to be moving. It wasn't very windy and anyway it was not that sort of movement. He climbed the gate and made his way along the hedge towards it. It soon became obvious there was something inside it trying to get out – some kind of small animal.

He stashed the biscuits back inside his coat and put his thick gloves back on. He was not happy about this: what if it was one of those exotic pets people go in for and then find they can't afford, something that really belongs in a jungle...with big teeth? He gave it a gentle kick and a meeow put his mind at rest. He ripped open the bag and the cat leapt out, using all four legs to propel itself straight upward. A split second after it landed it was off across the field like a furry missile.

Frank concluded, not for the first time, that his decision to detach himself from most of his fellow human beings had been the right one.

CHAPTER FIVE

A s Greg walked towards the front door he saw through the glass panel it was Kim who'd rung the bell. They smiled at each other and Greg opened the door. Kim gave him a kiss on the cheek.

"When did you get back?" asked Greg.

"Wednesday. I did mean to call you but…"

"No problem. Come and sit down. D'you want coffee or a proper drink? I've got vodka."

"Coffee's great, thanks. I have it black now."

"What's in the bag?"

"Prezzies for you and Roy. Merry Christmas." She held out the carrier bag.

"You're a bit organised; there's two weeks to go yet." Greg took the bag and pulled out one of the parcels. He remembered they had arranged for Kim to come for Christmas dinner. "Can you still make it for dinner?"

Kim's face showed a hint of exasperation. "Well, I think so. We've got a booking in Glasgow Christmas Eve and I've told the guys I want to be away straight after we finish. I might have to pull over and have a nap halfway down…could you ring me on the mobile and make sure I don't sleep right through the morning?"

"Yeah, sure. About nine?"

"Perfect. Will Mum be here?"

Greg picked up his present and squeezed it. "No, she's got the return match with Uncle Pete; remember he went to her last year. I'm picking her up from his place on Boxing Day."

"Oh God, yes. She'll meet...Rita...er...?" Kim knew it wasn't Rita. She was rolling her hand in a circle for the right name.

"Ruth," said Greg, walking towards the kitchen.

"Yes! Is he still going out with her? How old is she?"

"Forty-four. They were still together on my birthday. He gave me a ring and couldn't stop talking about her." Greg's birthday was on November the 19th.

Kim took off her coat, and followed Greg into the kitchen. "I think it's brilliant. That's the same age as you, isn't it? And he's got to be over seventy, hasn't he? Will she still be there on Boxing Day?"

"I don't know. Why?"

"I could come with you to pick Mum up and give Ruthy the once-over."

They walked back into the living room with the coffees and Greg shouted up the stairs, "Roy, Auntie Kim's here."

The thud of Roy's feet hitting the bedroom floor was an immediate response and he appeared at the top of the stairs dressed for his visit to the football match. He supported Sandford City and went to every home game. When he got to the bottom of the stairs he spotted the two newly arrived presents.

"Which one's mine?" he asked Kim.

"The biggest one, of course," she smiled.

He picked it up and shook it.

"Who are they playing today?" asked Kim.

"Barnfield Town. Dad, can I have money for a hot dog?"

"It's already on the hall shelf. What time's Adam coming for you?" Roy's friend Adam called for him on match days and they walked to the ground together.

"'Bout one o'clock." He put down the present without

making any guesses. Kim knew he wouldn't get it. She was quite proud of her choice this year and confident Roy would like it.

"That's a bit early, isn't it? Have you eaten anything yet?" It was 12.20 p.m. so there was still time for Roy to get something inside his stomach.

"We want to see the Barnfield players get off the coach. Micky Sloane and Jason Pitfield."

Greg understood. Sloane was an ex-Premiership player who had just transferred to Barnfield: one of those who was always in the news for reasons not usually connected with football. And Pitfield used to play for Sandford when Roy first started going to matches. He was eight when Greg first took him. His mother was alive then.

The train of memories Pitfield's name had set going in Greg's mind led inevitably to Stephanie. She had been to one or two matches with them and a recollection flashed into Greg's head: they were sitting behind the goal during the warm-up, Roy pointing out his favourite players and Stephanie asking what position they played. She'd made that old joke about left back in the dressing room, but it was the first time Roy had ever heard it and he'd laughed as if it was the best joke in the world.

Greg met Stephanie when he was twenty-six and she was twenty-three. He'd just started his own electrical retail and repair business. She was a rep for one of the big domestic appliance companies. They were married within a year. Roy was born a year and a half later and family life progressed through the stage Greg always remembered as 'totally knackered'. Some people seemed to enjoy bringing up small babies, and he supposed it made a big difference if your baby was a good sleeper. Roy was not a good sleeper and so Greg and Stephanie had not enjoyed being totally knackered every day. But other than that, they were thankful for the absence of any serious illnesses and disasters, and Roy grew up healthy, bright and strong.

Just after Roy's ninth birthday Stephanie felt ready for another baby and much thought was put into the future: planning of careers and finances, comparing schools, a possible move of house, the real life it's so easy to take for granted. Perhaps Arthur Toddingly was taking it for granted when he had his heart attack. Or was he savouring every moment in the awesome awareness that life and death are sometimes separated by a few seconds of random tragedy? Either way, his final thought probably had something to do with the impossibility of driving a vehicle when invisible concrete is crushing your chest. A confused and frightening death, followed by a quick and violent one, when his van smashed into Stephanie.

Roy was shouting from the kitchen, asking if anyone else wanted a sandwich. Very thoughtful, for a twelve-year-old, thought Greg.

CHAPTER SIX

KIM WAS TIRED AND BEDRAGGLED AND happy. The Christmas Eve gig had been one of her best. She hadn't come very far before the motorway became intolerable and a stop was needed. She was in a lay-by on a hillside about a mile from the motorway, somewhere in Cumbria. It was a clear night and she could see the lights from a small village in the middle distance to her right. A firework went up and squirted a sphere of green and red explosions above the community. Must be a good party, she thought, still having fireworks at three in the morning. Another one went up and sprayed silver stars in a ragged formation. There were bangs and blups from others on the ground and then a few more up in the air. Kim felt soothed and comforted. The band had done a few outdoor gigs where fireworks had been part of the final climax and they were no longer just the once-a-year treat she remembered from childhood. Their familiarity was a lift for Kim, somehow connecting her to the excitement she could imagine down in the village.

As the car started to cool down and the firework display concluded, she felt a certain oddness attach itself to the situation. There could not be many other people sitting alone in a car in the middle of nowhere at this time on Christmas Day. A memory of an old boyfriend sprang up...Gary. He had taken her to a firework display. It was a traditional one in the

November of…whatever year it was; it must be at least five years ago…no, more than that. Anyway, it had been one of their best dates. Crowds of good-natured people, hot dog stands, children, sparklers waving, music playing. The fireworks were special that night: there was something different and original in the way they had been done. Gary wanted to know who had designed the display and said he would ask the organisers later. They made love in the car on the way home. She couldn't remember what year it had been and her memory tumbled into one of those doomed cross-referencing sessions, trying to pin down the year in amongst a jumble of images from roughly the same time. She stopped it. Her mind irritated her when it did that. It felt like about seven years ago. That would have to be good enough.

As if to retaliate, her mind shot back at her with an almost vocalised question: What are you doing anyway, alone on Christmas morning, driving hundreds of miles, stopping here, getting cold?

The question wrestled with her feelings: the warm, tired-but-exhilarated feelings from giving a really good performance to a great audience, and then seeing some cute fireworks on the way home. Her feelings resisted and held Kim back from dark places.

Her fingers were in her bag, pulling out a can of Coke. She flipped the ring pull and drank. She turned on the radio, put the can on the dash and wound down the window. She could smell the fireworks. Her mind was almost back on track; just a bit longer. The radio was talking, talking, then music. Rolling Stones: 'Start Me Up'. Good enough, this would work, this would fortify and replenish. She started the engine and finished off the can of Coke.

Back on the motorway, she focused her mind on the band's performance. Carla had pulled off something really special on lead guitar. Her solo in 'Key to the Highway' had surpassed anything she had done before. She had created one of those extended moments, enclosing everyone in a bubble of ecstasy, where even between riffs the brief silences ached and moaned. And in 'Leaving Me', she had taken it down so quiet and gentle you could feel the audience wanting to hold its breath. Towards the end of that solo Kim realised Carla was crying; she panicked for a split-second but then knew it was the music, and when the drums came back in she ran over to kiss her.

Carla was from Chicago and her grandfather still played in a blues club there every week. They had plans to take a break and spend some time with him, maybe even do a couple of numbers if it felt right. It had been a while since Carla had mentioned it but Kim knew she was genuine and they would make it happen. They had only known each other for a year but the relationship felt solid, and the thought of playing a Chicago club with Carla and her grandfather's band began to make today feel a bit more like Christmas again.

An awful pop song from the seventies came on the radio and Kim stabbed at the channel buttons in search of something bearable. She found an old Free track called 'Fire and Water' playing on a local channel and left it on. Her drummer's twin brother was in a band called Water: he was a drummer as well. So was their dad. Their mum was an estate agent, which probably balanced out all that raw thumping rhythm.

Lloyd was her drummer and Ryan was Water's. She had stood spellbound back in the summer when the two had played on stage together at a charity gig. The other instruments had been there at the start but the last hour of the set, a full hour, was Lloyd and Ryan doing a drum duet. Two drum kits in a realm of perfection; two minds and two bodies playing as one.

It seemed so long since the summer.

Kim remembered, jolting herself up to date, that Lloyd, Micky and Jack had had a bust-up about a week ago. It was during a card game and they said it was just something that happened in the game, but Kim sensed there was something else. They refused to admit there was any more to it and it went away. Her mind trawled through yesterday's rehearsal and soundcheck, seeking something she had overlooked at the time, but nothing surfaced – they all worked fine together. Kim felt a glimmer of emotion towards Jack and admitted to herself once again that it was more than just a protective instinct. Musicians could be cruel to sound engineers and Jack had taken his share of flak over problems that were not his fault. Kim knew he was the best they had ever had and insisted he was treated as an equal member of the band. She had been having twinges of deeper emotion towards him all year but was trying to hold it back. Carla had probably noticed something. Jack probably thought she was just a pretty good boss. Lloyd and Micky would not have noticed anything.

Kim decided against parking up for a sleep; she wanted to press on to Greg's cosy Christmassy house. It was about 5.30 a.m. when she let herself in.

Chapter Seven

F RANK RANG MONA'S DOORBELL AND STOOD looking at the festive wreath hanging on the front door. It was a home-made one. There were bits of tin foil sticking out of it and in the centre was a sign Mona had obviously made in her pottery class – a small square of glazed clay with the words 'Merry Christmas' indented into it and painted white.

Mona opened the door and smiled enthusiastically. "Merry Christmas, Frankie. Get inside quick. The back door's open."

They hugged and Frank kissed her on the cheek. The hall was warm and someone on the radio was singing a Christmas carol at the other end of the house somewhere. Frank slipped off his rucksack and Mona dragged it to the space under the stairs. He unloaded his hat, scarf, and two coats, leaving just his boots to deal with. One of Mona's cats was sniffing everything he took off.

"Did you see the comet last week? I nearly missed it but Athene jumped on my lap and woke me up just in time." Mona was a keen follower of cosmic events.

"Missed it, I'm afraid. Heard about it on the radio though."

"Oh it was a beauty. Never mind. You've got Saturn giving you trouble at the moment. We'll sort you out later. Go in and sit down. You ready for a whisky yet?"

It was ten in the morning but it *was* Christmas Day. "Ah, go on then. Lot of cold needs driving out."

Mona went off to the kitchen and Frank smelled a powerful waft of turkey as she went through the door. This would be his first home-cooked Christmas dinner in six years.

Mona and Frank had met in the summer of that year. Mona's town had a very pleasant park not far from her house – a very large park for such a small town – where Frank could spend many hours with space all around. He was sitting on a bench in the sunshine when she came up to him and told him he had Mercury in his eighth house and his moon was on her ascendant, so they could talk if he wanted to. He hadn't got a clue about astrology and didn't feel a particular need to talk to anyone, but Mona had a childlike confidence and a look in her eyes that must have sent the right signals to him. He had looked up at her and in that second or two when we make up our minds about strangers he heard his voice saying "Mercury?" and felt a smile on his face inviting her to explain.

Mona was a few years older than Frank: about sixty-one. She had probably been very attractive when she was young and her face was lively and amiable. Her accent had traces of refinement but she was trying to hide it. He had listened to her patiently as she started by describing the probable features of his birth chart, and his main reaction was the question: How the hell could she know all this? She had known his birthday was in the first two weeks of March without asking him, and when he told her the day and the year she had plunged into copious detail, which Frank did not actually follow. But she was funny and he found her easy to listen to. He liked her enthusiasm and although at first she seemed interested in him only as a cosmic specimen, she did gradually allow the conversation to progress. They sat together on that park bench for more than an hour, and ended up chatting about the town, children, animals, the present state of society, the past state of society; and despite her zest for talking she allowed him plenty of time in return while she sat attentively listening to his ramblings.

Frank had found himself saying things to her about his time in the Navy. He slipped into naval slang a couple of times and she interrupted him and translated, confirming to him that she knew what he meant. He thought she must have connections with navy people but she denied it and he let it go. He came to realise later that Mona knew a hell of a lot about a lot of things.

Of course, for Mona, this immediate communication was a natural consequence of their two astrological personas having the right connections: she liked to listen to him because one of his planets was very cosy with one of her planets. But for Frank, whatever the reason, it was simultaneously weird and special and a little unsettling.

Their first encounter had ended with an invitation to Mona's house. She wanted to do Frank's astrological birth chart properly and she had given him an open invitation to come round whenever he liked, with a strong hint that he would be very welcome that evening. She had noted down his time and place of birth and said she would now do his birth chart anyway, but it was always better to talk it through with the subject.

As soon as they had parted Frank became aware that if he saw Mona again he would inevitably have to answer ordinary conversational questions about his lifestyle. During the whole of their park bench chat he had managed to conceal that he had no home. His appearance did not give him away and was more that of someone on a backpacking trip. He used laundry services if he had stolen a bit of money, or washed his clothes in rivers in the summer; he kept his beard trimmed; he washed himself although this varied according to what was available; and he brushed his teeth.

The absence of a home was bound to come up, and it took him many hours to make a decision. His first impressions of Mona were bedding in and proving a bit confusing. The idiosyncrasies on display while they had talked didn't seem too out of place at the time, but now, as that afternoon slid into evening, the scale of her quirkiness seemed to increase. She had kept on calling him 'Frankie', and her theories about astrology and the energy focused by each planet in its own special way were enchanting to listen to, but more than a little far-fetched. He had to get past her hint of madness and it had taken him a while, but really, Frank had no problem with people being slightly mad. She'd also revealed moments of humanity and Frank could cope with humanity.

He did go round to Mona's that evening, and stayed the night. He spent another day with her in October, and before they parted she had kindly invited him for Christmas dinner, if he was passing.

CHAPTER EIGHT

ROY WAS ECSTATIC OVER KIM'S PRESENT. It turned out that one of Sandford City's ex-players was now in a band, on bass, and back in the autumn Kim had found herself sitting next to him in a dressing room in Belgium. A month later she was in possession of a football autographed by all the current team, which now sat proudly on top of Roy's pile of presents.

Kim and Roy were in the living room, strumming their guitars. Roy had inklings of real talent but at twelve he was not really gripped by the discipline of regular practice. Whenever Kim got the chance she tried to encourage him.

Greg was in the kitchen doing the food. The TV was on in there and a news report was coming through about a fire in a night club in Florida. The BBC reporter was standing in front of a car park with very few cars in it but plenty of body bags. In the background the devastated building was surrounded by emergency vehicles and a dozen TV station trucks with satellite dishes on top. At least two hundred dead. The fire had started at about 1 a.m. and it wasn't clear why so many had become trapped in it. A lot were crushed to death rather than burned, some of their bodies having been pulled out by the fire department before the flames had reached them. There were still over one hundred not accounted for. Greg heard the unspoken footnote telling the viewers they were roasted beyond recognition and buried under rubble.

Greg felt his heart beating and heard a ringing in his head. The bereaved families would be engulfed in shuddering pain and a sudden thought flashed through his mind that perhaps some of the families were atheists or some religion that didn't celebrate Christmas. It really was a pathetic thing to think; as if something like that would make a real difference to unendurable pain. But his mind carried on casting around for some fragment of mitigation that would lessen the magnitude of their torment. Could there be anything that would prevent every future Christmas from falling into a dark aching pit? Twenty years from now the sisters and brothers, and fathers, mothers, sons and daughters of the dead would draw disapproving looks from their friends and workmates: 'What's he so miserable about?', 'I wish she'd sort herself out – it's Christmas, for Christ's sake'. Some friend would even say 'Cheer up, it might never happen', not knowing that it happened again and again every December.

Greg thought about Stephanie. It was the fourth time he had thought about her today. Her car accident had been in summertime, so he hadn't got the festive season anniversary thing adding weight to his pain, but a lot more time still needed to pass.

The news report gave a UK phone number for relatives to ring if they thought any of their family might have been in the fire. Then the programme moved on to a story about genetically-modified potatoes. Despite feeling hurt and upset about Florida and Stephanie he could not stop his mind wondering whether asbestos might have a gene they could put into human skin to stop it burning. He knew perfectly well there was no DNA in asbestos but the ridiculous gabble of consciousness had no respect for science.

The oven went ping, announcing it was hot enough for the turkey, and Greg slid the turkey in, screwing up his eyes against the heat. He reset the timer for a progress check in a couple of hours and set it going, grabbed a chocolate biscuit from the bread bin, and walked into the living room to the sound of Kim belting out 'So Many Roads'. He sat down by the window and munched on the biscuit, concentrating on the flavour of the chocolate and commanding his thoughts to put the pain of Stephanie's death to one side. He listened to Kim sing and let her beautiful voice join forces with the chocolate. She was astonishingly good. He wanted the song to last and last. Every time he heard her the experience gained a subtle newness, as if getting older not only developed the maturity of her singing, but also added something to his maturity of listening.

The verse ended and Kim nodded to Roy. She strummed the twelve-bar sequence while he jammed a string of lead riffs. Outside the window the cat was sitting on a pile of bricks, looking in at them. No doubt his feline ears could hear the music even through the double glazing. His expression said something like 'When you've finished having a typical English Christmas morning, are you going to let me in?'

Greg stood up and headed for the front door. The phone rang just as he was passing it. He picked it up and carried on towards the door. "Hello."

The caller's name didn't mean anything to Greg at first. "Jack Pearson? …oh right, yes, she is here. Hold on."

The cat meowed outside the door and Greg opened it up for him and left it ajar. He walked back in and waved the phone at Kim. "Jack."

Kim looked pleased and began a warm conversation with Jack. When Greg went back to the open door Fatty Tom was still sat outside looking into the hall, as if suspicious of Greg's sudden disappearance.

"Come on, Tom, all the cold's coming in." Tom took one more careful gaze into the hall, then began a steady progress in through the doorway. Under the circumstances he was not prepared to rush into anything. He wobbled on into the living room with Greg patiently following. Kim had put down her guitar and was curled up in a meaningful relationship with the phone, her body communicating that she liked Jack, perhaps more than liked.

Roy had put down his guitar as well. He saw Tom making for the kitchen and stretched out his left leg in front of the cat's face. "Hurdles, Tom."

The cat showed his disdain by sitting and twisting all in one movement, thrusting his back leg behind his head and enthusiastically licking his bottom. Roy laughed and retracted his leg and Tom immediately resumed his stroll towards the kitchen. Roy and Greg watched him disappear through the kitchen door and waited. A mental countdown began in both their heads that in all probability was uncannily synchronised. A couple of moments after zero, perhaps slightly longer than expected, Fatty Tom began a furious yowling. Roy and Greg laughed, their eyes meeting in mutual recognition of an accurate countdown. Greg went in to deal with the hungry cat, who continued to announce he could smell turkey right up until there was a bowl of substitute tuna under his nose.

It was time to start the vegetables so Greg stayed in there and began clearing a space to work. The TV screen had lost its colour. It was an old movie that Greg knew he had seen before but couldn't immediately name. Henry Fonda came on the screen and Greg got it: *The Grapes of Wrath*. The Joad family had all their home loaded up on their truck and were about to leave Oklahoma. A bowl of dust and wind. Bowl seemed a meek word to describe the annihilation of millions of acres of livelihood. Greg could not imagine being wiped out, forced away from home, driving off to total uncertainty with a truckload of family who would need nourishment and support and love just to stay sane. Was there anything to stop that kind of drought happening again? Greg didn't know but as far he could recall the dustbowl of the thirties was the only disaster of its kind in the USA. What did they do when the rains came back? Did they roll into action a massive civil engineering project providing contingency irrigation from miles around? Or did they just dribble back home and struggle on the way they had before? Did they fight the IDC or become part of it?

The sound from the TV suddenly seemed louder but disembodied. Greg realised the one in the living room must have been switched on and the same channel was on. He glanced round the door and Roy and Kim were watching it. Kim devoured anything to do with America and hardship because so much of the music she loved came from that combination, so she was probably keen to persuade Roy to stick with it. Roy would not have chosen it himself. Kim leaned across towards him and said something about California but Greg couldn't quite hear from the kitchen. He went back to the vegetables and began chopping carrots.

Just as the Joads reached California Kim came into the kitchen to get a drink. "He's really into it," she beamed to Greg. " He can't believe a drought could have been that bad and made everyone leave."

"It's a great movie. You ever read the book?"

"No, have you?"

Greg pictured the paperback copy of it he had upstairs in the bookcase. "No, not yet. It's one of those I bought ages ago, probably the last time the movie was on, but never got round to yet. Odd movie for Christmas Day, isn't it? They don't usually bother with the black-and-white stuff unless it's a Wednesday afternoon in February."

Kim explained, "It's the anniversary of somebody connected with it. They're having a 'season'. You having some of this posh red wine?"

"Yeah, thanks. I can probably leave this lot for a while now. I'll come in and sit down. Does Roy want anything?"

"No, he keeps grabbing chocolates off the tree."

Greg felt Stephanie's presence in his mind again. She always loved the Christmas tree to be adorned with plenty of chocolate decorations and it was the one thing Greg had forgotten the first Christmas without her. Roy had noticed and...well, that Christmas was a non-starter all round really.

Kim finished pouring the drinks and took them in, Greg followed and all three members of the Barnes family watched the rest of Steinbeck's story unfold. Greg hadn't grown the family's food or built their house, and they were not descended from oppressed American farmers, but as the movie ended he raised his glass to his lips, said to himself "Here's to you, Tom Joad" and took a sip of wine.

CHAPTER NINE

ONA'S HOME-MADE WINE WAS POWERFUL STUFF. They had only started the bottle half an hour ago, 6 p.m., but already Frank was pleasantly aware that it was topping up the effects of the beer and liqueurs they had imbibed over dinner, and he knew Mona had told him what it was made from but he couldn't remember. She was on the floor in front of the video recorder sorting out a tape she wanted to play him. While she was clattering her video cassettes he looked around at the room. He had been in it before on his other two visits but not really paid much attention to it. It was a much more lived-in room than the dining room where they had enjoyed dinner. There were piles of magazines on the floor and a bag full of knitting on the coffee table. And the bookcase immediately on his right was stuffed with all sorts of bits and bobs in between the books. There were rolled up tapestries he suspected were half finished, envelopes of every size and colour, a wooden geometrical puzzle, pots full of pens, ornamental cats made of porcelain or wood or stuffed fabric, and several other items he could not identify. When he looked at the book titles he was quite surprised. There were a lot of science books with very specialist titles – the sort you would find in a university. One of them was called *Dark Energy: Topological Modelling Principles*. Another was called *Multiple Phase Singularity Conjecture*, and another: *Quantum Multiverse Probability Transition*. Frank discovered that at least two of the shelves were entirely full of this sort of stuff before Mona interrupted his research.

"Here we go, Frankie, this is the one." The picture from the videotape sprang onto the TV screen and she began fast-forwarding it, muttering that she knew it was on there somewhere.

'It' was a concert from the Albert Hall featuring Chopin's Piano Concerto No 2, played by a young Polish woman. Mona found it and stabbed the 'play' button just as the prodigy walked on stage. She wore a long purple sleeveless dress and looked like a Hollywood star, except for her hands; as the camera focused on her head and shoulders she held her hands together just below her chin, as if she were praying, and Frank noticed her fingernails were short, unpainted and dull. Her hands and wrists were totally uncluttered: no rings, no bracelets, no watch, nothing. Perhaps it didn't mean much, perhaps it was just a comfort thing. Those fingers needed to travel light to reach the peak of their skill.

The unseen BBC presenter was giving a short history of her life as she walked on and readied herself at the piano. She was now nineteen; breathtaking repertoire by the age of six; giving concerts since nine; studied in Moscow, Paris, Chicago, London; professional at seventeen; unusually large hands from an early age but now elegantly proportionate to her five-feet-eleven stature. As he spoke of her hands the camera close-upped on them. They were flat on her thighs while the orchestra played the opening bars of the first movement. The shot zoomed slowly outward and Frank was moved by the beauty of her arms – her right arm to be exact, as the shot was in profile.

Frank waited for information from Mona. There was an astrological reason why she was so interested in this young woman and Frank expected a few snippets to be going on with. But as soon as the piece started Mona was resolutely silent. Frank had probably heard the piece before but he was far from familiar with it; he listened and sipped more wine, and his mind opened up to the bewitching realm of Chopin and Izabela Turowicz.

During the second movement Mona took a handkerchief from her handbag and dabbed her eyes, but that was the full extent of her activity throughout the whole piece. Frank took only half a glass of wine, and even the cats remained sound asleep.

On the final moment of music the audience exploded with joy. They knew she was a prodigy, they were captivated by her beauty, and yes, it was a sublime piece of music. But anyone with only half their senses could see that something extraordinary had been unleashed in the Albert Hall that night. The camera roamed among the audience as they clapped and clapped and Frank was astonished at how many people were crying. The BBC commentator was desperately trying to find new ways of saying that Turowicz could play Chopin with entrancing and mystical sensitivity.

As the standing ovation entered its tenth minute Mona lowered the volume a touch and leaned forward slightly. "That was the fifth of May this year. She began Chopin's concerto at 8.45 p.m. At seven minutes past nine Neptune and Venus were precisely in conjunction in the eighth degree of Libra, in her fourth house. On her birth chart she has Neptune, Venus, and Saturn in her fourth house. Guess which famous composer had a Saturn–Neptune conjunction on his fourth house cusp, in square to the sun and Venus?"

'George Gershwin,' said Frank mischievously.

Mona laughed loud and rampant. 'You're an old fart, Frankie, a pissed old fart.'

CHAPTER TEN

THURSDAY, DECEMBER THE 29TH HAD THAT slow-motion feel to it that sets in between Boxing Day and New Year's Eve. Greg was alone in the house for the first time in a week, and one hundred and forty pages into *The New Media Generation*. During the first ninety pages the author gave her views on news management and provided some good first-hand anecdotes about editors making perverse decisions on what was news and what was not news. Her argument was that a lot goes on that would be useful for the public to know if only the information made it into the bulletins or the news pages. She then went on to make a series of points about the use of language in news reporting and Greg found he needed to put the book down and hear a few examples for himself. He turned on the TV news channel and adopted a critical ear.

A mobile phone started ringing upstairs. Kim must have left it behind, was Greg's first thought, but when he got upstairs the ringing was coming from Roy's room. It was the new one Greg had bought him for Christmas. He obviously hadn't got used to carrying it around yet. It was beside his bed and it stopped ringing when Greg's hand was about nine inches from it. He picked it up anyway and it seemed logical to switch it off as Roy was out, but then he remembered Michelle from the admin office at work. Her son had forgotten his phone one day and she turned it off. He went bananas, apparently, when he came back because he couldn't find out who might have called him. If it had been left on there would have been a 'missed calls' list he could check. Roy left it on and put it back by the bed.

There was a piece of paper sticking out from under the pillow on Roy's bed. Greg didn't normally poke around at things in Roy's room, but he had pulled it out and looked at it before thinking about it.

It was a poem, handwritten by Roy. Underlined at the top of the page was the title: 'True Dreams'. Below the title: by Roy Curtis Barnes, and below that, the poem:

> *In my dreams*
> *Women in black play violins*
> *In reality*
> *Women in grey think I'm dead*
> *In my dreams*
> *The ocean is giving and restful*
> *In reality*
> *There are shivering fathoms*
> *In my dreams*
> *My guitar sings to you*
> *In reality*
> *The blues are black and real*
> *In my dreams*
> *My thoughts are new and fresh*
> *In reality*
> *My mind is full of junk*
> *In my dreams*
> *I understand and live your pain*
> *In reality*
> *I look and can't bear to see*
> *In my dreams*
> *Tomorrow will be different*
> *In reality*

Today will never end
In my dreams
I escape
In reality
The tunnel is dark.

After four lines the first bite of a tear was in Greg's eye. As he finished the poem he had to put it down quickly before he cried all over it. He sat on the bed and lined up the questions: Did Roy really write this? Has he written any more? Did it come from the grief of losing his mother? Does he need some help from a doctor, or me, or some kind of counsellor? How can I talk about it to him?

Greg was convinced the feeling of the poem was connected with Stephanie's death, particularly the line about women playing violins. Stephanie's mother played the violin and for a while she was a member of a professional orchestra. Stephanie would take Roy to concerts to see his Gran and, of course, they would always choose seats opposite the violin section. Roy was only five or six at the time but he enjoyed the spectacle of it all. The music itself didn't impress him much. He would get bored and wriggle around, and they did have to leave early once or twice because he disturbed the other concertgoers. But Stephanie saw it as a unique opportunity to expose Roy to high culture and Greg had no doubt she was right to give it a try. He had not gone along himself and Stephanie never appeared to mind, but after she died it was another of those things he felt guilty about. He could have gone, but he really didn't like classical music and he knew at the time that he might have influenced Roy against what his mother was trying to do. If ever he had fallen asleep and snored during a quiet bit Roy would have loved it and Stephanie would have gone ballistic.

The maturity of the poem troubled Greg as he read through it again. It expressed some pretty heavy stuff for a twelve-year-old and seemed to express it very well. Did Roy perhaps have some talent for this kind of thing? He did do well in English at school; perhaps it was a school exercise, perhaps they had been asked to write a poem about something personal. Greg couldn't imagine Roy reading it out in class, or even handing it in to a teacher. No, it just couldn't be a school thing. Most likely, it was a personal expression of something churning around inside Roy, which he had managed to perhaps resolve a little by putting it into words.

The temptation to hunt around for more poems was intense, but Greg resisted and slipped the poem back under Roy's pillow exactly as he had found it. He didn't know how he would bring it up with Roy but he knew he would do. He was sure an opportunity would come – he must make sure he didn't miss it when it did.

Back downstairs, the news reports were rolling along. A group of people calling themselves 'The Real Millennium Association' were planning a special New Year's Eve celebration for the start of 2001. One of them was explaining to an interviewer why 2000 had actually been the final year of the second millennium. The next item was an update on the total amount killed in the Florida nightclub fire. It was now confirmed as five hundred and eighty-one. Seventeen of them were British people taking a Christmas holiday in the USA, and a BBC reporter was interviewing the family of one victim from Yorkshire. Greg picked up the remote and tried another channel – he could not face any more news about that tragedy. It was so unbearably horrific and the news bulletins had of course been filled with it every day. Greg was concerned about the strength of the emotions he experienced as soon as any more mention of it came on yet again. It was kicking him right back to the level of grief he suffered over Stephanie's death, and he could not cope with it. His thumb pressed through the channels while his eyes rejected every image. His brain finally swung the thumb to the 'off' button and his legs took him to the window. Fatty Tom was outside, sitting in the middle of the drive, looking towards the road. There was nothing there, but Tom stared at it as if nothing was something. Perhaps there was something there; perhaps the road and the house opposite and the lime tree a bit to the left were enough for Tom. He was a wise fat cat.

CHAPTER ELEVEN

KIM HAD NOT BEEN BACK TO her flat since December the 23rd. When she pushed open the door there were several Christmas cards on the floor amongst the other letters. She scooped up the pile and picked out the cards as she walked on into the kitchen. She switched on the heating, filled the kettle and switched that on, threw a tea bag into a mug and started to open the cards. The first one was from Josh, the band's ex-lead guitar, now a family man with a respectable routine. He met a girl, they had a baby boy, they got married; and swanning around all over Europe with a blues band did not fit any more. The second one was from her upstairs neighbour, Bella. Kim had sent her one but she had not sent Josh one. One out of two so far.

The kettle boiled and Kim put the cards down. While she was swirling the tea bag around in the mug she thought about the last few days. She had not intended to stay at Greg's until Thursday, but when their mother had asked to stay until the 29th Kim felt the invisible finger of expectation pointing at her. Kim and Greg had fetched her from Uncle Pete's on Boxing Day and, disappointingly for Kim, Ruth was not there, which meant an intense interrogation by Kim all the way back to Greg's. That conversation had continued in the house and Kim now began to realise it was probably the longest chat with her mother she had had since the previous Christmas. It went a little way towards breaking down a small but problematic tension that always seemed to lurk between them, and the few days at Greg's were certainly more pleasant between them than usual. In fact, Kim had had a beautiful time at Greg's and when she took her mother home that morning the tension was still absent.

She decided to take advantage of her good spirits; she abandoned the cards and took her tea into the living room. She sat down at the piano, switched it on, and put her tea down on the floor beside the piano stool. She played a D Minor chord and began a sequence of experimental progressions. It was a good start: the timing and the chord changes felt good. Kim felt good. There was a melody in these chords, a divine melody beyond a subjective barrier: when fully created, it would seem as if its being filled a rightful place. When the barrier yielded it would fold into a cradle for Kim's newborn creation.

The building blocks of new music stacked up with pleasing shapes and sizes but progress was solid rather than lively, safe rather than thrilling. Every attempt at a final construction lacked inspiration. Any third-year music student could have come up with something similar. Kim wanted to astonish herself and feel the goosebumps tense her skin. She ploughed on, avoiding the traps of weirdness and radical combination, courting simplicity with intense passion.

The afternoon light listened and clenched its wintery fists for Kim, but its strength was fading. As it faded, Kim felt the lonely twilight drifting into the room like a ghost, but her concentration would not be disturbed. When the darkness came she pressed on inside its belly and closed her eyes against its empty drama.

Outside, the darkness was pierced by Bella's car pulling onto the drive. Kim felt a glob of frustration and disappointment throb in her stomach. She would have to lower the volume, or play through headphones, and it never quite matched up to the full glory of a roomful of resonating sound. Not that Bella was some kind of tyrant about it – she would probably say nothing – but Kim liked her too much to risk causing annoyance. Anyway, she had been playing for nearly four hours and this enforced pause had allowed fatigue to make itself known. She picked up the cold mug of tea off the floor and drank a couple of sips, immediately wishing she had made coffee. Black coffee tasted pretty good when it was stone cold but tea was nauseating.

Those drops of tea sliding down her throat awakened her hunger. She had eaten nothing for nine hours and stomachs tend to lose their sense of humour when they are ignored for that long. Kim gave in and headed for the kitchen, switching lights on as she went.

The world at the piano was replaced by a different world of light and sandwich making. She noticed the unopened cards near the kettle and found herself thinking that anyone else would have paused and opened them. But she finished making her sandwich and pouring her Coke into a glass, and took her meal right past the crisp envelopes back into the living room. If the phone rang, she would ignore that too. It wasn't that she was so hungry she had to eat before any other activity: it was a state of mind she was in. She had been in it many times before and rejected similar everyday matters until her mental landscape found its horizon again. She didn't understand it. Was it connected to this obsession with melody? If she couldn't compose an inspired melody, did something inside her want to pretend it didn't matter because she didn't belong to this version of reality anyway?

Crazy thoughts that she didn't belong to the world were always a part of it. Where did she belong, in that case? There was never a real answer to that – only a feeling that it was somewhere she hadn't found yet. She liked to think she would have belonged in one of those early blues bands in Memphis in about 1932, but she was a white English woman. She wouldn't have belonged, a black Tennessee woman would have belonged.

The whole idea was illogical as well as impossible.

She had belonged as a little girl. Kim and Greg had had a pleasant childhood and they had slotted into their small-town English culture with all the belonging children could wish for. Nasty things happened of course, but Kim had no memory from her childhood of ever sensing any evil or malice or injustice – nothing that would put up a barrier or distance her from things she loved. Perhaps if something really traumatic had befallen her she would have been attacked by emotions that were too harsh for a little girl, but nothing did. Perhaps the older version of herself was so long removed that she was simply a different person from her childhood version. People tended to quote that old 'people never change' mantra, meaning you are basically the same as your childhood self but, like all well known phrases and sayings, the grain of truth in it was always an oversimplification. Kim felt very different from her childhood self and knew that somehow her route into adulthood had taken a confusing detour.

Her torment over the creation of a sublime melody did occur to Kim repeatedly as a more than likely contender for the key to it, but then again, perhaps she just needed a proper relationship with a man. One option made her feel that her mind was doing spooky things that she didn't want it to, and the other made her feel ashamed that she might actually need a traditional romance with a man: was she just playing at being a blues singer until Prince Charming came along and swept her into suburban contentment?

CHAPTER TWELVE

On New Year's Day Frank said goodbye to Mona and headed south. It was a cold dry morning and mostly downhill to the town boundary. His clothes held their warmth as he made good progress along the tidy suburban pavements. Some householders were outside on ladders taking down their outdoor Christmas decorations: long strings of fairy lights on green cable and giant plastic snowmen. The Twelve Days of Christmas had been a strict timetable when Frank was small, but now convenience probably dictated matters.

He reached the edge of town and the pavement dissolved into a muddy track along the grass verge, then after a bus stop the track vanished and the grass verge became a ditch. He stepped into the lane and began to enjoy the fact that no more windows looked out at him, fewer and fewer signs of civilisation were in view, solitude became more real with every step. The occasional car passed by but drivers were so cut off inside their tin boxes that their noisy but brief interruptions barely affected him.

Frank reflected on his stay with Mona. She was certainly an odd character but he liked that. There was a lot he hadn't worked out about her but he liked that as well. He distrusted that feeling of 'knowing' someone as if they'd been around all your life and was glad Mona did not inspire it. The astrology was a problem. He didn't believe in it but he was open-minded about how some of it might work. He did believe in intuition, and he was playing with an idea that maybe there could be some way that intuitive people bounce their ideas off the astrological framework and manipulate a few right answers out of it sometimes. It was a wild theory, more of a question really: Could something like that be happening?

A very large lorry was trundling along the narrow lane and Frank decided to head for a nearby farm entrance to get himself off the road. There was a low brick wall curving in on both sides of the farm driveway and one section had its pointed coping stone missing. He sat on the flat bricks and looked across the road at the view beyond a low hedge. It was a pleasing view, nothing spectacular, but reassuringly familiar: a distant farmhouse to the right and further on, straight ahead, another smaller building partly obscured by the curve of a hill; otherwise, uninterrupted fields and trees and hedges. His eye caught sight of a red-and-gold object sticking out of the roadside hedge just to the right of where he'd been scanning the distant horizon…a beer can.

Frank's belief in intuition was no longer under constant review. The verdict was in and the evidence had been archived. He got hunches about things and, so far, they were always right. In his previous life he had made a point of asking friends to report their hunches; they had forecast fragments of this or that which sometimes proved accurate far beyond coincidence. Not very often, he had to admit, and all of it put together still came a very poor second to a couple of dreams experienced by a childhood friend of his. But those dreams were solid gold.

Ben Kirton's dreams were remarkable by any yardstick, and a cornerstone of Frank's conviction. A pair of inexplicable mysteries within his own direct experience: not something he had read about or been told about, but involving his life as much as Ben's.

Frank and Ben met on their first day at Tudor Road Infants School and progressed together through the Infants and

Juniors, then on to Weyford High School, where they were split into different streams for classroom work for the first two years. However, they were still in the football team together. They had never been all that close until the end of those two years. The football coach sensed that they 'clicked' when they played in midfield together (they called it centre half and left half in those days) and a strong partnership on and off the field gradually developed.

One Saturday morning in 1960, when they were fourteen, Ben rang Frank and told him about a dream he'd had the previous night. The first and certainly the most bizarre thing Ben reported was that he knew the exact date the events in the dream were happening: it was two weeks in the future on Saturday, March the 25th. He said that Frank, his big sister, and his parents were on a train and it would not arrive at its destination. He didn't know why it wouldn't get there but things would be all right in the end and a woman in brown and pink would tell them what was happening. It was a long journey. That's all he knew.

Frank had tried to laugh and get Ben to stop kidding, but Ben couldn't hide how frightened he was and kept repeating how different it was from other dreams – nothing like anything anyone had ever had before, he said.

Frank did the obvious things like asking his parents if they were planning a train trip on the 25th and did they know anyone a long way away they might visit. He asked if any aunts or uncles had a birthday coming up, or was the Queen visiting somewhere they might go to. Frank's mother was a loyal follower of all of the Queen's travels and always talking about going to see her.

The answers were all negative except that of course they had one or two relatives who lived a long way off, but nobody they had spoken to since cousin Celia's wedding in 1954. In fact, it was downright certain that they would *not* be going anywhere on the 25th because that was the date of the Law

Society conference. Frank's dad was a solicitor and nothing was going to stop him performing his duties as this year's delegate for the firm. So that was that.

Frank's parents of course prised it out of him why he was asking all these questions and to be fair to them they were quite concerned. They liked Ben and knew he wasn't the sort to make up stupid pranks. But rational thought and the insurmountable edifice of the Law Society conference soon blocked their brief encounter with the supernatural and it was all pushed to the back of Frank's mind; inert but quietly waiting for the 25th.

At 9.30 p.m. on the 24th the phone call came. Great Uncle Simon, in Carlisle, had been arrested. The police advised Frank's dad that he was requested as Simon's legal representative, but no need to travel up until the morning because Simon was too tired and distraught to be interviewed tonight. There had been some kind of incident between Simon and his wife, Hilda, and she was dead.

Well, Simon was Mother's uncle so she was certainly not going to be left behind and if they might be gone for several days they couldn't leave Frank and his sister, Maggie, down here on their own. And so the McCombie family succumbed to the fateful 25th and caught the 6.10 a.m. to Carlisle, changing at Crewe.

Frank was like a firework trapped in a barrel. He didn't sleep after the Friday night phone call and it took him all night to convince himself he wasn't dreaming. The train journey was the most exciting and frightening and powerful experience he had ever had by far, further than far. Every single second of it had been foretold, destined, meant to be. After they had changed at Crewe he began the search for the woman in brown and pink. He announced his need for the toilet and walked towards the front of the train as far as he could get – no brown and pink females that way. He came all the way back and wanted to carry on towards the rear, but knew this would seem odd, so he sat down for a while. He toyed with the idea of coming straight out with it and saying he wanted to look for her. After all, his family knew about the dream and they must have been expecting her just like he was. Maggie was the problem. He knew she would make a big fuss and ridicule him loudly, even though it was obvious the dream was coming true. She was nineteen and her boyfriend had finished with her only last week. She was in a right mood about everything. Frank worked out later in life that this was quite likely the main reason their mother wouldn't leave them at home together. The mood Maggie was in she might well have throttled Frank if he had put a foot wrong. Well, certainly not looked after him properly anyway.

Another thing that probably held him back, although he was not conscious of thinking it at the time, was that he must have been aware of his parents' intense distress over the reason for their journey. Uncle Simon might get charged with murder or manslaughter and even if he didn't, the whole ordeal of Hilda's funeral had to be survived.

After a suitable interval he informed his family of his need for the toilet again and this time went towards the rear of the train. The sun was shining by now but still low in the sky. It was slicing straight through the corridor and into the passenger compartments. Some of the passengers had pulled the blinds down, making it impossible to complete an effective search. Frank trooped on and looked as far as possible but the mystery woman could not be found.

He realised that, in fact, she may not even be on the train yet. They would probably stop two or three times before Carlisle and she could board at any of those stations. When he got back to his seat Maggie and his father, both sitting opposite him and his mother, had fallen asleep. He turned to his mother and asked if they been asleep long; he deliberately pitched his voice so that it might wake them if they were only dozing.

"They both dropped off as soon as you went to the toilet. You were long enough. Is everything all right? You haven't been sick, have you?"

Frank knew he could tell her what he had been doing. "I've been looking for the woman in brown and pink." He glanced opposite: no response. Good: they were both in a deep sleep.

"What? Looking for who?"

"You know. Ben's dream. He said we would get this train. It's the 25th."

His mother didn't respond for a second and he looked at her face. She was pale and unnerved. "I'd forgotten about that, but...well, coincidences do happen, Frank. You mustn't take this too far. I'd be very surprised if this mystery woman turns up."

Frank was not put off at all – he was certain she would appear, and he knew it was more than a coincidence. "What if it's more than a coincidence. Does that mean Ben is some kind of prophet?" He knew prophet wasn't the right word but they'd been talking about the Old Testament at school in Religious Education and his mind went straight to the word because of that.

"No, no, not at all, dear. We don't have prophets these days. People have strange dreams sometimes and then something happens which is like their dream, and well, you know, they read too much into it." The colour had come back to her face now and she was sounding a bit more convincing, but Frank knew people didn't dream an actual date and then the thing actually happened on the actual date. And he knew his mother didn't fully believe what she was saying either.

Somewhere between Preston and Penrith the train suddenly slowed down. It almost stopped but then seemed to maintain a steady crawl. Frank's father said it would pick up again in a minute but it never did. After twenty minutes of crawling they pulled into a tiny village halt called Lower Shapton. The train was much too long for the platform and Frank's carriage was just short of the level crossing, which they were blocking completely. A frantic session of window opening and sticking out of heads began; and a young man in a grey suit from their compartment announced he would go and find out what was happening, and wandered off down the corridor.

Nothing at all happened for at least fifteen minutes – not even one car pulled up at the level crossing and Frank thought it must be a really quiet village in the middle of nowhere. Then a police car appeared at the level crossing gates and the officer got out and went through the pedestrian gate towards the front of the train. After five minutes he came back and drove off.

Another fifteen minutes went by and an empty double-decker bus came almost to the level crossing but turned off into the service road towards the back of the signal box, stopped just inside the junction, and then reversed back up to the level crossing gates. A second bus did the same and parked in front of the first one. In Frank's town, the buses were painted dark blue and cream. These buses were a pleasant mid-brown colour, like a certain brand of very milky milk chocolate.

Another vital part of the dream was becoming real. Ben had said that the train would not arrive at the destination, and now it had stopped and empty buses had come. They were all going to get off and be bused to Carlisle; he knew it. He turned from the window back to his family and couldn't speak for a few seconds, then he made eye contact with his mother.

"The engine must have broken down. Buses have come for us," he said, pointing out of the window.

"Damn and blast it!" blurted his father. "That means we'll be late. I'll have to get a message to the police somehow."

Frank glanced at his father but his wide eyes went back to his mother, straining to impart the meaning of the situation. She had realised, and he knew she had now remembered the dream's details as clearly as he did.

The door of the compartment had been left open since they'd stopped and the female bus conductor eased past people standing in the corridor and swung herself into the open doorway. "I'm afraid the train has broken down and they can't get another engine to you. We have provided buses and if the Carlisle passengers could transfer first, please; and those for Penrith remain in your seats for the moment. Thank you." She smiled and moved on towards the next compartment. Her uniform was brown and she wore a pink blouse underneath it.

Unloading a train and filling up several buses was a messy business. Buses don't really have anywhere to put luggage and Frank ended up with his feet on one suitcase and another suitcase on his lap. His father managed to telephone the police station from the signal box before they left and when the bus crossed the Cumberland border there was a dramatic rendezvous with a police car. Mr McCombie was transferred into it and whisked off, looking very important.

Frank found he couldn't remember much about their stay in Carlisle. He recalled being bored and feeling trapped in the hotel by bad weather. They kept Uncle Simon at the police station for two days while other enquiries went on and the results of the post mortem tests came through. On the third morning Maggie woke Frank up to tell him that Mum and Dad had gone to see Simon, who was back home again. They thought it would be too much for him if all four of them descended on him so soon after all the upset. Maggie and Frank were not allowed to know the details of what had happened until they were on their way home later that day.

Uncle Simon had not been charged with anything and they hoped the inquest would come to an accidental death verdict, but there was still a lot to sort out before then. Everything seemed to show that Aunt Hilda had fallen down the stairs but two aspects of the tragedy gave rise to suspicion and led to Simon's arrest: the strong smell of alcoholic drink from Hilda's body, and the fact that Simon did not call an ambulance. A delay of thirty-five minutes before he called the family doctor was also very unwise of him.

Hilda had been a secret alcoholic, apparently. Simon knew

of course but the couple had managed to keep it from everyone who knew them, and Hilda had not been ill for years so the family doctor never had occasion to discover it. When the doctor came on that Friday evening and found she had allegedly fallen down the stairs a routine issue of the death certificate was out of the question. When he found the body reeking of drink he refused to believe Hilda could have willingly got herself into that state, and dialled 999 immediately.

It wasn't long before the police found the receipts. Hilda would not throw them away in case the dustbin men noticed them, and used to burn them every few weeks. It was a while since the last bonfire and the left-hand drawer of the Welsh dresser in the kitchen was crammed full. She and Simon must have visited every off-licence in Carlisle, and a few in surrounding villages; never the same one twice in a fortnight.

"Why didn't they just throw the receipts away in the street as soon as they got outside?" asked Maggie at this point in the story.

Mrs McCombie understood the old-fashioned ways of Simon and Hilda. "Well, there is hardly ever a litter bin outside these places and it would have been vulgar and common to litter the ground."

Maggie found this hilarious. "They don't mind getting plastered every day but, oh no, one can't possibly disfigure the street with litter."

"Not 'they', only Hilda. Simon hardly touches the stuff," corrected Mr McCombie, and felt the need to add, "Don't ask me to explain it: they were a funny old couple and no mistake."

Hilda's alcohol problem having been established, the police then had to clear up the ambulance issue. This was where Simon came very close to a court appearance. His only explanation was that he knew she was dead so he couldn't see the point – he had seen enough dead people in the war and that was that. After several interviews with no change of story the benefit of the doubt was eventually given to him and the police unhappily released him. The coroner would now consider all the evidence.

Frank was interested to hear all this but he was still in a state of rapture over the fact of Ben's dream coming true. His parents and Maggie were subjected to several further attempts during the journey home to enthuse them with the same amazement, but they seemed determined to write it off as a coincidence: an early lesson in Frank's life that people will see what they want to see, and hear what they want to hear.

The second time one of Ben's dreams came true was many years later, when their lives had taken separate directions. It was not directly connected to Frank as he played no part in the dream and he was not even in England when Ben dreamt it. He didn't find out about it until three months later.

Frank joined the Navy when he was eighteen and naturally saw a lot less of everyone in his home town from then on. Ben was already two years into his electrician's apprenticeship when he was eighteen and playing football for Colverton Town, the local semi-professional team. He took his football very seriously and was one of the four or five in the team who stood a genuine chance of being scouted for a professional team.

It would not have been unusual for the two to have drifted apart completely over the next few years but in fact they kept in touch quite consistently. Whenever Frank came home on leave they would always find time to have a few pints together and Frank would go to the game to see Ben play. Neither were any good at letter writing so in between there was no contact at all, but this didn't matter: they had one of those friendships which just picks up where it left off.

In the spring of 1971, just after his twenty-fifth birthday, Frank came home on a few days leave at Easter and found a letter waiting for him. It had arrived only a few days previously so his parents had not sent it on to the ship. It was from Doctor

Rosemary Moss who, it became clear, was Ben's general practitioner.

She explained that Ben had given permission for her to contact Frank so she was not breaching confidentially. She had seen Ben five times since January and felt Frank could possibly be helpful in connection with a dream Ben had reported to her. She did not describe the dream but cited similarities with a previous one as the main reason for contacting Frank. From what Ben had told her she felt sure Frank would have a clear recollection of this matter even though it was eleven years ago. Ben had told her he was due home on leave at Easter and she wanted Frank to visit her at home; she'd given a suggested time and date if he could possibly manage it at short notice.

His first reaction was the urge to blurt out his surprise to his mother, who was in the kitchen with him when he read the letter. An instinct stifled this reaction and replaced it with a 'steady on, this sounds serious' kind of feeling. He calmly read the letter again and made a mental note that the time and date she wanted were no problem, quietly replaced it back in its envelope, and opened the next one from the small bundle of recent arrivals.

He arrived at the requested time the following week and Dr Moss, late thirties, Scottish, showed him into her living room. She made coffee and began their discussion by getting a bit of background out of the way: she'd known Ben quite well since he was fifteen, not that he was ill a lot but he had developed an allergy that they'd worked on over several months. It took a series of tests to figure out what was causing the reaction and by the conclusion of all that, Ben was one of a small number of patients she knew well. Frank vaguely remembered his friend going through these tests; it turned out to be certain types of cheese he was allergic to.

She didn't see much of him over the next couple of years – just the odd infection and vaccination for foreign travel – but enough to maintain an accurate estimate of his general health and, more important, his solid level headedness.

So when he presented her in January with what amounted to a warning to her about a dream he had had, it was not an option to throw him out as some kind of weirdo. In fact, she had been impressed with the articulate and mature way he had explained it, apologising in advance for what he was about to unload on to her. As with the earlier dream he had given an exact date for the events to happen: three weeks away, on February the 2nd. The details concerned Dr Moss visiting a vet with a sick or injured dog, and then subsequently entering into a long-term relationship with the vet. Ben had then apologised yet again and said that there had been an 'emotional atmosphere' to the dream which was hard to describe but boiled down to a kind of instruction to him to warn her about this relationship. He didn't know why, and he of course had no idea where or who the 'instruction' came from, but the strength of conviction he felt gave him no choice but to tell her everything, particularly in view of the dream he had had in 1960.

He had then told her all about Frank and his family unexpectedly going on a train journey on March the 25th exactly as his dream had predicted, the train not arriving, the woman in brown and pink, and in spite of all that, everyone except Frank trying to fob it off as a coincidence. This was, for Dr Moss, a crucial point in the interview with Ben. The possibility that another person could verify the authenticity of an earlier example added weight to Ben's ominous tones.

"But then he told me you were in the Navy and it might be hard to contact you before February the 2nd, which turned out to be true, so all I could do really was wait for it to come along."

"Have you got a dog?"

"No, no pets at all. It's impossible in my profession if you're a single person. I easily spend more time out of the house than in it."

"I get the feeling something did happen though, on

February the 2nd?"

"Indeed. I hit a dog with my car. It just came out of nowhere. I didn't have time to brake or swerve or anything. I didn't kill it but it couldn't move so I waited and looked for its owner to appear, but no one did. It had no collar on and, well, I ended up asking passers-by where the nearest vet was; it was mid-afternoon so there was a chance one might be open. As soon as I said the word vet to the first man who came past I remembered the date and the dream and everything. I must have turned white as snow. He didn't know any vets and he scuttled off a bit sharpish but there was a bit of a crowd gathering by then and somebody else gave me directions."

"Can I ask you something?"

"Certainly, Mr McCombie."

"Were you tempted, at that moment, having realised about the dream, to just avoid going to the vet at all costs? You know, to stop the dream coming true?"

"I never really, not seriously, at that moment, believed that I could be fulfilling some kind of fated moment. My scientific training took over really. I just had an injury to deal with and a vet was on the agenda one way or another. There was no practical alternative."

Frank nodded. "While I was in Carlisle, and after we got back, I spent a lot of time wondering if anything could have stopped the details of the dream becoming real, you know. Maybe if, before we set off, I'd have persuaded the train driver to check everything over he might have found the fault that caused it to break down. Except that he would never have listened to a teenage boy trying to tell him his job. But, theoretically, could a change have been made, was the future absolutely fixed or, now that we knew it, could fate or whatever allow us to change it? D'you know what I mean?"

Dr Moss looked at him as if reaching a conclusion about something. "Ben said that you had been strongly affected by his dream coming true, well, if I recall, 'completely freaked out by it' were his words. That's true, isn't it?"

Frank laughed. "I became like a mad scientist. I wanted to know everything about predicting the future. I read book after book and wrote notes and asked people questions. I wrote letters to universities. I thought that Ben would do it again quite soon and I wanted to be the one to reveal it to the world. I wanted to know what I was talking about when it happened again and to be able to prove to everyone that Ben was, well, that he'd got a genuine gift."

"He's already told me it never happened again until the dream about me."

"Yeah, it's been a long wait. Well, I gave up waiting ages ago, about two years after the Carlisle thing. I began to feel it had been a freak of nature that would never repeat, and I got older, things moved on, my first steady girlfriend cured me of it all, really. She got sick of me going on about it and I realised how boring it was for other people."

Dr Moss smiled. "I imagine other interests became more exciting…with your young lady?"

"Yes. Vanessa, she changed my priorities, that's for sure." Frank picked up his coffee and took a sip. "But anyway, did you want to know some more details of Ben's dream about me?"

"Yes, if you could go through it in as much detail as possible while I compare the notes I took from Ben's account, is that okay?"

Frank recounted the entire sequence of events and Dr Moss made a few notes in amongst her earlier notes, but she remarked afterwards that there was nothing at all in conflict with Ben's version. She put the notes aside and returned to more recent events.

"I haven't told you about the vet, have I?"

"No, not yet. So you did take the dog to one straight away?"

"Yes. He's called John Russon, and we are still in touch, all as predicted. He couldn't save the dog and the owner never did come forward so that side of it was all very straightforward. He arranged for the disposal and I only spent about half an hour there. Then about ten days later he telephoned me and asked me to go to a dinner party with him. He was very charming and a bit tongue-tied at first, in a boyish, endearing kind of way, but I've got to admit I didn't enjoy that phone call. If Ben hadn't told me about the dream I would have loved it. My last relationship ended last summer so being asked on a date should have been splendid for me, but five seconds into the call Ben's concerned face flashed into my mind and I was just a confused heap."

"But you went on the date?"

"Yes." Dr Moss paused for a fraction of a second to consider the possibility of clearly articulating how complex her feelings had been when she accepted the invitation, but decided it was too intimate to explain to Frank at this stage. "We had a lovely time."

The video recorder under the television set whirred into life and displayed a colourful array of symbols and numbers. The time on it said 20:59.

"I'm taping a documentary," explained Dr Moss. She then continued with the final details about John Russon. "I saw John again a week later and…things have developed quite well. There's nothing about him so far that needed a warning, but obviously now that reality has accurately reflected Ben's dream, I'm being very careful. The problem is there were no time parameters attached to the warning part of the dream. It could be a warning about something that will emerge months or years from now. I'm hoping you can help me a bit with this but what I've got in mind is terribly vague, I'm afraid."

"I can feel all my mad scientist tendencies stirring again."

"Could you meet with Ben and go over the dream in detail with him; try to 'tune in' to each other, if you know what I mean. You might draw out a detail that Ben suppressed or simply forgot. He tells me that you've always had a good rapport with each other mentally, so I think it's well worth a try."

"Yes, we always were on the same wavelength. How about you and the vet ...does he know about the dream?"

"No, no, not at all. I considered telling him for about two seconds but my instincts kicked in strongly against it. I don't know, it just seems like something I need to sort out in my own mind and you are part of that, but not John or anybody else."

"I know what you mean. I always see Ben every leave I get anyway, but I take your point. We need to get in a quiet room together – no interruptions or distractions."

"Thank you, Mr McCombie. I appreciate your concern, and you are clearly interested in this for its own sake, but can I make one more request of you? Please say nothing to anyone else about this. If any members of my profession got to hear that I was researching paranormal phenomena it could be intensely embarrassing for me."

"Of course. No problem."

Frank walked home feeling connected to something meaningful. Ben had now done it twice, giving the exact date both times and giving specific details about what would happen. He felt sure he could coax a bit more out of Ben's unique mind, and if it had happened more than once it was not just an isolated freak any more: it could happen again. There may even be something significant about Ben's ordinary dreams if they could be understood in the right way. Frank resolved to take a fresh look at all of it: not just Ben but anything recently published in specialist publications, and when he went back to his ship there was something he could try. They were sailing to Singapore, which meant several months with the same crew. He would have to be low-key about it but he might be able to persuade a few of his mates to report their dreams on a daily basis. Perhaps Ben was not unique. It just needed somebody to connect it all together.

When Frank met up with Ben to go over the dream it was a

fascinating experience but ultimately disappointing. The only new aspect that came to light was that the voices in the dream did not appear to match the real voices. Dr Moss did not speak in a Scottish accent in the dream, and the vet in the dream spoke in a strange accent that Ben could not identify. Ben had apparently not discerned this detail until the discussion with Frank and was very dismissive of it. He said that the important parts of the dream had an 'immediate' feel about them and this accent thing did not: it was just part of the non-real experience of any dream. When Frank went back to Dr Moss about this she confirmed that John Russon spoke in a mild southern English accent – he was originally from Hampshire. This would have sounded as ordinary to Ben as it did to every other English person so his voice was obviously quite different in the dream.

Frank had telephoned Ben to tell him about John Russon's normal accent and they chewed it over again but Ben insisted he could not link the accent in the dream with anywhere in particular. Not of UK or Irish origin was all he would say if pushed. As for Dr Moss losing her Scottish accent in the dream, Ben said her voice just seemed ordinary, local to their home town.

Apart from his two extraordinary dreams, Ben was a very down to earth man and did not enjoy the involvement in something unnatural. He did not want another prophetic dream and dreaded his life being punctuated with them every few years. The upsetting atmosphere of the second one, compelling him to warn Dr Moss about the relationship, had deeply affected him and it was perhaps a blessing that when this puzzle was eventually solved, nine years later, Ben was not around to hear about it.

Rosemary Moss and John Russon married in 1973 and a year later they emigrated to Kenya. Ben was a professional footballer by then, for a northern Division Two club, and hardly ever came back to his home town. He probably didn't know about the marriage or the emigration. In 1977 his club went on a pre-season tour in Holland to play a couple of friendly matches and their team bus crashed on the first day. Ben and two other players were killed.

Three years later, in August 1980, John Russon was at home with Rosemary and their two small sons, Adam and Michael. In the evening when the boys were asleep he went upstairs and loaded two shotguns. He killed Adam and Michael while they slept. When Rosemary started up the stairs to see what on earth was happening, he shot her dead before she had taken five steps. He killed himself downstairs at his desk. Perhaps he had intended to write a note but no evidence of it was ever found. As far as Frank could ever find out, there was no reason or explanation anyone could satisfactorily offer.

Frank stood up and stretched his arms out sideways. Time to make some progress. He walked across the road to the hedge and pulled out the discarded beer can. He emptied a dribble of liquid from it – dregs of beer mixed with rain water – and put it into his jacket pocket. Thirteen miles down the road he put it into a litter bin outside a shop in a village called Bratton Wergs.

CHAPTER THIRTEEN

G REG HAD TOO MANY JOBS AND not enough engineers
again. He was out on the road covering a few calls he
had chosen for himself in the better parts of town. On
the way to Tromaine Gardens the radio news was beside itself
with excitement over the main story. Evidence had come to
light that British soldiers, probably the SAS, were responsible
for killing the Italian billionaire, Marco Columbari, and his wife
and her brother. Apparently, an international team of marine
scientists were testing a new robotic underwater camera, and it
had captured images of divers attaching the bomb to the hull of
Columbari's luxury motor cruiser. The divers would have had
no idea the camera was watching them as it was at least forty
metres distant, and twenty metres below the surface. It was
being controlled from the scientists' boat moored in a Tunisian
port fifty miles away. The beauty of the robot's design, reported
one of the scientists with innocent enthusiasm, was that it lay
dormant at great distances from its control centre and detected
any unusual marine activity within a hundred-metre radius.
It would then switch on and propel itself towards the activity,
turning on its high-definition camera when visual images
were possible. Military experts had studied the remarkably
clear images and pointed out various technical details about
the divers' equipment. The conclusion drawn was that this was
an SAS team or a team using equipment deliberately designed

to implicate the SAS if detected. A response had been sought from the Defence Minister but he was currently on holiday in Dubai and unavailable.

Greg's call to the brand new Tromaine Gardens estate was to a long-established customer who had moved there two months ago. She showed him into the kitchen, where the portable was on the blink. It was an old one and as soon as he switched it on he could see that the tube was well on the way out; in which case it was more economical to supply a replacement set rather than repair it. He explained that to the customer and went out to the van to get a few brochures on the latest selection of portables. When he came back she had put the kettle on and invited him to sit down in the living room. He found a small boy in there watching the main set. He was about six.

"Hello," said Greg.

The boy looked round and smiled briefly, then turned back to the TV.

"Not at school today, then?" asked Greg, trying to be jolly about it.

"Training day," said the boy, steadily focused on the screen.

Greg was a bit puzzled for a second. "Oh, the teachers, yes, right." He was about to make a joke about staying in bed longer but remembered that six-year-olds get up as soon as they wake up, usually about an hour before the parents.

His mother came in with the coffee and they began going through the range of portables on offer. Most of them now had built-in video recorders and Greg explained that this would be an upgrade so her rental would need to go up a few pounds to cover it, but then again it was useful having a second video in case you wanted to record something while you were watching a tape on the main TV. She started to browse through the brochures and then the phone rang. While she was chatting at the other end of the room Greg looked up from the brochures at the programme the boy was watching.

It was one of those American daytime chat shows with a permanent caption along the bottom of the screen. This one said 'My wife left me for a lesbian'. The host was a tall attractive forty-something woman with a Spanish look about her, apparently named Ursula. Two blonde women about thirty sat on one side of the stage and a row of five men sat on the other. It was man number three's turn to tell his story and the two women were his ex-wife and her lover. One of the women was saying that she wanted her son to come and live with her and her new partner, and she went into detail about the advantages he would have. While she was talking the camera flicked to man number three, who was vigorously shaking his head. Man number two was also in shot and shaking his head in sympathy.

Greg was appalled by the amount of detail being spilled out by the participants and concerned for the customer's son, who sat watching it all with a disturbing level of concentration. What could he possibly be making of it all?

Surely it was common sense that a boy of his age should not be exposed to issues like this? What kind of questions would it raise in his mind?

It turned out that the partner's five-year-old daughter was already living with the couple and, it was casually revealed, she often slept in their bed with them.

Greg found within himself that two things were going on. He had not got a problem with lesbians and when some marriages broke up it was probably going to be hell for the children whatever the reason, and sometimes it would be because mother had met another woman. That was reality. However, the additional issue of all of this being on television at ten o'clock in the morning was making him tense and angry. The need for it to be on television at all was probably also up for debate, and to top it off, the showbiz freak-show way it was being presented was winding him up as well. People in the audience were raising their hands and being invited by Ursula to make a point or ask a question. Somebody asked if the two women had sex while the five-year-old girl was in bed with them. Only if they knew she was asleep, was the answer, which both of them clearly felt to be mature and responsible behaviour. At this point, man number three stood up and announced there was no way his son was ever going to live in that house. The audience applauded. Ursula saw that as a suitable moment to bring man number three's turn to an end and break for some commercials. She put on a tantalising voice and promised that after the break, man number four, Clifford, would reveal how he found his wife naked in their pool with two other naked women, one of them (Ursula could hardly contain herself) his sister!

There was a very strong smell of the IDC about all of this. Why do they make these shows? Would the producer say something like "My show gives ordinary people a chance to tackle important issues in a controlled environment. Nobody is forced to come on the show. In fact there are many *many* more people who want to be on than we can fit in?"

What would Fiona Voden say? An imaginary quote ran through Greg's head: "These shows pander to the lowest tendencies of prurient humanity. If people can see that someone else's life is much more of a mess than their own, it makes them feel they're doing okay. Or if they see someone on TV getting away with doing something awful, and even being allowed to be famous for it, they feel empowered to do the awful thing they want to do."

Greg knew what to say. "I've come to fix the TV in the kitchen but do you mind if I just have a look at this set while your mum's on the phone? I'll need to change the channel."

Greg flicked through the channels and found a wildlife programme about penguins. "Wow, look at them jumping out of the water. Do you know what they're called?"

"No."

"Penguins, they are. They live in a really icy snowy place near the North Pole."

"That's where Santa lives."

"That's right. What did he bring you for Christmas?"

"A bike and a CD and some videos and some games and jarmas…"

He would have listed much more but when he paused Greg said, "What do you like best?"

That was easy. "Fish fingers."

Greg laughed. He knew it would spoil the moment if he tried to explain what he meant and he had no intention of trying to. He just said, "Me too, with chips."

Mum was off the phone. "You'll look like a fish finger if you eat many more of them," then to Greg, "I think we will have one with a video. Which one is the easiest to programme?"

Greg picked up a brochure. "I'd go for this one. The remote control is laid out much better than the others. The programming buttons are in a colour-coded group at the top."

"Pengins, Mummy," said the boy, pointing at the screen.

"That's right, Russell. Aren't they having fun. Yes, that would be fine. When can you bring it?"

"Later today possibly, as you're quite near the depot, but certainly tomorrow."

"Make it this time tomorrow if you can. I'll definitely be in. I might be out this afternoon."

"Okay, no problem."

"Pengins walk funny," chuckled Russell.

CHAPTER FOURTEEN

Kᴵᴹ's ʙᴀɴᴅ ʜᴀᴅ ɴᴏ ᴍᴏʀᴇ ɢɪɢs until February and only a week into the new year this was already the longest chunk of time she had spent at home since last summer. She had the classical channel on the radio and they were playing Haydn's 89th Symphony. Lots of tunes were stolen from classical pieces, sometimes without any cosmetic changes at all. The right lyrics and, bingo, an ancient melody hits the charts. Kim had never seriously looked into it but she guessed that the best classical tunes had probably been used for several different songs. She didn't want to steal one: she wanted to be inspired, she wanted something in her mind to be switched on by a quality piece of music. She liked the Haydn a lot. It didn't trigger anything off but it was oozing with talent and stature. When it finished she wanted more of the same, but it was a commercial station and a torrent of adverts came grating out. She pressed the mute button on the remote. Now might be a good time to get out of bed and have the pee she'd been holding in.

On the toilet she made up her mind to go straight back to the warm bed. But then the heating would still not be on. Switching on the heating meant going into the kitchen and if she went into the kitchen she would want coffee. Now that she had thought of coffee she definitely wanted it. She was not going to stand around naked waiting for the kettle to boil, so that meant going back into the bedroom to get her robe. If she went back into the bedroom she would dive back under the duvet. She looked around the bathroom at the towels. They were all small ones: the bath towels were all in the washing basket in the spare bedroom. She couldn't go in there because the curtains were open and the room was overlooked by neighbours' windows. Perhaps she could put one small towel round her waist and another one over her shoulders; that would take the chill off while the kettle boiled.

Ten minutes later she was back in bed with heating on, coffee at bedside, and she had even picked up the mail from the doormat. Two small towels, a green one and a pink one, were on the floor. She unmuted the radio but it was a soprano being very forceful with something dramatic, so she muted it again straight away. Opera singing had never quite clicked with Kim.

There was a letter from Greg. He was worried about a poem Roy had written. He had wanted to talk to Roy about it but just couldn't find a way of bringing it up. Then he wanted to reread it but couldn't find it and was afraid Roy had thrown it away. Then he felt guilty for searching Roy's room. He had resolved to write to Kim about it but needed to show her the poem. He explained a few more points of concern because he wanted to get them down while they were in his mind, but then repeated he couldn't send the letter until he found it and copied it for her. A gap of three days had elapsed after this paragraph but eventually he'd found the poem and resumed writing. A handwritten copy was with the letter.

Kim read the poem and immediately saw why Greg was in a state. Her first reaction was to connect it to Stephanie's death. She remembered all the well-meaning but trite comments that children are tough and adaptable and Roy would soon get over it. Kim never believed that, but wanted it to be true, and only a few months after the tragedy Roy did begin to show a tenacity about getting on with his life. Greg had many conversations with her during the first couple of years, along the lines that Greg was nowhere near recovered from Stephanie's death, so how could Roy be? But he seemed as if he might be, so Greg needed Kim to say he could be. They were bizarre interchanges of reassurance that skirted round the truth but Kim knew she'd always stopped short of saying that Roy was fully recovered. She also knew that Greg stopped short of convincing himself Roy was recovered. They both knew he wasn't. But they both hoped that one day he would wake up and be more recovered than damaged.

Greg's letter revealed that he seemed to have let himself think that the recovery had finally conquered the damage. Perhaps over the last year this thought had taken root. Their lovely Christmas probably nurtured it a little more, but then he'd discovered the poem.

Greg explained that Roy didn't know he'd found the poem and insignificant as that detail might be compared with the issue of Roy's emotional welfare, it was proving a stubborn obstacle to deal with, for if Greg instigated any discussion of the poem, this would unavoidably reveal that he had looked at personal stuff in Roy's room. That could cause damage before they got anything off the ground. Greg had to be Roy's friend over this and rummaging secretly through the contents of his room was not a good place to start from.

The rest of the letter was Greg being confused about what to think. Kim finished it and put it down. It seemed clear that Greg would have to talk to Roy about Stephanie's death: find some excuse to mention it as delicately as possible, choose his moment, and hope that Roy was open to it. Try to steer the conversation round to methods of dealing with grief, just hope that something would connect with how Roy felt when he wrote the poem, and perhaps he would feel comfortable enough to speak up about it.

Kim's thoughts flowed easily to this solution, but she felt she'd better mull it over a bit before launching it at Greg. There might be other ideas that would come to her if she gave it time.

As she was mentally changing gear back to her own endeavours, a rogue thought flashed from nowhere: she could put a melody to Roy's poem. The recoil from this cognitive intruder was physical; her spine straightened and the fingers of both hands splayed out. She was appalled at herself. She reprimanded herself and tried to kill the thought before it lodged in her memory. Her conscience chased it round her head like a wasp being pursued with a swatter. She screwed up her eyes and shook her head. It was a truly hateful thought and nothing would induce her to accept it. But it wouldn't go away.

Okay, so there it was. It had now existed for several seconds so, short of reversing the flow of time, there was nothing she could do about it. It was another reason to hate herself. Not only was she incapable of writing a decent melody and was seriously considering stealing one from classical music, she was now also deluding herself that the heartfelt grief of her nephew could inexplicably inspire her. Insensitive, disgraceful, and pathetic.

CHAPTER FIFTEEN

ROY WAS WATCHING A TV DOCUMENTARY about the search for planets outside the solar system. He'd never really been interested in space and stars and rockets, and he wasn't quite sure why he was watching it. It was something to do with the way the narrator was explaining it: his voice was exciting and Roy wanted to know what he would say next.

He'd heard of a light-year but it meant nothing to him. It cropped up quite a lot in this programme and he wanted his dad to come in from the kitchen so he could ask him what it was. There it was again: they had discovered a star that wobbled, which meant there was probably a planet going round it, and it was forty-three light-years away. It was a star roughly the same size as our sun. That was familiar, he knew the sun was a star and Earth went round it; he had a vague memory of having a primary school lesson about that.

They had now found eighty-one wobbling stars and were certain that planets must be commonplace, but it was too soon to tell if any were like Earth. At last his dad emerged from the kitchen.

"Dad, what's a light-year?"

Greg had read a bit of science fiction and seen a few space movies. He liked it when Roy asked him questions. He liked to answer as educationally as possible, but Roy would get bored if he went into too much detail. "It's how they measure distances in space."

"Why can't they use miles or kilometres?"

"They could do, but the numbers just get far too big and difficult to work with."

Greg noticed the TV and listened to a few seconds of the commentary. "See, he's talking about twenty-eight light-years, if you tried to say that in miles it would be millions and billions."

Roy was a bit shocked. Not even the moon was millions of miles away, and he had always assumed the sun was closer for some reason. "How big is a light-year then?"

"Well they call it that because it's the distance light travels in a year." Greg knew he had better get to the point quickly on this one. "Light is the fastest moving thing in the universe. It's incredibly fast – a ray of light moves at 186,000 miles a second."

"So when I shine a torch it goes that fast?"

"Yes. Now think how many seconds there are in a year… thousands, and it's gone 186,000 miles for every one of them. I've never worked it out but it's a gigantic distance."

Roy was feeling as if something important had been lying around with everybody stepping over it and now someone had stopped and pointed at it. He couldn't quite believe it, or imagine it, but a new picture was forcing its way into his mind. "So the light from the sun is shining into space that fast and going on for years and years – billions of miles every year?"

"Yes."

"And if a star is forty-three light-years away it would take us forty-three years to get there if we went as fast as light?"

"Yes, that's it. Except we can't go that fast. Only light can."

"How fast does a space rocket go then?"

Greg was getting out of his depth. "We'll have to start looking things up if you're really interested, but it's nowhere near as fast as light. They go about 18,000 miles an hour, I think. It would take us hundreds of years to get to other stars in the spaceships we've got now."

"But in the future they'll go faster? Maybe in twenty years they'll have incredible engines we haven't thought of yet?"

Greg smiled, remembering how long twenty years is to a twelve-year-old. "Maybe, but there's another problem I've never really understood myself. Have you heard of a man called Einstein?"

"No."

"He's dead now but he's still pretty famous. You'll probably hear about him again at school. He was a genius who worked out loads of stuff about light and space and gravity and everything. It's a bit hard to imagine but apparently strange things happen when something goes incredibly fast. He proved that a normal object, like a spaceship, cannot actually go as fast as light, or even nearly as fast as light, no matter how good its engines are."

"How did *he* know, if they've never invented it yet?"

Greg wanted to be encouraging at this point, for he could see Roy was getting frustrated. "That's a good question, Roy. He couldn't really know, could he? Nobody can really know what might be thought of in twenty years."

Roy seemed content with this. He turned to the television again and listened to more commentary about stars and planets. Greg watched it with him.

At the end of the programme Roy said, "I didn't know it was all so big, no one could even live long enough to get to most of it."

Greg saw excitement and awe in Roy's face and began to sense that maybe he should build on it. This was the first time Roy had ever given so much attention to anything not connected with football and he didn't want to waste an opportunity. He mustn't overdo it though: cosmology was not exactly straightforward, and it would be easy to get bogged down in abstractions. "Did it say how big the whole universe is, you know, all of space as far as it goes in every direction?"

"Not really, I was waiting for that but he only talked about our own galaxy. What's a galaxy?"

"It's like a clump of stars – millions of them, mind, not just a few. Most stars are in galaxies rather than drifting about on their own, and there are massive gaps of empty space in between them. Maybe we could find out how big the whole universe is?"

"Is it in one of your books?"

"Well, not that I know of. Might be hidden away in one of them somewhere, but it's a bit late to start searching tonight. We'll have a go at it after tea tomorrow."

Chapter Sixteen

Frank had eaten all the food Mona packed for him and lasted another day on nothing. Now he was hungry and needed to steal food. He was in a small town with a traditional high street and his objective was to find a grocer's with no security camera. Tiny shops just outside the main town centre were the least risk, and food theft was not a massive problem anyway, so shopkeepers were seldom on high alert. It took him an hour to find one but the theft was easy. He got three apples, four bananas, two packets of biscuits and a large bar of chocolate.

He had no criminal record other than a couple of cautions for drunkenness when he'd been on runs ashore in his navy days. That was many years ago so Frank figured he might well get another caution if he slipped up again. He decided to add to his stash a bit more tomorrow. Tomorrow was Saturday and Saturdays were good days for stealing. If he got arrested on a Saturday the police would be annoyed at him for being No Fixed Address. It meant that if they were going to charge him they couldn't give him bail. They would have to keep him in custody until court on Monday morning. All that for a few mouthfuls of food? Not very likely; much more probable he would get a caution. He would risk it and stock up.

He ate as he walked and thought about where to head for. He wanted to be somewhere tomorrow that would have the right type of shops for stealing. He had never been this way before and didn't know the towns very well. He had worked out a rough direction from Mona's road atlas before he left but he wanted to refresh his memory. He was heading out of the town now: the centre was too far to go back and look for a shop that sold maps. He would look out for a petrol station. They usually had maps. A quick glance at one was all he needed. If he stuck to the main road for a while he was bound to come to one. They would probably fill his water bottle as well.

Frank walked for five hours and did not come to a petrol station. The main road became a winding lane and the signposts said the next village was another four miles. It would be dark when he got there so he would rather, if he could, find somewhere to bed down while it was still light. The air and the sky had the feel of snow about them, which added a bit more urgency to his quest. He scanned the fields on either side for some hint of a forgotten hut or ruined cottage. Another half an hour passed by.

He turned a bend and saw up ahead that a railway bridge spanned the lane. Railways had been good to Frank and were always promising for long-forgotten sheds or large chunks of discarded pipe and suchlike: things he could crawl inside or squeeze underneath. He scrambled up the bank to the left of the bridge and looked both ways along the rails. It was a modern electrified line so risk of passing trains was high but he had done it before. He picked a direction and carried on walking, over the bridge and beyond, in roughly the same direction the road had been taking him. The track continued to be elevated for as far as he could see and he felt very exposed up there. He didn't want to spend long beside the electrified rails.

Only ten minutes along the line, the tracks began to whisper and Frank looked for a place to hide from the approaching train. The first flakes of snow were falling and the light was very poor. It would be here any second. He plunged down the embankment through the nettles. He felt one brush above the sock on his left leg and knew he was stung. Half a second later he was face down in them but luckily his hands took most of the stings. The invisible ground beneath the nettles hid a small vertical drop which had thrown him forward. He glanced back at the train as it rattled past. All the lights were on inside it. No one would be able to see him.

Frank pulled himself round to a sitting position and braced himself against the stinging pain. A bad night was ahead. He had more or less conquered self-pity and negative thoughts. He knew why he had chosen his life on the road and he knew what he thought of the alternative. But a small eruption of weakness was inevitable occasionally and he heard the words 'fuck this for a game of soldiers' blurt from an angry part of his mind – a mental stinging nettle trying to provide guerrilla support for its organic comrades.

He stood up and assessed his options. He was not inclined to scramble back up onto the track. Instead he looked in the opposite direction. About a mile away was a small wood, standing out from the open fields in that defiantly quirky style the English landscape sometimes conjures up. It was the only chance of shelter he could get to before dark.

About halfway to the wood it struck Frank that this was a very remote spot. He had not seen any signs of humanity, apart from the railway, since he left the town about six hours ago. He supposed he was on someone's land but it had a neglected appearance and there were none of the usual telltales of activity he tended to encounter. Perhaps it was just the snow, still falling delicately but persistently in flakes that disappeared when they touched something. Snowflakes tended to muffle every trace of human presence so perhaps they were just exaggerating the isolation of this place.

Frank had almost reached the wood when the ground began to shake. He had been about to take out his torch ready for entering the wood, and his first reaction was a gut feeling that he needed light to see what was causing the shaking. It wasn't yet totally dark but it was much more night than day. His head darted around for less than two seconds before he realised that he was not going to see the cause of this. The magnitude of the vibration swelled rapidly and Frank toppled over. His mind flashed back to shore leave in Istanbul in 1968. Luckily he'd not been in a building when that earthquake hit, and the same pang of thankfulness ran through him now.

He grabbed onto the long grass and felt absurd. This was England. The earthquakes here were feeble. It would only last a few seconds. Probably already had the worst of it.

A thudding, roaring rumble seemed to come from his right and explode underneath him. He was thrown off the ground and landed on his back, his rucksack absorbing most of the impact. He was jostled and flipped and saw trees falling on the edge of the wood. Then something hit his head.

He woke up with a bitter coldness gripping his face and hands. He tried to look at his watch but it was now total darkness. He needed light urgently. He needed to put himself in a recognisable place. He moved to grab at his rucksack and a dizzy reaction sloshed through his head. He ignored it and fumbled idiotically for his torch. Eventually it was liberated and switched on. He shone it on his watch and felt immediate relief: he had only been unconscious for half an hour at most so the intense cold should not have penetrated his body to any serious extent. Apart from the fallen trees, his torch beam would not reveal any other features affected by the earthquake. It was a moonless night and the light beam was simply too weak to travel any decent distance.

He stood up and patted his head where the impact had been. The hood of his jacket had fallen back but his tight-fitting woollen hat was still on. His hand was a bit numb but as far as he could tell there was no blood. He didn't want to take the hat off because of heat loss, it was best to preserve every bit of warmth in his body. He flicked the hood back on and tightened up the drawstring around his face. He also took out his gloves, which he wished he'd put on before he fell into the nettles, and tried to convince himself their cold lining was actually soothing to the stings.

Frank congratulated himself on surviving and set off towards the wood, reaching it in less than ten minutes. It stopped snowing during this short walk and the light dusting on the ground was no hindrance. He picked his way over and under and around the fallen trees, pushing them and pulling them to test for safety. Only one failed this test, a small one resting precariously across two others and which slid off as soon as he touched it. He only went in as far he needed, and got on with building a shelter. The fallen trees made this quite easy. He found one that had fallen right down flat on the ground and then just collected enough small leafy branches to make a leaning roof against its trunk. He tried to wedge them against things and interweave them a bit and as long as no strong winds got up the whole structure should last the night. It was the best he could do by torchlight.

Frank's sleeping bag was the most expensive thing he owned. It was a waterproof cocoon; a professional job, designed for arctic explorers and Norwegian soldiers. It had cost him several hundred pounds at the start of his 'freedom' but it was well worth it: it was still in excellent condition. He slid it under the lean-to roof and threw his rucksack in after it.

He decided to keep his boots on tonight and worked them down gently inside the bag. As he zipped up the heavy duty fabric and lay back he tried to remember previous English earthquakes. He could only recall two being reported on the news during his lifetime. This one had been powerful: shaking trees down took a hefty force. He wondered how long it had lasted while he was unconscious. Maybe it had done serious damage or even killed people. He fell asleep concluding that he must have been near the epicentre to have felt it so strongly.

The morning was sunny and crisp. When he emerged from his bag and took a few steps away from the shelter, the devastation was appalling: at least half of the wood was less than upright. He could see out beyond the wood in the direction he had walked and was surprised that he could not see the railway embankment in the distance. The flat fields he had plodded through the previous day now seemed to have a raised plateau stretching as far as he could see to left and right. It wasn't a particularly tall feature – just high enough to block the horizon beyond, where the railway was. He made his way a little nearer to the edge of the wood to get a better look and this confirmed his eyes were not playing tricks. A swathe of land about half a mile wide had become a long low hill.

Frank was intensely curious about the new hill and determined to inspect it. In fact, it was the best direction he could choose in any case. He needed to get water very soon: his last half a pint had served as breakfast and nothing was more important. He knew the road was there beyond the fields and the short stretch of railway, and there had to be a house or a farm or some inhabited building along it somewhere. He had never been refused a refill of water, and quite often had a handful of biscuits thrown in as well. As long as he kept up his 'seasoned old hiker' image, people were fine.

He got packed up and trudged out of the wood. The land began to incline straight away and was very uneven compared with its pre-earthquake uniformity. He headed to the left of the highest point and soon began to warm up. When the railway appeared over the ridge he was thankful it was still there but it seemed further away than he remembered; he must have misjudged the distance in the dismal winter light. As he made his way around the new hill a line of blackness began to appear on the ground running along the slope at right angles to his approach, upwards and down. As he came nearer to it the line thickened up and then revealed its true identity: it was a crack in the hillside.

It was too wide for Frank to jump across, about ten yards at its widest point, and it was too deep to scramble down and up the other side. He could not really see the bottom but the sides appeared to converge about forty feet below. He could see the full extent of it at ground level, and a detour down the hill was probably the quickest way past it. Frank was no geologist, but it seemed remarkable that he was looking at solid rock. The topsoil was a thin veneer and, if the crack was anything to go by, the whole of the new hill might be made of rock.

Making downwards along the edge of the crack gave him a better view inside it and presented him with more to excite his interest. He could see the bottom now and he could see an intriguing blackness just big enough for a man to pass into. The crack had now become more than a passing curiosity – its newly exposed cave was exactly that: new. It meant that, if he chose to, he would be the first person to look inside it, and if there was anything interesting in there his torch beam was going to be the first to find it.

He scrambled down towards it, hoping it wasn't just a glorified hole. He paused at the entrance to take out his torch, and put spare batteries in a convenient pocket. The entrance was tall enough to walk into with only a slight stoop and immediately progressed inwards away from the crack. It appeared to Frank that he was following a flat course and might well emerge again at any moment from the side of the hill. Then a sharp downward right turn began to take him deeper. The cavity opened out briefly and then closed right down to a hole on the floor, but Frank could see there was a larger space below the hole. He dropped through and slid for a few yards. He shone his torch back up to the hole, making sure of his chances of scrambling back up when the time came. It was more spacious now but he still couldn't stand fully upright. He made his way inward and downward for about half an hour along a very twisty stretch and became aware of a trickling noise. Water. He couldn't see yet but now that he was down here he needed to find it. He couldn't afford the luxury of impromptu potholing without basic supplies of water. He would have to exit the cave very soon and get on with his life if he didn't find it quickly.

The floor levelled out and an illusion bewildered Frank for a couple of seconds. His torch beam seemed to vanish into nothing as the wall of rock in front of him disappeared. He flashed it all around and realised that an enormous cavern was opening up just beyond his present position. The light beam could not reach the opposite side.

He stepped out into the dark space and turned right to stay close to a wall. He dislodged a small pebble, which made a splash directly in front of him. Water, right there on the ground – two small pools of it, fed by a steady rivulet bubbling out of the rock.

With his water supply topped up Frank felt relaxed and focused on what he was doing. He felt that this cavern must have existed before the earthquake but obviously his route into it was new. Perhaps the crack on the surface was the only entirely new feature and somewhere nearby there may well be another way in that had existed for centuries. He had no sound basis for this assessment of the situation and, strictly on the evidence observed so far, the whole thing could have been created by the earthquake, but that just didn't seem likely somehow. Equally, there did not necessarily have to be an older way in. If the cave was an ancient feature it may have been cut off from the surface for the whole of its existence. It was still possible he could be the first living thing to enter it. He hauled his rucksack into a more comfortable position and pulled on the adjusting straps to fix it there. It was a lot heavier now all of his bottles were full.

Making his way around the edge he tried to estimate how far underground he had come and guessed it was certainly more than fifty feet but perhaps not as deep as a hundred. The floor was strewn with rubble and he had to place every step carefully so as to avoid the risk of a twisted ankle. His torch beam flicked rhythmically up and down between the floor and the wall. He sensed he was following a curved route and would eventually come back to where he started if it continued. The ceiling of the cavern now seemed a bit lower but the impression of size was strong. His torch beam still faded into blackness when he shone it towards the centre. The lower ceiling seemed to coincide with less rubble on the floor and now he noticed that the wall was smoother. The next flick of the torch beam also revealed that someone had made good use of this stretch of smooth rock.

Frank stood square on to the wall and scanned the beam over it, working from top to bottom. He had only seen cave paintings once before, on a tourist visit decades ago in southern France, and the one before him now was nothing like those. He remembered the French tour guide describing them as remarkable and his response at the time being lukewarm. They had been very faded and brown, depicting several different types of animals. But the scene he looked at now was strikingly colourful. There were two shades of blue, a deep orange, a yellowy-green, and black. There were seven figures standing in a circular formation but only four of them appeared to be ordinary humans. The other three had human bodies but their heads seemed to be representatives of the animal kingdom. One was clearly a bird's head but the other two were less distinct. There was very little detail, no recognisable expression on the faces and no attempt to show clothing, unless they were all naked, in which case there were no clues as to gender, except one of them had a dark feature coming from the bottom of the face, which could be a beard. However, the lack of detail was compensated by what Frank would certainly describe as artistic ability. The scene was beautifully drawn, managing to convey dignity and an impression of respect for the purpose of the group, whatever that might be. Above the seven figures was a circle and some dots, drawn simply in black, which Frank imagined to be the moon and stars. He supposed the whole purpose of the painting was to record some form of worship ceremony but he checked himself and tried to keep his mind open. It would be lazy to slap a ready-made meaning onto it; what did he know about prehistoric cave dwellers?

He made a wider search around the painting but this was all there was, on this section anyway. He realised his discovery meant he would have to search the rest of the cavern at least, and maybe other tunnels running off it. This was tricky. How long would his batteries last and how long would he last without food? He would need to limit himself and perhaps come back another day. He began making his way further round the cavern, sweeping his torch like a World War Two searchlight, until he came to an obstacle. The wall stuck out and the floor trailed down to his left, becoming an impossible gradient, This was as far as he could get without risking a treacherous drop towards the centre of the cavern, and his torch again failed to register any bottom to the gradient. It was too much of a risk. He turned back feeling thankful his exploration had been limited by external circumstances, relieving him of decision.

He shone his beam a bit higher on the way back in case he had missed any tunnels leading upward from points above his head, but he was now hoping he didn't find any and was keen to get back out onto the surface. He felt lucky to have seen the cave art and imagined there must be photos of it in glossy books somewhere. Two steps more and the logic of the situation engulfed him like a fever. He stopped and retraced his three-second mental journey: there would not be photos in books because other people *did not know* about the art; the earthquake had revealed the entrance; he was the first one down it; he had discovered the art. He was the only one who knew about it.

He would have to do a thorough search on the surface for any other entrance, or any feature which might have been an entrance before the earthquake, but he was already convinced he would not find one. An instinct told him he was the first human down here for a very, very long time.

Frank arrived back at the painting with new responsibility. As the discoverer of this ancient artwork he felt that some form of record was needed. He searched his rucksack for the pad and pencil he knew were in there – items he rarely used. He positioned the torch on a waist-high rock to maximum advantage and settled down on the cold floor to make a drawing of the cave art.

CHAPTER SEVENTEEN

KIM PRESSED THE 'END CALL' BUTTON on her phone and placed it silently on the window sill. She stared out at the garden and wished she was a crocus, peacefully caressed by the February sunlight. The words of an old blues song entered her mind and began the inevitable haunting she must now suffer:

> She lied to her mother
> She lied to the county judge
> She lied to Billy and Joseph
> She lied to everyone she could.

Her lie was an all-time platinum chart topper, destined for classic status. She had lied to a reporter, Suki Tomkins, and the reality of what she had said was rumbling in her ears like someone had just started a truck engine. It would have consequences: it would do damage and it would hurt more people than just the one person it defamed. Suki had been insufferable, but that was not unusual and did not begin to offer the slightest glimmer of mitigation. Kim knew this was her own evil.

Suki rang Kim because she was doing a profile on Tara for a magazine called *Rockissed* and the history part needed a bit of colour from previous band members. That's the phrase she had used – 'members from Tara's previous bands'. *Tara's* bands. The hackles had risen like a flick-knife. It had been *her* band, not Tara's band. Anyway, she had let that go, mainly because Suki had babbled on with her spiel before it could be corrected. As she ran through what she had already researched Kim detected something ugly about Suki, apart from her name, that could not be allowed to thrive without some form of attack. This girl suffered from knowing everything. It might be possible that she was short of detail in one or two areas and things just needed fluffing up a bit, but really she knew everything worth knowing about anything that was important, and as well as knowing it she was rarely wrong about it either.

She asked a few questions about which countries the early band had toured in, and whether any famous record labels might have made the embarrassing mistake of seeing Tara and failing to recognise her obvious talent, then she said, "After Tara wrote 'Snowfall' how do you remember the impact? Was it immediate?"

The demon had seized Kim at that moment and armed her with perfect timing for the attack. "Er…well, yes, the impact was immediate, but can I correct something that's been bothering me for years, if you promise not to use it?" She knew that a pretence of naiveté about what reporters would use or not use would make Suki feel even more superior. By then telling her something she had been wrong about all these years, her superiority would be satisfyingly blown out of the water.

"Strictest confidence of course. Off the record completely," said Suki, about as convincingly as a cartload of manure promising not to smell.

"Tara did buy the rights off me, for quite a substantial sum, and it's quite legit she puts her name to it. All part of the deal, but…"

"You mean you wrote it?" Suki was salivating.

"Still got the original notes." What? Where did that come

from? Oh, crap!

"But why on earth would you part with it?"

"Well, obviously you know all about Tara's rich family…"

"Stinking," said Suki deliciously.

"…Tara had access to a good bit of the family cash and, well, I needed money for something I'm not proud of – please don't ask me what. Tara was sort of connected with it but she could never have used the money out in the open for something like that, so we concocted this deal so she could pay me a lot of money for something innocent."

Suki was a bit suspicious but still hooked. "Why did her family believe that she needed rights to a song and you didn't?"

"Come on, Suki, I'm a hardcore blues singer. 'Snowfall' is not really me, is it? It was just a one-off and I had no ambition to build on that kind of image. But Tara, well, it was a perfect launchpad for her and, as you know, she has got a certain talent of her own for that sort of music, as she's gone on to prove. We were good mates, y'know. I was happy for Tara to use it, and her family saw it that way as well." Kim thought she had overdone it with this claptrap.

Suki loved it. She was almost cured of her affliction. "You know, Kim, I've always had doubts – her later stuff was never quite in the same mould – but you have really put things in perspective. Thanks."

"No problem."

The remainder of the call reverted back to the boring background stuff she had wanted in the first place and Kim heard her voice providing all the information while her mind was in a storm of noisy recrimination. 'No problem': that was as wrong as it's possible to be, and then more wrong. This was a big problem, and she had unleashed it into the real world for stupid reasons. At last the phone call ended.

Kim thought she understood why she had done it. It was not just the insufferable haughtiness of smarmy Suki, Kim had also hit a crisis of self-belief. She was bereaved from the loss of a question mark. Previously there had been the question: When are you going to write a good melody? And now there was just the answer: You are never going to write a good melody.

She felt blocked in and burdened by her limitations. She wanted to destroy what there was and force something else to take its place. The destroying part was easy. The something else was the problem and until it arrived, destruction was rumbling towards her. She had an image of herself standing in the road with a huge black truck about to flatten her. She had reinvented reality and she wanted to uninvent it again. It did not feel like she wanted it to: it was her first try at being dangerous and she had been too dangerous, obscenely dangerous. She wanted to rub out that obscenity and put something less offensive in its place. Her petty jealousy towards Tara now seemed childish and pointless; she wanted to put it back in its playpen and make it play nice. But it was out there, driving a rumbling black truck with 'fuck Tara' all over it in blood red, about to run down a naughty childish girl.

CHAPTER EIGHTEEN

G REG WAS HAVING AN OFFICE DAY. Head office had reminded him of their existence with a torrent of emails. The firm had recently decided to start hiring out the new DVD recorders and first on the job list was training all the staff to have some idea of how they worked. Two-day courses in Leeds for every one of his staff, but not all at once, of course. He was ploughing through the dates of the courses and trying to match them up with holiday dates and other courses some of the staff were already committed to. A little voice inside him was suggesting he ask the staff which dates they wanted first, and then try to match them up with the required level of cover, but he knew it would take forever to get straight answers out of everyone. Doing it the other way round meant he would probably get half the dates accepted without quibble, and he would only have to wait for the other half to finish doing swaps with each other until everyone was satisfied. When his first attempt at matching names with dates was finished, he had a stack of statistical information to compile that would fill up the rest of the day.

Francine Pike put her head round the door and asked him if he wanted a coffee. He said yes. Fran was one of the four female engineers on his team. She was having a workshop day.

When she brought the coffee back she had hers with her

as well. She put them both down on the desk and sat down opposite Greg. "You've been hiding in here all morning. Is it something we've said?"

He smiled and looked up from his lists. "Thanks, Fran. I'm ready for this. The DVD recorder courses have come through – two days each in Leeds."

"Two days? I thought they'd just be a bit more complex than the players?"

"Well apparently we haven't been making too good a job of the players, nationally I mean, not us here. Too many being sent back to the factory when we could have fixed them."

"We haven't sent any back, have we?"

"Only that one the customer took to Turkey and plugged in to the dodgy supply."

Fran smiled. "It was not delighted by Turkish electric at all, was it?"

Puzzled by her strange language for a split second, Greg looked up from his papers and found Fran holding a cherubic straight face. Did she just make a joke? Turkish delight... of course. Their eyes met and he felt his face displaying uncertainty. A split second later he rebuked himself for being caught out by Fran's sense of humour yet again.

She knew she had got him and let her face crack into an evil chuckle.

"I'll get you at playtime," said Greg, wishing he could think of something better.

"You can't, you're the boss. That would be inappropriate," retorted Fran, pronouncing 'inappropriate' like a hoity-toity personnel officer.

Greg was still holding his list for the Leeds courses. "Okay, Miss Pike, how about I send you to Leeds with...ooh, let's see...Trevor and...Ernie. Yes, that would make an ideal team dynamic...what do you think?"

Fran's glare was glistening with icy menace. "I know where you live, y'know."

Greg couldn't help laughing, and he held the list out to her. "D'you want first pick of the dates?"

"Naah, you pick for me. Any time will suit me." There was a slight edge to her tone.

"You okay?"

Fran picked up her coffee and held it in both hands just below her lips. "Nick and me broke up yesterday."

Greg felt uncomfortable: Fran and Nick had been together for years, living together for the past five or six. This was quite serious. Fran could see Greg was having trouble saying the right thing. She carried on.

"He's moved out, so I'm not homeless or anything, but I do feel a bit strange. Still coming to terms I suppose."

"Well, you must be. I mean you and Nick were…did something happen suddenly? I had no idea things were going downhill."

"Neither did I, Greg. It's classic really, he's been shagging someone else, I found out, world as I know it gone to hell."

Fran was a tough woman. Her face told Greg she was not about to be the victim and her next move was going to be positive and decisive. "Will you have to see him again, sort out his stuff from yours and all that?"

"I've already boxed it up and texted him to fetch it while I'm at work. There's not much. I'm going out straight from work tonight just in case he tries to catch me later. Trish was the first person I told and she insisted we go out tonight. I didn't take much persuading, mind. Might even end up crashing at her place."

Trishia was Fran's sister. She picked her up from work occasionally and Greg had met her briefly in the car park. "Have tomorrow off if you want, Fran. You know, if you make a night of it and need to recover, you'll at least have to go home and …whatever…if you've stayed at Trishia's, so have the morning off at least."

"Yeah, maybe… I'll give you a call in the morning if I'm

having the whole day."

"Don't worry about it. See you when I see you."

Fran stood up to return to her work and Greg was relieved the conversation had not delved into the details of Nick's misbehaviour. He was weary of hearing about people being shitty.

He was pleased he'd been able to do something practical to help Fran but already a little niggle was starting. Why did he always get this notion that he was only nice to people so that they would be nice back? Was he flirting with her, trying to get his leg over? He honestly didn't think so: he was still not right in that department even though it was years since Stephanie had died. And in any case, as is well documented in almost every art form and factual analysis of human nature, this theory is total bunk. Some people are pleasant in return, but many are not and never will be. The worst of them look upon pleasant behaviour as some kind of weakness, marking you out as a possible target for their manipulations. In the consumerist utopia to which we have allowed civilisation to aspire, the gullible customer is an essential component, and being a pleasant person in this environment is all a predator needs to move in for the kill.

Greg was pretty sure he was not gullible, and certain that he was not always pleasant.

Fran was on her way to the door. "Thanks, Greg, I owe you a pint."

"Have a good time tonight."

CHAPTER NINETEEN

THE DOOR OF THE MUSEUM HAD clear glass in the top panels and Frank could see there was a member of staff inside behind a reception desk. It had taken him two days to reach a city which he knew had a museum. He could have diverted to a couple of small towns that might have had one, but he felt a big city museum was a better bet anyway. He had washed in the toilet of a large pub, one of those where the car park is at the back and the toilets are just inside the rear entrance. A surprising amount of big pubs have this layout, which allowed him to slip in to the gents without actually passing through the bar, and leave again totally unnoticed.

He hesitated at the door, looking down at his clothes. He was irrevocably scruffy but hoped with fresh face and combed hair he could again pass for an eccentric hiker. He entered and strode confidently up to the reception desk.

"Do you have an archaeologist or palaeontologist who works for the museum?"

The young man behind the desk shot a brief glance at him and immediately started tapping on a computer keyboard, his eyes scanning the screen. Without looking up he said, "The curator who covers palaeontology matters is in a meeting at present. Should be free about four o'clock."

Frank didn't respond immediately, which was enough to drag the young man's eyes away from the screen. He was looking at Frank with an empty expression. Frank didn't like 'curator': that seemed like a museum word for a manager. He wanted a scientist. "Is he a scientist, you know, an actual palaeontologist?"

This completely flummoxed the receptionist, so Frank kept talking before the young man could fill the conversation with waffle. "I think I've discovered something important so I need to talk to someone who actually works out there on ancient stone-age sites and suchlike."

A flicker of neural activity slightly changed the young man's expression. "We have a university professor who brings stuff, and takes exhibits away to work on. She doesn't actually work here, you know, we have a …we liaise with her at the university, anything to do with fossils and ancient history."

"She sounds perfect. How would I get in touch with her?"

The young man's face swivelled to the screen again, fingers tapping. After a slight pause he announced that she would be visiting tomorrow for a meeting and may have some time after it. Her name was Alison Branmarsh. Frank decided to try for it and wrote a note for the museum to give her as soon as she arrived. He was sure she would be interested and would want to know more from him after her meeting. The receptionist read the note when Frank passed it over, and promptly burst into life.

"Hey. The earthquake! You were there when it hit?"

"Right on top of it."

"Just a few hours ago we had some seismologists on the phone about that. I think one of our staff is going up there with them next week. I know Professor Branmarsh would be keen to beat them to it if there's anything, you know, to be discovered."

"Tell her she won't be disappointed. See you tomorrow at 11.30."

CHAPTER TWENTY

J ACK HAD TO GO AROUND LUNCHTIME and after he'd left Kim thought back to the sex that morning. She couldn't believe she'd done what she'd done. She feared it might be too weird for him and that it would be the end of their... whatever it was; that they would awkwardly go back to being mates in the band.

Up until this morning their new sexual relationship had been much less adventurous. She was still surprised at herself for initiating it in the first place; after all, they'd been friends for years, since before he worked with the band.

She agreed with the thinking that any form of pleasure was okay if they both wanted it but this morning's adventure might have been pushing her luck: it did not seem right to have made such an exhibition of herself this early in their new thing. If she'd been intimate with Jack for a few years she'd be a whole lot more comfortable with it. If things ended with him tomorrow their sex would slide into the 'casual' category and she had visions of him laughing at her preferences with his mates.

But this morning something had snapped and she'd thrown herself into it with complete debauchery. Ever since she'd come out with all of those lies to the magazine reporter her head had been buzzing. She had betrayed an old friend and stolen the credit for something in a reckless outburst of stupidity. She had done bad things before, the kind of stuff that gets you out of doing something you don't want to do, or takes advantage of a misunderstanding – lazy stuff. But until now she had never coldly manufactured something that she knew would cause serious harm.

The thing she had done was a shock to her own image of herself. She'd built up a picture of herself as a serious musician who'd worked hard to keep alive the music she cared about. She wanted the people who knew her to respect her for that. The obsession with writing a good melody was a personal flaw she'd always wrestled with, along with her other personal failings. She drank too much, she didn't contact her family enough, she wasn't putting enough money away for old age, she had a confused attitude towards men... the list went on and on. But now one of her personal blemishes had escaped into the outside world, and it looked different. When it was inside her head she had not really taken a critical look at it and seen it clearly. Now it was out there it was uglier than a mere blemish, it was a grotesque part of her character. It might be an indication of a nasty streak that could get worse and seeing it staring back at her had knocked her sideways. She was not the person she thought she was and she didn't like herself.

She knew it was dangerous to dislike yourself. The mind finds ways to make you suffer. If she had made a fool of herself with Jack and he dumped her, it was what she deserved.

The rational part of her mind, what was left of it, kicked back in and got to its feet like a defence barrister. The argument to her inner jury was based on the premise that this was not the real Kim. The real Kim was serious about her music and caring about her friends. She was usually honest and had been reprimanded by her conscience over much lesser lapses than the current incident. Unfortunately of late, she had become too serious about her music, to the point of obsession, particularly in matters of melody. While the balance of her mind was disturbed by this aberration, she had allowed herself to be beguiled into a mischief that was not only reckless but doomed to certain failure. Miss Barnes knew that she would be found out. The lack of premeditation, indeed the total absence of it, was surely evidence that the lies emanated from an emotional maelstrom rather than a rational intention to inflict harm. In the aftermath of the fateful phone call, now four weeks ago, she has sought solace in many ways. She has eaten chocolate twice daily, bought strange choices of clothing, imbibed too much vodka, said risky things to the audience between songs, and initiated a sexual relationship with Jack Pearson during which she enjoys behaving like a depraved tart. Members of the jury, who among us can be certain we would never fall into similar degradation if we were in a similar position; if we had to cope with the certain knowledge that on the appointed date, now only two weeks away, the magazine containing the falsehoods would be published.

It wasn't working. It made no difference that she wasn't normally a bad person. Nobody is a good person or a bad person – it's all mixed up inside everybody, along with a whole warehouse of other baggage. A suitcase full of sibling issues, a heavy duty trunk labelled 'parents', an entire crocodile-skin range of hideous holdalls bulging with adolescent demons, and a large wooden cargo crate sealed with black-and-yellow chevron tape bearing the words:

RELATIONSHIPS - BEWARE - MAY BE
FATAL IF YOU ARE HUMAN.

The next two weeks were going to be torture, and when the magazine came out the torture would become a crisis she would have to deal with. Everyone who knew the slightest thing about Tara Pentire or her music would crawl out of the swamp and start digging for the truth. It could affect the band and their bookings. Kim stopped herself now: this was too painful. She had to do something, or go somewhere, but not shopping again; somewhere with no people, somewhere quiet.

She grabbed her bag and her walking boots from the bottom of the coat cupboard and left the flat, intending to find a walk by a river. She drove a hundred yards down the road and stopped. She took her phone out of her bag and switched it off, stuffed it at the bottom of the bag, and drove on.

CHAPTER TWENTY-ONE

THE BOOK ROY FOUND IN THE school library had too many scientific words and even had bits of maths amongst the writing, which were meant to help you understand it. They had only just started doing algebra and equations and he was getting on well with it, but these were like a different language. He skipped over them and skimmed the text for the answers he wanted.

It took all of his lunch break but he eventually got what he wanted. The most far away objects were at least ten billion light-years away and the universe was about fourteen billion years old, according to most estimates. He was beginning to discover that scientists didn't always agree with each other. This size was bigger than anyone could possibly imagine. He tried to picture how far away the sun was and where it sat in our own galaxy, which itself was thousands of light-years across, and then where our galaxy sat in the big emptiness of intergalactic (he loved that word) space. He pictured the whole scene beginning to move, as if he were looking out from a spacecraft, speeding away from the galaxy towards the next one, faster and faster, a blur of immeasurable speed, but at the same time trying to grasp how far he was travelling. Even if he went a million times faster than light it would take weeks of imagining like this before he reached the next galaxy. And the edge of the universe was still a lifetime away. It was awesome.

It made everything around him seem like a toytown full of ants. The whole world was a tiny ants' nest floating in the sky far away from much bigger and more important things.

His next lesson was English and after the spelling test the teacher instructed the class to take out their reading books for silent reading. Anyone who needed to change their book could do so as long as there were no more than three pupils at the bookshelves at any one time. Roy did need to change his book and glanced round to the rear of the room, where five bookcases ran the whole length of the back wall. No one was there yet so he sprang up and walked calmly in between the tables. The English teacher, Mr Walton, was a strict man and any hint of horseplay was harshly dealt with.

Emma Tatchbrook stuck out her ruler as he walked past and he nimbly dodged the playful jab in the leg, or somewhere more personal. He gave her a look and carried on towards the books.

There was a good choice and his eyes drifted around for anything new. As he slid his old book into a space he noticed the cover of a book a bit further to the left on the same shelf. There was a gap next to it so he could see most of the front cover. It was a picture of outer space with a large colourful planet in the foreground with moons close to it, and in the background were a few galaxies and stars. The title was *Intergalactic One*. It was his favourite word again and even though it wasn't a new book his new interest in space made him look at it for the first time. It was a collection of science fiction stories by an author named Dylan Zanuck, and their titles sounded brilliant to Roy: *Voyage to the Edge*, *Hyperspace Contact*, and especially one with another one of those awesome numbers, *Three Hundred Million Years*. He turned to that one and started reading. It was about an alien civilisation on a distant planet. He slipped his thumb into that page and made his way back to his seat, skirting Emma by an alternative route.

Back in his seat he continued reading, firmly gripped

by the story. They normally had about twenty minutes for silent reading so he hoped he could get well into it before Wally Walton announced the next bit of the lesson. Towards halfway through the story he realised the main point of it was that this alien civilisation was very, very old. Their planet, called Vortus, from its earliest times had developed a very stable ecology that had allowed them to evolve in a remarkably fruitful and uninterrupted way, and they now had a continuous history stretching back three hundred million years. They were obviously extremely advanced and one of their main occupations was detailed research of the universe. There was a character called Tijen, who wanted to explore in a new way and the others were not happy about it. It sounded a bit like mind-reading to Roy but Dylan Zanuck was using some invented language for it. It had been made clear that this race was long past the stage of zooming around in spacecraft: physical journeys like that were a thing of their ancient 'First Age'.

He didn't get much further before Wally instructed them to get ready for a comprehension exercise, page 43 in the blue textbook. While he was shuffling his books around it dawned on Roy that although three hundred million years was a long time he wasn't sure how it compared with humans: was it twice as long as us, or three times, or a hundred times? How long had we been around? He had no idea, really.

CHAPTER TWENTY-TWO

Having a day off during the working week to compensate for working at the weekend was allowed within Greg's employment contract but up until recently Greg never used to take them. It usually meant that stuff would just pile up at the office and he would cram the same amount of work into fewer days. Since the company's pay structure review about six months ago his ideas had changed and he was going through a bolshy phase. They had effectively frozen his salary by restructuring his job at a lower scale. He was safe on his present level but any successor in his job would be employed at two thousand per annum less. The extra little jab in the ribs was that he would not now get any rise in salary until the cost of living index decreed that the new rate had overtaken where he was now stranded, which could take years. So he took his weekdays off when he was owed them and tried to be as clever as he could with the piled-up work.

If he were honest he didn't always enjoy weekdays off, but today he was feeling good. It only took a few little things to cluster together to have an effect on Greg's mood, especially at the start of the day. If they were pleasant things he became reassured the day was set fair; if they were unpleasant things the day was put on probation, with a duty to prove it was not out to get him. Pleasant things had happened this morning, starting with Roy getting up on time, eating his breakfast and going to school with no last-minute panic over something or other (it was football kit yesterday morning). Then Fatty Tom's morning bowel movement had produced a nice solid dry poo on which Greg could use the carrier bag disposal method. As long as the litter tray was reasonably dry underneath, the cat poo could be scooped up by first placing a hand inside a carrier bag (not one with little anti-suffocation holes in it). Then, using it as a glove, the poo and surrounding dry litter could be grabbed and held secure while, with the other hand, the bag is turned inside out around it. The bag can then be tied off and temporarily dropped outside the back door to await the next load of rubbish taken to the bins. This is a lot quicker than having to empty the whole litter tray and replenish it with fresh newspaper and cat litter.

The next thing was the arrival of a postcard from Glenda Gadby. She was an old friend of Stephanie's who had kept in touch in a sparse but consistent sort of way: a kind of every-few-months letter or phone call, or in this case a card from Austria, where she was on a skiing holiday. She put on the card that they must 'get together' sometime this year. It was well over a year since Greg had actually seen Glenda and John so that would be good; just before he put it down he noticed she had signed it 'Glenda', not 'Glenda and John'. Intriguing.

And the current pleasant thing was an interview on the radio with an 82-year-old woman called Madeleine Harvey. She had been a music teacher until her fifties, then written three novels, and then, while she was in hospital for a minor procedure but which needed a lengthy recovery, she had spent her time reading *War and Peace*. After loving this book she learned Russian so she could read it in the original language and eventually went to university to study Russian. In her seventies she went on to achieve a PhD in Russian and won a prize for her translation of Pushkin. She was a delight to listen to, an inspiration in the truest sense. It wasn't just her achievements: it was the unassuming way she talked about her children and grandchildren. If there were more like her, thought Greg, the IDC would not be happening.

The rest of the morning and afternoon settled into a peaceful plod through the housework, ending up in Roy's room for the ultimate challenge. While he was wiping sticky marks off the top of the bookcase where Roy put down his drinks of pop, the poem he had first seen under Roy's pillow attracted his attention again. It was now inside a plastic sleeve on top of a row of videotapes just below where Greg was cleaning. He pulled it out and had another look at it. After rebuking himself for not doing something about it sooner he began to weigh up the possible reasons why Roy would write a poem like this. He lifted it halfway out of the plastic sleeve, as if this would enhance his chances of guessing the truth. The thickness of the paper seemed significant: it was very good quality plain paper, and perhaps this was the main reason it did not seem connected with Roy's schoolwork. It was clearly Roy's handwriting and he had made a very neat job of it, but after reading it through carefully six times Greg was convinced that it was not in fact Roy's own creation, even though Roy had put his name to it. This was a relief and ruled out a minefield of speculation on the state of Roy's mind. However, he *had* copied it from somewhere and the neatness of his writing showed some respect for it, or perhaps an empathy with its sentiments.

Greg was not aware of how he knew it was not Roy's, but he did feel a real certainty about it. It was a bit like his book-buying trance: while he was reading it the same unconscious mechanisms had kicked in, and made their decision. The rational part of him still had to concede there was no evidence either way, but Greg trusted his instincts.

Perhaps it was the work of a precocious friend, or friend's brother or sister or even parent. Perhaps this friend or acquaintance had been successful in some way with it, winning a competition maybe? But why would Roy want to copy it out and pretend it was his own work? Perhaps it *was* that thing about the female violinists. It certainly would make a strong emotional connection with Roy's mother and grandmother.

Now he had convinced himself Roy had not actually written it, it seemed easier to mention it to him, and he felt confident that a useful conversation would happen soon.

Greg was also confident he had remembered Kim's movements this week. She was in between two local gigs so it was likely she was staying at home at the moment. He dialled her home number and she answered straight away.

"Hi, Kim, how's things?"

"Oh, y'know, ups and downs."

Greg knew straight away this was code for 'all screwed up', but he pressed on with his own agenda first. "I just thought I'd let you know about that poem of Roy's, the one I found a few weeks ago just after Christmas."

"Oh, right, yeah." Kim's voice was odd.

"I just found it again and, well, I'm pretty sure he didn't write it. I just can't see words like that coming from a twelve-year-old and you know how you get a feeling about things? Well, it hit me and I know I'm right. You were just as disturbed as me about it so…"

" Yeah, certainly, it's heavy duty stuff, so where do you think it came from?"

"I don't know, but instead of being terrified to mention it I feel okay about it now I know Roy must have copied it from somewhere. And it wasn't hidden under his pillow this time, it was just slipped in his bookcase so, y' know, it's not that dramatic that I just came across it while I was cleaning."

"Yeah, you can ask him about it now, casual."

"That's why I ringing, really. I'll probably mention it tonight so I wanted to check if you'd had any more thoughts about it. I dunno, maybe it's a song rather than a poem and you know all about songs I've never heard of…"

"Naaah, don't think so, Greg. I'd have clocked it straight

away if it was already a song. A lot of poems do get used as lyrics though – bits of poems anyway. Maybe that's what Roy's intending. Has he been practising his guitar?"

"Not all that much. He's gone mad on space and planets and stuff lately. Last night he asked me how long people had been on Earth."

Kim laughed and Greg felt her mood had lifted a few notches. "Does he think we came here from another planet?"

"No no, I don't know. Maybe, but he didn't mean it like that. He wanted to know how long it's been since we were savages and cavemen."

"Tell him from Aunty Kim, there are plenty of savages playing the drums in plenty of bands right across Europe."

They both laughed and then Kim spoke first. " I'm really glad you've rung, Greg. You've cheered me up."

Greg took his cue. "You did sound a bit glum when you answered. Man trouble, is it?"

Kim made a sort of 'hmm' noise, acknowledging that Greg could be forgiven for thinking that yet another boyfriend had turned out weird. "No, for once it's something totally my fault and nothing to do with men… I'm sure I've told you, quite a while ago probably, that I'd like to write a song with a good melody…"

"Yeah, sure, you even told Roy, when you were strumming away with him at Christmas, showing him a couple of new chords. I was listening."

"Did I? I can't remember… Anyway, I love the blues and it's my life and all that but, oh God, do you remember Tara Clitheroe? I was at school with her and she was in the band when we left…she's famous now: Tara Pentire?"

"Blimey, is that the same Tara? Yes. I've got one of her albums."

"Hasn't everybody…but the thing is, I mean we're still quite good friends. I could ring her up now and meet her for a night out, but I've done something really nasty to her and it's all because of this obsession with writing a good melody. There's a magazine coming out tomorrow with me in it telling the world it was me who actually wrote her first big hit."

"I suppose the reporter has made a big deal out of some passing remark?"

"No, Greg, it's as bad as it gets. It was me. The magazine rang me at a bad moment and I just made up this pack of lies. The song was nothing to do with me but it's such a special melody I went stark raving jealous and just claimed I had really written it and not her."

Greg was bemused. "Couldn't you have just called back the next day and said you were drunk or something?"

"Oh, believe me, Greg, I went over and over and over trying to find a safe way to undo it, but journalists like that know the score. Those conversations are always taped. If you try and change things they just write you up as some kind of saddo or nutcase or pisshead. She might even know I was lying but she's got a great story on tape and she'll use it one way or another. The only small comfort is that it's just a specialist rock music magazine and as long as none of the big time reporters pick it up it might just…well, as long as my whole career's not ruined I'll be able to get over it, I hope."

Greg asked his next question carefully – he was just trying to understand; he was not being judgemental or scornful. "So you were so jealous of Tara, or her good melodies, that you couldn't help yourself?"

"Yes."

"Have you told Tara this article is coming out?"

"No. D'you think I should? That's another agony I've been wrestling with. The journalist might have told her straight away depending on how she wants to play it, but then I'm sure Tara would have rung me up and…"

"Kim, calm down. Don't let it rip you apart…are you on your own?"

"Yes, but my boyfriend's coming round later."

"Good...I can't really come round now because Roy's due home in half an hour, but look, will you be okay until your bloke gets there?"

"Yeah. I've been like this for weeks now, well, y'know, it's okay as long as I don't talk about it."

"But look, Kim. If you're going to be on your own tomorrow when the magazine appears we need to arrange something. I can take some time away from work and be there if you want?"

Kim marshalled her thoughts and tried to visualise the next twenty-four hours: Jack would probably stay tonight, then they would get up about nine-thirty. She remembered he was going to a trade demonstration of some new technical sound gadget tomorrow lunchtime over in Worcester, so he would have to leave about eleven. If the magazine had posted her a copy she would avoid opening it until he had gone; if nothing arrived by post she would go out and buy one. "Could you come round to my place about eleven? They might send one by post because I'm in it, but I won't open it until you get here."

"Sure that's early enough?"

"Yeah, Jack...my boyfriend, will be here 'til about then. He doesn't know anything about it so I won't open it while he's here, and if I have to go and buy one we can go when you get here."

"Fine. See you tomorrow then, but if anything goes crappy later, give me a call, okay?"

Again, Greg was forgiven for thinking that a boyfriend situation could 'go crappy' at any moment. "Don't worry. Jack is a good guy. I'll be okay."

They said goodbyes and Greg came off the phone feeling stunned. It reminded him of a situation Stephanie got into at work not long before she was killed, only in reverse. Stephanie was the talented one and several people working close to her had become infected with a malicious strain of jealousy. Three separate incidents occurred over the span of two years that were impossible to explain unless envy or jealousy played a large part. Greg had been in love with Stephanie so his view of her was understandably favourable, but trying to be ruthlessly objective about it still led him to the conclusion that she possessed talent and charisma and was very good at her job. She got things done; high-powered people phoned her or arrived for meetings and progress was made, and the rest of the team were reminded of their limitations and frustrations.

It took Stephanie a long time to believe that this jealousy affected grown-up professionals so powerfully, and she wouldn't accept Greg's ideas on it. He could detect it and explain it after only nine months into that horrendous period, just after the second of the three incidents. Not being talented or charismatic in any way, it was easy for Greg to see why the rank and file became jealous, devious and manipulative: it was their only hope of crawling a bit nearer to corporate Shangri-la.

He couldn't help feeling some sympathy for Tara Pentire; she would suffer pain and confusion because of Kim's stupidity. But he loved his sister and understood how she had driven herself into this mess. He would not criticise her or get drawn into unanswerable questions; he would go there tomorrow and attempt to be supportive, understanding; and hopeful that a way out of the mire was possible.

CHAPTER TWENTY-THREE

ARCH THE 29TH WAS SIX WEEKS and two days after Frank had first taken Professor Branmarsh and her assistant, Angus, to the cave paintings. They had agreed to meet up again at the museum on this date because she estimated her preliminary findings would be ready by then. It was a wet day and Frank would be glad to spend some time under the museum roof.

Their initial trip to the cave had gone well. She had a long look at his drawings before they set off, and asked him a lot of questions. It was hard to tell what she thought of his answers – she was a bit like a robot gathering information for someone else. But when the three of them finally arrived at the paintings and got the lights fired up she bubbled into life, and intense discussions with Angus flowed on for over two hours with very few gaps. They wanted Frank in some of the photographs, which he thought was very gracious. When they parted and made the arrangement to meet again, she was keen to emphasise it had been a very worthwhile investigation.

The same young man was on the desk when he entered the door. This time he was beaming. " Mr McCombie, good to see you. Professor Branmarsh is looking forward to your visit…do you want me to hang your coat up? Filthy day, isn't it?"

Frank slid his rucksack to the floor and took off his dripping coat. The receptionist walked out from behind his desk and took the coat by the hood. Frank pre-empted any move to relieve him of his rucksack. "I'll hang on to the rucksack, thanks."

"My name's Paul, by the way. Do you want coffee or tea?" He was treating 'Mr McCombie' like royalty.

"Coffee would be fine, thanks...you don't make it with hot milk, do you? I like it black."

"No problem. I'll bring a pot up to the meeting room." He disappeared into the office behind the reception area and returned minus the coat. "Right, follow me. It's upstairs."

Professor Branmarsh and Angus were seated in an impressive room at one end of a boardroom-style mahogany table. An open laptop plus folders and files and assorted papers were arranged in front of them. Angus stood up and greeted Frank warmly and Alison Branmarsh pulled out the chair next to hers and ushered him to sit there, again with generous warmth. As he sat down she placed a bound file of papers in front of him. Beneath the clear plastic cover the first page contained only a title: 'Dallag Stead Site'. He noticed they each had an identical copy.

Angus repeated the offer of coffee and it was clarified that Paul already had it organised and would be bringing a pot. Angus then looked at his boss and there was a meaningful pause before she began to speak. When she did begin to speak it gave Frank a sudden memory of Mona. Not that she sounded or looked like Mona – it was that way Mona had of imbuing her astrological explanations with the sense that she knew more than she was saying.

"I'm really pleased you could get back here today, Frank, and I must repeat our thanks that you chose to share your discovery with me. I think, when we parted after the first visit, I did give you some idea of the possible importance of the site...well, obviously there's a long way to go, but several things can already be confirmed. The main one is that you have discovered an entirely new site. We've checked every possible reference and it's clear that Dallag Stead was completely unknown until the earthquake uncovered it."

Her face was on fire with excitement; she was a different woman from the anorak and corduroy academic who had followed him down the hole six weeks ago. He noticed her hair was newly cut with a chestnut colouring very subtly and professionally added; she was wearing make-up, and she was wearing expensive clothes – a pale yellow short-sleeved top with a lacy edging round the neck and sleeves. Her left arm was on the table very close to him. It was a very feminine arm, slender with a smattering of freckles. He thought she was about forty-five when he first met her but now she could easily be six years younger.

She was pressing on. "Your name is heading for the archaeology textbooks, Frank. That must feel, I don't know, weird?" She glanced into his eyes for a reaction and he felt himself give a kind of eyebrow shrug, but then she was talking again without waiting for a spoken answer. "...But I haven't told you the real... This is nothing short of a bombshell in my profession and I can't believe it's happening... It's looking to be certainly the oldest site of its kind in the UK and Ireland, and possibly amongst the oldest in Europe. We've got people coming from all over Europe, and the interest is global. There are comparisons with sites in Africa and South America."

"Tell him about Jane," prompted Angus.

"Yes, of course...before I launch into all the scientific stuff. As you can see, Frank, we are somewhat excited about all this, and I don't want to assume anything about you but, well, you have made a remarkable discovery and, if you agree, there is something else you can be involved in. We've been approached by a television company – one of the better production teams actually – who want to make a documentary. The producer is a woman called Jane Greegan. I've worked with her before, and she'll do a good job. She's not pushy for anything to be dumbed down, and clearly, Frank, you would be an essential part of the story."

After a pause that felt like it wanted to be part of a much bigger pause Frank said, "I don't know... I've tried to be independent of big organised modern life. I don't want to drift into a situation that might compromise... or...you know what I mean?" They probably didn't know what he meant.

Alison took a shot at it. "Well, you said a few things about your lifestyle when we met before but, to be honest, when we got to the cave art everything else went out of my head... Your no-fixed-address thing I took on board and we made the arrangement for today because you can't be contacted, and I suppose I was left with an impression that...well, as soon as the TV thing came up I somehow knew you might have mixed feelings about it, but I'm not quite sure why."

Angus remembered a snippet. "On the way to the site you said you keep on the move because of a dream you had."

"It started with that, years ago. I dreamt a kind of escape dream. I won't bore you with all the details but I suppose, basically, I'm a bit of a misfit. I don't believe in modern values. I sometimes feel like I'm from another planet and I was never meant to fit into the human community."

Alison was interested. "That's an interesting phrase, 'the human community'?"

"There are certain people I like, people I visit sometimes. I suppose you'd call them non-threatening people. They think they understand me and they never try to dig into me any further. But as a whole, I see the human race as a bit of a mistake."

They both laughed agreeably. Alison said, "You might find there are people who agree with you on that score."

And Angus asked, "What would you do to change things, y'know, if you had omnipotent power?"

"I'd go back in time and fix it so the animals got a better deal...so that none of them evolved into an intelligent dominant species. I know animals kill each other and even their own kind sometimes, but their lack of consciousness about what they're doing while they grind away at the survival struggle has an untainted purity about it... I don't think animals have consciousness in the same way that humans do. Maybe I'm wrong about that?"

"The jury's still out on that one, for a lot longer, probably. Consciousness is nowhere near being figured out yet. So how long would you give the animals to scuttle about in their ignorance?" Alison had inserted a note of disdain.

"Millions of years, for as long as the climate was stable. None of them would have enough dexterity to build things that threaten the planet like we do, so life and death would carry on according to the natural ecology, unless a giant rock came down from space and disrupted everything. But even then, things would eventually pick up again."

"Bit ironic, Frank. On your alternative planet Earth, your fantastic discovery would not have been put there in the first place."

"True, but I wouldn't be here to discover it either."

Alison didn't want to go any further with this; she probably had a certain enthusiasm for her own existence. "So anyway, do you want to know a bit more about the art? I must admit a lot of it has got us baffled." She flicked over a few pages of her copy of the main file. "Page 7 is the first photograph."

Angus started flicking to page 7, so Frank complied also. He felt the conversation had been cut short a little. Perhaps they were pushed for time. Or perhaps he *was* a misfit. He had never had a conversation like this with anyone before and found it difficult to imagine how his odd views had sounded to people who had careers devoted to human development. He hoped they didn't feel insulted. He didn't think his idea was that outrageous, but perhaps it was. How could he know?

Their attitude towards him appeared to maintain the warmth of his initial welcome as they discussed and explained the details of the discovery, so apparently his mad idea did not appear to have caused any lasting damage. Their investigation was a fascinating story: how they dated it, how they checked with colleagues all over the world, how they interpreted the art, theories of how the colours were made and what they signified. At what point did the cave become sealed up? Was there a previous earthquake that caused it to be buried and lost before it had ever been found? The geologists and seismologists were working on that. What were the people like who lived there? Are they buried in there or nearby? How many of them were there? There were decades of work ahead and towards the end of the meeting the television programme was mentioned again in terms of when it would actually be made. Somewhere between four and seven months was the answer, and as it was a new discovery, already covered by some of the news channels with regular follow-ups likely, an early broadcast date was feasible; perhaps over Christmas. Frank was reassured by this: he knew he would have time to think about it and expressed his wish to do so to Alison. He reminded her he had not actually said no in the first place – he just wanted to think about it.

As he left the building with another firm appointment to return in two months, Frank judged his choice of this particular museum to be one of his better decisions.

CHAPTER TWENTY-FOUR

S UKI TOMKINS HAD DONE SOMETHING ODD with Kim's revelation. It was not included in the feature article about Tara but made the subject of a separate piece two pages further in. There was a photo of Kim and the headline 'Blues Girl Claims Tara's First Hit.'

Kim was not sure if this was better or worse. More people would read the big feature about Tara because, after all, she was internationally famous. But to give Kim's story a separate piece with a headline certainly upgraded the chances it would be noticed by the general reader. Perhaps it didn't make much difference: the lie was out there and there would never be another day when it had not been said.

Kim and Greg read through both pieces carefully, looking for any surprises or unexpected angles. The only one they found was that Suki did not appear to have told Tara about Kim's lie. At least, there was no mention of any reaction: no quote from Tara being outraged or indignant. Nothing. It was as if the magazine had decided just to publish it and sit back and enjoy the fight.

Kim decided to phone Tara. She dialled the number and Tara's husband answered. He was as friendly as usual and they exchanged pleasantries of the 'How've you been' sort. But Tara was out of the country and not back until the weekend, and the signal on her mobile was rubbish every time he had tried it.

Kim did not fancy a difficult broken conversation with her so she tried for a long shot. "Larry, do you know if a reporter called Suki Tomkins has called her in the last few weeks?"

Larry was immediately disgruntled. "I hope to God she hasn't. We had enough trouble with her last year. Has she been bothering you, then?"

"Nothing I can't handle. Did she upset Tara, then?"

"Well, yeah, she became more of a pain than most of them. It started about this time last year but I didn't know about it until nearer the summer. She wanted to write about Tara's childhood and early family history and it was all done by phone and email at first, but then they met up and it comes out this Suki reckons she's discovered something…if you don't mind, Kim, I won't say what it was, bit personal, you know… anyway, Tara was pretty rattled."

"So this was last summer, you say?" replied Kim, concluding with relief it couldn't have been anything to do with her.

"Yeah, that's right. So after that Tara went cold on the whole project and contacted the lawyers to try and stop her publishing any of it. Then she started sending letters – nothing threatening or anything but just kind of manipulative…you know, snidey ones trying to get herself back into Tara's good books. But there was something about her that Tara, and me, found really creepy, so we got the lawyers to send one more letter telling her she was not wanted, you know, in lawyer language."

"You got rid of her, then?"

"I hope so. Nothing else from her since about November. We managed to stop her publishing anything other than the usual bland profile piece, and I was a bit worried because reporters and editors can be a bit vicious when you prevent them going about their lawful trade – free speech and all that crap, you know… If she's been after you, Kim, I would be very careful."

Kim decided to play dumb. "Well, just one phone call so far but thanks for that, Larry. I'll make it the only phone call."

They promised to meet up soon when Tara was free, and said their goodbyes.

Greg had been watching Kim's face intently. "That seemed interesting."

Kim was feeling an unsettling mixture of relief and guilt and fascination. "A whole load of stuff's been happening with Tara and that reporter. Could be that she didn't tell Tara about me because of that... It might be that she only rang me in the first place to get back at Tara, y'know, to dig for some dirt. Handed it on a plate there, didn't I? Shit, Greg, I feel even worse now. I've added to a pile of grief Tara was already suffering from this bitch and snidey Suki didn't even have to lift a finger to drag it out of me."

Greg followed as Kim shot off into the kitchen. She pulled a bottle of vodka from the cupboard and started to pour it into a used glass sitting by the sink. It looked as if it had previously had orange juice in. The clear vodka became tainted with cloudy wisps as the remains of the juice mingled with it.

"At least put some more orange juice in there," said Greg.

Kim responded and headed for the fridge but her mind was not on her drink. "Larry said she'd unearthed something horrible about Tara, from when she was...well, much younger, I think, but obviously he didn't want to say too much."

"Something horrible?"

"Yes, well. Sorry, d'you want one?"

"Bit early for me. There's more coffee in the pot, I think." Greg grabbed the coffee pot and they both headed back to the living room, where he topped up his half-empty mug.

Kim took a big gulp of her drink and continued, "He didn't actually say what kind of horrible, just that it was very personal, but it had to be some kind of secret she didn't want people to know – that was obvious – and they got the lawyers onto it to stop it coming out."

"Oh, right. So snidey Suki didn't take that lying down I suppose?"

"Apparently she tried to wheedle her way back into their favour but it backfired. Larry said she came across as really creepy and they got the lawyers to warn her off once and for all."

"Not wanted on voyage."

Kim smiled. She hadn't heard Greg use this catchphrase for a while but she recognised it from way back. He picked it up from an ex-navy guy he used to work with…must be twenty years ago now.

Greg had come full circle. "Ah, so then she called you, knowing you as Tara's friend from way back, no doubt hoping you'd be aware of this horrible secret and she could get you to blurt it out…"

"…Because if it came from *me* , she might be legally okay to report that and get round Tara's lawyers."

"But then you gave her something else: as good as, or better maybe than this other thing."

"Which Tara still doesn't know about, by the way. She's out of the country."

"So we've still got that bridge to cross. What about your band? Don't a few of them know from personal memory that you didn't write the song?"

"Only Micky would know for sure. He wasn't actually in our band then but both of us have known him since college, and he played on a couple of Tara's early CDs before he joined me. He won't be easy to deal with – he can be an awkward sod."

Kim's head dropped forward. She was sitting in a hunched position with her drink clutched in both hands on top of her knees. Her hair fell down around her drink and one strand fell into it. Greg moved over to the sofa and sat next to her, putting his arm round her shoulders. When her head lifted there were tears on her face.

They sat in silence for a few minutes and Kim overcame

her sobbing. It occurred to Greg she had probably not eaten properly for days and when he asked her she admitted it. There was no food in her flat so he persuaded her to have lunch at a pub. This would have the added benefit of getting her away from her phone for a couple of hours. He knew she would never leave her mobile behind but maybe she would agree to switch it off while they were eating. She changed her top and put on some make-up before they left, which he thought showed she wasn't completely bereft of self-respect.

CHAPTER TWENTY-FIVE

A FTER A MAIN COURSE OF CAJUN chicken and new potatoes Kim was much brighter. When the coffee arrived Greg felt it was safe to ask her something that had been niggling at him for a while. "Kim, can I ask you a question? …I know you've already said stuff about it, but I haven't really grasped it, to be honest."

"Sure. Fire away."

"Why does it mean so much to you to write a good melody?"

She looked at her brother in the manner of a detective making an assessment of a suspect just before interrogation. "You want this without any crap, don't you?"

"Heavy duty as possible, please."

"Up until I lost my sanity with snidey Suki the answer was a lot simpler: I thought I understood it but I'm a lot more confused now. I thought it was all to do with my musical ability, my understanding of music, my fine tuning of the whole musical range. I was arrogant enough to believe that if you have a deep relationship with music it should give you a way in to all the different styles. I did pretty well with my classical training, if you remember, but that wasn't the main thing that put the belief in me. It's the blues…being able to sing and play blues is like having a reservoir of musical expression implanted in your soul: when you tap into the reservoir the sound of your voice or the instrument expresses precisely what you want it to express… Oh shit! This must sound bizarre. What I mean is that when you have always been able to find a musical way to express pain or longing or love or anything you want to, it seduces you. It brainwashes you so that music is like your own magical language and my problem was that I thought I knew the whole vocabulary. I thought I could translate my blues ability into any other form I wanted…rearrange the phrases into a top quality melody. You're looking sceptical, Greg."

"Only about the translating bit. I get what you mean about your inner bond with your musical talent…but it *is* different, isn't it, composing a melody? I suspect you've realised that now?"

"Yeah, don't worry, reality has landed…having the blues in you is like knowing one musical language. Composing a melody requires a completely different one that not many people can learn, the same as not many people can successfully learn the blues: it's either in you or it's not. But anyway, this nightmare with Tara has taught me that I've been deceiving myself with all this musical ability stuff. It's odd really because I've always known that I envy her talent with melodies and the jealousy over it has been driving me mad lately, but I always thought it was a sort of side effect of my frustration with my own ability."

"It's the other way round, isn't it? …Sorry, I'm jumping the gun."

"It's okay. You can probably see it clearer than me. Yes, I appear to have admitted to myself that I told that ridiculous lie because I am insanely jealous of her and always have been, and all that guff about translating my musical ability into other forms was just froth… The weird thing is though, Greg, part of me still believes I could do it one day, and the even weirder thing is that I cannot for the life of me work out why I am so jealous of her. I mean, y'know, fair play, I'm a damn good singer and musician and in certain ways I'm in a different league. She's one of those musicians who's got blues ability but doesn't appreciate it. Y'know, she can use it or lose it, move on when it suits her. I don't think she's done a blues number for years now."

"Now that you understand it better, is it easier or harder? I mean, just because you know you're deeply jealous of her, has it ended one set of frustrations but thrown up loads of new questions?"

"Well, the immediate mess I'm in has taken over now. I feel scared that I'm going to lose everything, be disgraced and disrespected and suddenly find I can't get bookings. And it'll take ages to sort itself out. Some people away on tour won't hear about it for weeks and just when I think I've had all the bad reactions, someone else will lash out."

Greg didn't know enough about the music business to fully understand how that side of it would all pan out. But he had seen Kim perform and now might be the right time to say something he'd long been mulling over. "Well, let's hold on to the fact that you're a brilliant live singer; the last time I saw you the audience were ecstatic. And you're a gorgeous woman. I know you hate being rated by your looks but it's the way you move and express the song and all that kind of stuff. People are looking at you as well as listening to you, Kim and...you could make more of that if you wanted to."

There was a bemused and slightly resentful frown on Kim's face. "How did we get...make more of what?"

Greg knew he'd gone off at a tangent but it came from a gut feeling he always had when he saw Kim's band and never quite knew how to put into words. In the desperate bleakness of the current conversation the words were forcing themselves out. "The best thing all round is for you to concentrate on what you do best: audiences are not going to care about Tara and this songwriting thing, honestly they're not, Kim, and if you just get out there and give them everything a blues fan really needs, plus a little bit more, they'll stick with you. Venues and booking agents are not going to shun a cast iron guaranteed audience and you've got everything an act needs to pull them. Like I said, Kim, they look at you as well as listen, and well, whenever I've seen you on stage I always thought your clothes …I know you've got to feel comfortable about the way you look and the whole image thing is mainstream blues and all that, but you're a terrific-looking woman, Kim, and you could _ "

"If you weren't my brother I'd have the sisterhood hit squad round here like a shot. You can't say stuff like this, Greg, it's…"

"I know, but that's the whole problem, people …men…can't say this stuff anymore, even if it's meant in the most positive way. Has no one in the band honestly never said anything remotely like this before?"

"Not since that so-called manager we had a few years back." Kim had got rid of him in acrimonious circumstances and managed the band herself for the past four years.

Greg was determined to get his point home. "Just think about it professionally for a minute. I'm not saying you should dress like a tart or completely change your image, just a subtle shift in style to a kind of naturally sexy look." Greg knew this had come out hilariously badly as soon as he'd said it.

Kim's laughter took about fifteen seconds to die down and people in the pub were looking at her. Looking at her and smiling. She sat up straight, flung her hair back and her arms out in a mock catwalk pose, and her voice was direct from London Fashion Week. "And here we have Kim in this season's naturally sexy ensemble of faded denim and off-the-shoulder lilac chiffon."

They both laughed and Kim took a long drink from her vodka and orange. Greg needed to make her grasp what he meant. He was feeling an upsurge of confidence that this was one of his better ideas and could make a real impact on the band's success. "Okay, I'm not getting this across very well but you must know what I'm getting at. There are shades of grey between where you are now and looking like a total slut. I'm trying to think of another female singer who might be in the same sort of slot but actually it's pretty difficult – not many of them get it right, if you ask me."

"You're serious about this, aren't you?"

"Yeah, I suppose I am. If you're going to survive this mess you've got to pull out all the stops, and it can't do any harm to be devastating when you're on stage – there's no rule that says a female blues singer can't look sexy. A lot of the songs are about sex and lust so what's the problem? I bet some of the old-time women singers were really raunchy when it was what the business expected of them."

Kim was still resisting but knew his last point was the truth. "You're right about the old way of doing things but that was an exploitation thing. The women were just…well, to be fair, I know the best ones did get past that stuff and managed to get work purely for their voices even in the thirties and forties."

"But I bet they didn't suddenly start dressing like nuns and wearing no make-up. Surely they could enjoy the glamour of it as well as the music?"

"I suppose so. Like you say, it was expected that performers looked the part on stage so I suppose they didn't think about it like we do: there was no divide between commercial pop and more serious stuff like there is now."

"Really it's more of a divide between big studio conveyor belt chart crap and bands who can play really well in live venues. All I'm saying is don't compromise on your devotion to the blues and the skill of your musicianship, but don't look like a bunch of students who can't afford proper clothes; especially you, as the lead singer."

"Okay, okay, right, let me get my head round this. It's a long time since anyone told me I look sexy…Jack's not much of a charmer in the compliment department…I'm not too fat?"

"You're not fat at all, you've got a perfect shape…remember

Jill's wedding we went to last year; you wore that pale green dress and high heels, and make-up?"

"I hated it…surely you're not – "

"No, I'm just saying that you looked feminine and sexy and there were plenty of heads turning and when everyone got pissed in the evening the blokes were firmly focusing their fantasies on you. The bridesmaids didn't get a look in."

"Now you mention it, I remember thinking that if you weren't there I might have had trouble with one or two of them. The guy who had the last slow dance with me was definitely *up* for anything on offer, if you catch my drift."

"Well, there you go. He probably wasn't the only one, and that was just you in a nice frock. You just need to come up with something for your gigs that's…I dunno, somewhere between Elkie Brooks and Tina Turner …maybe?"

"Elkie Brooks! Blimey, Greg, drag yourself into the twenty-first century at some point, you old fart."

He smiled at her justified amusement – he was harking back perhaps a little too far. "She had a great voice though, didn't she?"

"Alright, I'll give you that, and to be fair, she is still working. Shame she doesn't do more blues; anyway, I think I get what you mean. Can't say I'm sold on it though, Greg. You'll have to let me talk it over with the band."

"Course, obviously."

"Let me just clear something up…you weren't thinking of going round telling any other women they should wear different clothes, were you?"

"Only the ones on my list…you know: dental receptionists, barmaids, and that girl in the florist with the big boobs."

She landed a very hard fist on his right shoulder.

Chapter Twenty-Six

FOR THE PAST FEW WEEKS Roy had noticed something going on in the bedroom of the house opposite. The houses across the road all had drives sloping down from the pavement whereas the houses on Roy's side were all slightly uphill from the pavement. This meant that the bedroom opposite was much lower than Roy's room and he could see right into it. He knew that it was very wrong to spy on people and his conscience was firing warnings at him, and he genuinely tried not to look at all when people were in there. But when he opened his curtains every morning the bedroom opposite was an intrinsic feature of the landscape and he could not help glancing into it. It faced east, which made it a particularly bright room on sunny mornings.

The people opposite were always up before Roy and the man also left for work very early. The woman usually set off in her car about the same time as Roy left for school, but she was always dressed before him. The first time he noticed her was probably when she opened her curtains just as he looked out while opening his. He couldn't specifically remember that time or recall anything significant. She was always smartly dressed in 'office' clothes like the reception women at school so there was nothing about her appearance that intrigued him. He couldn't quite understand why he had only noticed the bedroom recently: it and its owners had been there for as long as he could remember so he was puzzled about that. Perhaps they had recently redecorated it or rearranged the furniture. The double bed opposite the window was the focus of the daily ritual responsible for his attentions, so maybe it had been in a different position before. Anyway, now that he had noticed it, the morning routine seemed to touch him and trouble him at the same time.

She always opened the curtains before making the bed and Roy noticed there was always a small brown teddy bear somewhere on the bed, in amongst the rumpled duvet, or sometimes on one of the pillows. She would straighten out the duvet and the pillows, lifting the teddy bear and then putting him back on the made bed. She then went out of sight for a moment, somewhere in the room on the left of the window, and reappeared with three cushions, which she arranged on the bed where the duvet began its incline over the pillows. They were small plain cushions individually coloured yellow, purple and green. Next, the teddy bear was carefully placed against the cushions and, again from somewhere out of sight, she would carry two companions over to join him. One was a white teddy bear the same size as the first one but wearing a dress, and the other was a much smaller bear of a darker shade of brown. Usually, the two larger bears would be side by side and the smaller bear would be cradled on their laps. It was a source of some anguish for Roy that following his first observation of this ritual he had found it an irresistible necessity to fetch his dad's binoculars and clarify the descriptions of the three bears. He had known they were fluffy toys of some kind but the distance was too far for him to see details, and it was only after he had fetched the binoculars and focused into the room that it occurred to him how bizarre it was that he needed to know more. Also, how reckless he was being when the woman might easily catch him. He had stepped back and lowered the binoculars as soon as these thoughts entered his mind, but he had seen enough to satisfy bizarre curiosity and thereafter visualise the family of bears in their luxurious setting.

Roy had several memories of his mother doing things with his teddy bears when he was small: putting them in bed with him, choosing which one to take on holiday, pretending to feed them. So he knew his recent observations must chime with the pangs of emotion he lived with whenever his mother came to mind; but it seemed to him there was a more mature curiosity coming into play, not connected with his own long-gone teddy bears, or his mother. If it was only about missing his mother he would not want to look – he would avoid seeing the bedroom opposite.

This morning there was a new development. When he opened his curtains the cushions and one bear were already in place, with the morning sunshine flooding in on them. The woman appeared a second later with the other two bears and carefully placed them in position. Roy expected her to disappear from the bedroom as usual so he continued idly gazing at the bears, touched and troubled as usual, with no particular worries that the bears would be offended by his intrusion. But then she sat down on the bed next to the bears, her face turned towards them.

Roy took a step to one side and peered round his curtain and an intense wave of guilt filled his mind. She could not see him because her face was towards the bears, but she might stand up at any moment and turn back towards the window. Her hand was gesturing and gently touching the bears, and the tiny movements of her head gave away the confirmation that she was talking to them.

She sat there for at least a minute, perhaps two, talking the whole time. Roy was now firmly overbalanced in favour of 'troubled'.

Three hours later, at the end of the English lesson, a memory came into Roy's head of Emma Tatchbrook rummaging in her schoolbag. She kept a small teddy bear in there. It was one of those things he knew about Emma but never thought about, in the same way that he knew Adam Dobson would always refuse to play in goal, once to the point of storming off in a tantrum. He looked over at Emma, who was standing up and packing books into her bag. As she put the last book in she held it back slightly and reached down with her other hand. All in one movement she lifted her bear – his head bobbed up just enough for Roy to see him – and slid her last book down underneath him. She did not want to squash him with her book. Could this possibly mean she also talked to her teddy bear? The question slid into Roy's mind like a circus clown bursting into the ring. It had every right to arrive there but it still seemed ridiculous. Just because she was careful with her bear it didn't mean that she talked to it.

They were leaving the classroom for morning break now and Roy was following Emma. If he could catch her on her own for a minute he might be able to solve the mystery. She walked outside with two of her friends and he stayed well back as they slowly ambled to a low wall near the staff car park. They sat down on the wall and took drinks and snacks from their bags. It didn't look promising for a one-to-one chat. Roy waited the entire fifteen minutes and when the bell went he saw his chance. Emma started off one way and her two friends went another. They were obviously in different groups for the next lesson.

He caught up with her and immediately heard himself saying, "I saw something really weird this morning."

She was surprised by his sudden appearance and abrupt announcement. She looked at him with suspicion. "What?"

"A woman talking to teddy bears."

Emma's suspicion was deepening. "You trying to wind me up, Barnsy?"

"No, honest. I saw her and she's, like, a normal woman, not mad or anything but – "

"What did she say?"

"Eh?"

"What did she say to the bears?"

"Oh, I dunno. She was in…she was too far away, but then

just now I remembered you've got a teddy bear – "

Emma stopped walking and became aggressive. "Has Lee Billingham been blabbing to you? What's he said? I'll kill him if he's been blabbing."

Roy realised he had been too hasty and the mention of Lee Billingham had now rearranged his priorities: he did not want to get on the wrong side of Lee Billingham, no matter how urgent his need to clarify the teddy bear issue. "No, it's nothing to do with Lee. He hasn't said a word about you, honest. I just saw this woman and then I wondered – "

"You better not be winding me up, Barnsy. You sure Lee's not been saying stuff?" She was walking again, faster than before.

"Totally definitely not said anything. I don't hang around with him anyway."

She threw him a sharp-eyed glance and if Roy had any understanding of twelve-year-old girls he would have been able to tell that she didn't believe him. The only thing he actually felt was utter confusion. They were now entering the classroom for their next lesson and the teacher, 'Lofty' Vernon, was already barking orders in his broad Yorkshire accent. Emma found her usual spot with another group of female friends and Roy took his place on an all-boys table. It was a demanding lesson and his one final thought on Emma's bear did not come until afterwards when he was about to play football in the lunch break. All that stuff about Lee Billingham must mean that he knew she did do something funny with her bear. *Talking* to bears was the only thing he had said, so that must be it. Lee Billingham knew she talked to her bear and he must have teased her about it and now she was worried he was telling everyone.

The serious matter of lunchtime football then commenced and all ponderings on teddy bear communication were dispelled completely, not to return until the following morning.

CHAPTER TWENTY-SEVEN

As Greg walked through the workshop saying good morning to everyone his mind was again wrestling with Roy's poem. He arrived at his office and allowed the thoughts to unfold before he tackled his desk. It was four days since he had rediscovered the poem in Roy's room and he still hadn't mentioned it to him. Maybe tonight might be a good time. Tomorrow was his last day at school before the Easter holiday: this year they were having the week running up to Good Friday and the week starting with Easter Monday, which Greg preferred. Sometimes school went right up to the day before Good Friday, which always seemed wrong somehow. With one day left at school it would give him the option, if the poem was connected with school, to perhaps clarify things with the teacher if necessary. If he left it until the holiday he would have to wait until school came back and then he might have gone off the boil about it or forgotten what he wanted to ask, so best talk to Roy tonight if at all possible.

He sat down and stabbed his computer's power button. As the icons began to appear on the screen everything suddenly stopped, with several icons yet to materialise. He slid the mouse from side to side but the pointer remained unmoved. He waited. Sometimes it started going again after these inexplicable freeze-ups. He opened the post and scanned the letters for any nasty surprises, keeping the corner of his eye on the still-frozen screen. All the letters were routine bumph and he placed them on his in-pile. Okay, restart the computer.

He went off to the kitchen to get coffee while it went through its restart. Fran was already in there with a tray full of mugs, making coffee, or tea, for everyone; his own mug was already washed and waiting on the tray. He informed her she was an angel, which she chose to enjoy rather than feministically resent, and Greg returned to his office.

Everything looked normal on his computer screen and he logged on to the firm's intranet to get his emails. As the screen started to fill up there was an ominous pause and a box appeared in the middle of the screen telling him there was an error. It helpfully gave him the number of the error but as he and everyone else he had ever asked had no idea what these numbers meant, it boiled down to another restart.

Greg had never made a written list of things that contributed to the irreversible decline of civilisation, but he was very close to starting one, and computers would be very close to the top. He knew this was contentious – many important advances could not have happened without computers, but this went to the nub of Greg's perspective: scientific advances did not necessarily equate to an enhancement of civilisation. What did civilisation mean? Surely it wasn't just technical virtuosity?

Fran came in with his coffee and put it on the folded-over paper towel he used as a coaster. She had hers with her as well and sat down on his spare chair.

"The IDC has struck again," Greg gestured at his computer screen.

Fran was vaguely familiar with Greg's civilisation thing, but not as familiar as he thought she was. "Frozen up again? I nearly threw mine out the window yesterday."

Greg shook his head at it and jabbed the power button. He couldn't be bothered to try and 'control, alt, delete' his way out of it. Switching it off would give it the pleasure of gloating at him that he had not shut it down properly, and consequently, it was now going to run an exhaustive check of itself to see if this irresponsible action had corrupted any of its files. He switched it back on and awaited his reprimand.

"Where did you get this IDC thing from?" asked Fran. "It sounds like something off one of those 'Was God an Astronaut?' documentaries."

Greg knew he had told her before, but he also knew he could be boring when he went on about it, so he didn't blame her for forgetting. "It was a letter in a magazine. When I was at the police station about three years ago, after we had the vans damaged in the back yard that night. There was a law-and-order type magazine in their foyer and this retired police officer had sent a letter in about the 'yob culture', you know. He said there was no real answer to it and it was all part of the irreversible decline of civilisation."

"Bit dramatic."

"Yeah, I suppose so. I didn't think much of it at the time but afterwards, whenever something negative came on the news or whatever, I found myself repeating that phrase in my head. It got to the point where I wanted to go back to the police station and read it again. I never did but, you know, there's such a lot of crap we all have to live with in the name of progress, and it just might be true that we are actually messing it up."

Fran had always been a glass-half-full person. "I know what you're getting at, but just take something like medical advances. We are much more civilised in looking after our health."

Greg wanted to mention the AIDS pandemic in Africa, but he knew that Fran had a point. "Fair enough. Hard to deny we have better medicine, and better conditions in other ways, and we live longer; but that sort of stuff is not really what makes us civilised, is it? It's more to do with doing the right thing, trying not to damage people, trying to build a community with some kind of justice and security… Sorry, I'm getting heavy now."

"No, no, it's okay… So, really, as long as we have criminals, selfishness, greed, all the bad stuff, and we're not doing enough about it, it doesn't matter how healthy we are, we're still not much better than Attila the Hun?"

"Well, it's obviously much more complicated but something like that is how I feel… It's the bit you said about 'not doing enough about it' that really gets me. What's stopping us from doing something about it? "

"Stopping us?" Fran wanted clarification.

"Yes, we should have cracked it decades ago. Philosophers and poets and all sorts of people with a bit of grey matter have been working on it for centuries. Everything we need to know about overcoming our defects has already been written many times. Why don't we get wise and do it?"

Fran looked at Greg and couldn't work out whether he knew the answer or not. Something sprang into her mind. "Okay, what about a situation like the one I'm in, where my bloke has betrayed me and it's all ended in disaster and the emotions are torn to shreds and a woman in my position could react in several different ways. Some women would boil with anger for months, might even seek out the ex and his tart and attack them or something. Some women would become victims and lose their self-esteem and become useless blobs. Others might throw themselves into work, or into a mad round of dating. The thing is, in every case, it's the emotional burden of it that's the mountain they're all climbing.

"But, given that horrible doom inside them, if you asked them to calmly state what would be the most sensible way for them to get on with their life, nearly all of them would know the mature thing to do. We know what to do, but doing it is a different thing."

Greg was close to bursting. "Exactly! That's it. Couldn't have put it better. What stops us is something about ourselves that is fundamentally dysfunctional."

"Hang on, Greg, you can't get carried away just yet. Some of those women in my example will deal with it maturely and calmly. I like to think I'm doing pretty well."

Greg was not fazed. "Good point. Some people get through life in an orderly way, and usually get labelled as 'dull' for their trouble. But if it's possible for some to do it in a civilised way, what is it that makes them different?"

Greg's boyish enthusiasm for his pet subject was starting to make Fran feel maternal. She smiled at him. "You've put a lot of thought into this, haven't you?"

"Okay, I'll stop now. Enough IDC for this morning."

"No, tell me, what makes some of us civilised?"

"You sure?"

"Tell me, tell me, tell me."

Greg finished his coffee and adopted a measured tone. "Well, clearly, it would be the miracle of all time if I had the answer, but I have read a lot of stuff by those geniuses I was on about just now, and some things seem pretty safe to assume. A lot depends on your childhood. If you are loved and made to feel secure and looked after properly it has a profound benefit on the rest of your life, the love and secure part being by far the main thing. We don't have a particularly good record of parenting in that way, in my opinion, and schools have now become part of the penal system. Compulsory education was brought in to stop ten-year-olds being sent up chimneys by monsters making money out of them. Now the whole thing has become bizarrely reversed. If you want to have your children at home and love them and let them have a bit more childhood, rather than expose them to the sarcasm of weary, stressed-out teachers, you get threatened with prison.

"But it's obviously much more involved than just parents and schools. I suppose there are bound to be people with inherited genetic baggage that dominates their lives. Even with a perfectly-balanced child with no inherited problems, a sudden tragedy or serious illness could jolt them into bitterness or resentment or some sort of negative attitude."

"Sounds like a bit of a lottery, then?" said Fran.

"Yeah. And it's the way we're programmed as well. The competitive thing behind the struggle for survival. It's all set up so the strongest come out on top, and these days that's been translated into politics and big business. We don't really need to be competitive any more in the sense of struggling to stay alive but things are still organised so that the most selfish individuals get the most power. And when they get it, they just want to hang on to it for its own sake."

"No, I don't agree there, Greg. You need the entrepreneurs to take the risks and get things moving in the economy and all that."

"Well yes, I can't disagree, up to a point; but don't you think the balance is all wrong? ...For every entrepreneur who spreads a bit of wealth and does a bit for the community there seem to be ten who are just ruthless bastards, and it's usually one of those ten who ends up running more than his fare share, strutting around like king of the jungle until they get arrested for stealing the pension fund."

"You hear about stuff like that quite often, I suppose, but I don't follow the news that closely."

"Sometimes I think a revolution in the way we bring up children could make a real difference, but when I have a bad day I remember millions of years of survival by aggression and ruthless instinct; I look at their faces when they show a stock market trading room on TV and I feel like a misfit, totally divorced from that world. You know me, Fran, I'm not especially competitive, so it's hard for me to imagine. What *is* it like to be so instinctively competitive that you must win, you *must*, like it was life or death? You think of athletes and boxers and stuff but they don't run the world...the people with the money run the world, and where money is manipulated is where you get the worst kind of uncivilised lust for power."

"Is it that bad really? I don't know anything about how all that works."

"No, it's a bit of a closed world unless you avidly read the

Financial Times, which I did for a while, when it was all flavour of the month in the eighties... You were still at school then, weren't you?"

"Yep. Hey, Greg, tomorrow you can tell me what you did in the war?"

"Ha Ha! Anyway, after it all went pear-shaped in the nineties I read a few books about it. One was by an ex-trader who made a fortune and then ended up in prison."

"Sometimes they hype it up a bit though, Greg. Books have to sell and all that."

"Even allowing for that, there was a lot of checkable information in there, and well, I've read a lot of books and you get a feel for phoney crap. The thing about this guy's story is that it was so logical. To him it came naturally to be totally focused on profit no matter what, and he rejected every factor of his life that posed any risk: no feelings of any kind about his colleagues, no personal interruptions of any kind while he was working, and no compunction whatsoever about taking advantage of a colleague's weakness. He mentions later on that the prison psychologist diagnosed him as psychopathic. He explains it's not always to do with violent behaviour – it's a kind of mixture of selfishness and complete absence of conscience. Anyway, he was wildly successful and the scary part is that all the successful ones are exactly like him, and so are the managers and the directors and the chief executives. They all stab each other in the back and bend the rules, and it was only because of a random audit that he ever got caught."

"So all those hard-working wealth creators are psychopaths?"

Greg did not want to sound like the typical anorak conspiracy theorist. "Okay, okay, there's a good test you can apply... Who benefits?"

"Eh?"

"The individual trader benefits, his company benefits, the banks who hold the wealth benefit, the accountants who find ways round the tax laws benefit, and if any tax is paid to our own government rather than a foreign one then some slight benefit might just filter down to ordinary mortals eventually. They are like modern lords of the manor fighting over territory and power and we are the peasants catching a few crumbs. What do you think?"

"I think my brain hurts. Doesn't all this drive you crazy?"

"Probably will do eventually."

"Why do you care about it so much, Greg? ...Sorry, that didn't come out right...I'm making you sound like some kind of obsessive."

"No, it's okay. That's a fair question... I haven't got a very good answer... To me it's just natural curiosity. If we are so intelligent, why is most of the world in poverty? If we are an advanced civilisation, why are we incapable of spreading the benefits of civilisation evenly?"

"Yes, but most people stumble across those questions when they're about seventeen and...well...write them off as unanswerable."

"I suppose it was round about then when I stumbled across them, but I liked reading, Fran... I liked history, I liked biographies of people who kept on going when it was hopeless... I was a right little nerd really in some ways, but I played rugby for the school so I got away with it. But the thing was, I discovered that those questions had been answered...lots of times. Different answers of course and I didn't know who was right but I suppose I thought that all the best ones added together would make a pretty good manual for civilisation.

"So then I was up against a new puzzle...if all this wisdom was out there, why weren't our great leaders making use of it? That question seemed answerable; it seemed there were things you could point to and say 'why don't you do that?' So I read more biographies...of great leaders, and found out what made them tick...reading about Churchill or Ghandi was fairly safe of course and my parents could understand my curiosity in that direction, so I just kept on going and here I am, still trying to figure it out."

Fran was frowning slightly and Greg was worried he had gone on too long. Without looking up she said, "We did Romeo and Juliet at school. It was wonderful...y'know how sometimes you'd get a really good teacher and everything is much better than it would have been?" Fran looked up at Greg, no longer frowning.

"Yes, I know what you mean... Go on."

"Well, the year we did Romeo and Juliet we had Miss Redfern for English and she...she was great. I loved every minute of it, Greg. We went to Stratford to see it, we had videos...really up-to-date ones where they've set it in modern times, and we did a performance for the rest of the school; she cast me as Juliet... Me! Can you believe that? Anyway, don't answer that, but she was inspiring like teachers are meant to be and Shakespeare went from being some dead old fart into the best experience I'd ever had... I actually understood a Shakespeare play when I was fifteen. I still go and see it whenever it's on. You ever seen it, Greg, properly, in the theatre?"

"Not at Stratford, but I have been to a half-decent amateur performance of it, couple of years ago." The memory of that night sprang back: Kim was going out with the actor who played Tybalt – another one of Kim's excellent choices. It was a good night though: they put the story across well.

"What you said a minute ago, about lords fighting with each other, it made me think of the Capulets and Montagues. They had to hang on to their pride and their position, their little chunk of power. People died because of a silly quarrel that had grown out of all proportion; they had to hang on and never give an inch, like stubborn children, with disastrous consequences... It's exactly what you're saying, isn't it?"

"Pretty much, yes," said Greg.

CHAPTER TWENTY-EIGHT

"LAST DAY AT SCHOOL TOMORROW, MATE." Greg was trying to start on a positive note.

"And we're away at Newcastle on Saturday!" For some reason Roy had a real soft spot for Newcastle's ground, and enjoyed every minute of their trip. They were taking the coach this year so Greg could also look forward to not driving.

"Yeah, brilliant." There was a natural pause and Greg went for it. "Roy, I was cleaning your room this week and I came across a poem on your bookcase…"

Roy was holding the remote control for the TV. He switched from one sport channel to another sport channel. The sound was already quite low and the cricket match now on was accompanied by a pleasantly hushed commentary. He turned his head and gave the tiniest of nods towards his father to acknowledge he had heard him.

Greg continued, "It's quite a sad poem and I was worried you might be depressed. It's about dreams, well, dreams compared with real life, sort of."

"Yeah, I found it at school."

"Ah, right, I thought it might be a school thing. You *found* it. How d'you mean?"

"The English homework was to find a poem and make a few notes about it, so I went to the library at lunchtime."

"So you didn't write it then, only it's got your name on the bottom."

Roy was clearly uncomfortable for a second or two. "I didn't like her name, the real writer. It sounded like a horror film, so I put my name instead."

Greg was trying hard to stay with Roy on this, but alarm bells were ringing so he decided not to push it. "Okay, so, what was it about that poem that you liked?"

"It was short and clear, and I liked the bit about tomorrow – it never comes, it's always today."

"Bit sad though. You sure it didn't sort of grab you because you were already sad about something."

"I'm okay, Dad, honest. Can I ask you about something else?"

Greg was not finished with the poem by any means but he could see Roy was desperate to change the subject. "Yes, fine, fire away."

"You know that woman across the road, right opposite, with the little green car."

"Megan?"

"Well I don't know her name but anyway, is she like… normal?"

"Normal? You mean, just…ordinary….like most people?"

"Yes."

"As far as I know she is. We haven't had a conversation for ages, other than shouting hello across the road. Why? Has she said something to you?"

"No it's…well, I couldn't help it, Dad, because my room looks right into theirs, and I know you shouldn't spy on people, but I don't think she'd mind that much, if it's normal."

Greg was having horrendous images of what Megan might have been getting up to in her bedroom, witnessed by his twelve-year-old son. He cleared his throat. "What did you see?"

"She was talking to her teddy bears." Roy looked up at his

father with the expression of someone who has uncovered a secret cult.

Greg tried to hold it back but the laugh sucked in its own energy from somewhere, and let it out again in a spluttery, guffawry chortle. Roy began chuckling as well and Greg forced back his self-control before he gave the boy a fatally irresponsible impression. "Look, Roy, I know it's got a funny side but really you have done something a bit wrong, y'know. If she saw you looking in at her, whatever she was doing, she could make quite a serious complaint to me or even the police, except I don't think Megan's like that. But some people would be on the phone to the police like a shot, so be careful, okay?"

Roy nodded.

"So, is she normal? It's a good question. Depends whether she was expecting them to talk back, I suppose."

More laughter.

The obvious question sprang into Greg's head, "How could you tell? You couldn't hear her from that distance."

"You can tell someone's talking without hearing them. She was making hand gestures at them, and sort of patting them like a pet."

"Yeah, fair enough. Well maybe that's her version of having a pet. We talk to Fatty Tom. She might just be taking her imagination one step further. If she had a happy time with her bears when she was little it might be her private way of remembering happy times."

"Shouldn't she have grown out of teddy bears?"

"I suppose so, but it doesn't mean she's mad if she wants to keep one or two of them. It's a harmless bit of fun, I suppose."

Roy was having trouble accepting his dad's explanation. "I saw an old film once where a vent...ventilli...quist?"

"Ventriloquist."

"Yeah...he talked to his dummy when they were in private, you know, not doing the act or anything, just talking like two people, and he made the dummy argue back and it drove him mad."

Greg knew that movie. "Well, you can take anything to an extreme and make a good story for a film, but as you get older you'll discover that most things, and most people are fairly safe and boring really, with just a few silly secrets here and there. Some people go mad, obviously, but I think you have to look at everything, take in the bigger picture as far as possible, the overall impression. Megan's got a responsible job and a nice house, and I know she does voluntary work for a charity; and her husband, Gerry, is a good bloke. If she were losing her marbles you'd see signs of all that normal life starting to fall apart."

Roy was softening a bit. "What d'you think she was saying to them?"

"You've got me there, mate. Could be anything, her little secret… You're not expecting me to ask her, are you? On your bike!"

"No, course not."

"That's a relief. Now promise me you'll stop looking, and if you see her in the street just smile normally or whatever. I don't want you to react to her like she's escaped from the madhouse, alright?"

"Yeah, course"

"Good. Can I have the remote? It's time for the news."

Greg flicked over to the news and the Florida nightclub fire was the headline story again. It had emerged during the investigation that the manager and the local fire chief had both been notified several weeks before the tragedy that the building was breaching safety standards: an ex-member of staff had written three letters to the manager and a current member of staff had emailed the fire chief, all of it apparently ignored. Five hundred and eighty-one deaths could have been prevented.

CHAPTER TWENTY-NINE

THE BAND REACTED WELL TO KIM's plan for a change of image, especially Carla, who revealed she had already thought they should 'raunch it up'. She had plenty of ideas for stage clothes, for herself as well as Kim, and two shopping trips later the new image was ready for a dress rehearsal.

They agreed from the start that it would be too naff for her and Carla to match like a pair of twins, so when decision time came there was plenty of flexibility. The rehearsal day turned out to be one of the first warm days of the summer and the guys were concerned about the stock of beer in the fridge. Micky decided to go for more supplies, which gave Kim and Carla another twenty minutes to get down to specifics.

Kim had dyed her hair blonde. Her natural colour was a mediocre light brown but her hair was thick and shoulder length with an attractive wave, and now it was blonde it looked stunning. She decided on the midnight-blue skirt and matching stilettos, with a white cap-sleeved top. The skirt was tight, longer than a mini but with a lengthy slit over the front of her left thigh. The top was quite conservative with a wide neckline, not too low, and it clung to her figure but not too tartily. Legs had been a bit of an issue but with the summer starting it had to be bare skin plus fake tan, which was expensive but beginning to deepen nicely.

Although Carla was black she had a Portuguese grandmother and her hair was shoulder length, straight and full of body. She chose a red sleeveless minidress with matching high-heeled shoes. The shoes were not quite as high as Kim's: she could be quite mobile on stage and didn't want to be distracted by having to concentrate on staying upright. Both pairs of shoes were stage versions so they had a more tailored grip round the foot, but high heels were high heels.

Make-up would be another factor on the night, but they made do with standard stuff for this rehearsal. The guys had been very patient, puzzled at first why clothes had to be tried out but eventually persuaded you couldn't just leap on stage as a new person without getting the feel of it first.

Kim and Carla were behind a full-length four-panel art-deco screen at the end of the room and they heard Micky return and start filling the fridge at the other end. Time to make their entrance.

They tottered out and stood in front of the screen.

The men were visibly taken aback. Lloyd was the first to speak. "Can you two groupies see if Carla and Kim are ready yet?"

Kim was staring at Jack, focussing her intuition on his true reaction. He smiled and put both thumbs up. Micky said something about Hollywood, then Lloyd said to Kim, "You sure you can sing at that altitude?"

They got started and Kim found she was feeling absurd. Carla seemed to be far more at home and looked impressive. The music began to take over and Kim soldiered on. The second song turned into a bit of a jam when Carla took off on a slightly weird improvisation and Kim felt inspired to grab a harmonica. Blowing on the harp made her forget herself completely and unconsciously she discovered a posture that suited the high shoes. When Carla took the lead back and Kim began to move around as if on stage she realised something had clicked. A nugget of confidence edged into the absurdity and she glanced at Carla for reassurance. The glance was returned with scintillating eye contact and a surprisingly lecherous grin, which Kim took as confirmation she was raunching it up in the correct manner.

In the fourth song, a slow number, Carla launched into her solo and Kim turned to watch her. She noticed Micky was also focused square-on to Carla, with eyes wide open. She looked electrifying and she had done something with the controls of her guitar to make it sound a few notches more dirty and raw. She compensated for this by playing short, gut-wrenching riffs with long sustains to finish. This was the blues of unbearable pain, the pleading of a despairing soul.

By the end of the session there was full agreement that the music would not be betrayed by the new look – if anything it provoked an overcompensation towards even more hardcore blues. On the first gig with Kim and Carla raunched up to the eyeballs they would be extra vigilant with the audience, prepared to be flexible, ready for anything. When you worked it out coldly, they were a very experienced professional band who had the repertoire to deal with the quirks of any audience.

On the way home Kim could not help feeling a little bewildered. She knew this was going to work but she was reluctant to acknowledge that her initial sense of absurdity had now been completely disarmed by sexual confidence. She was going to play the part of a sexy blues singer and a voice was telling her that, actually, she *was* a sexy blues singer. Don't be absurd and ridiculous, said another part of her mind but mostly, and guiltily, she knew that her stage sexuality was a genie well and truly out of the bottle. After all, blues was a very sexy form of music. Sex and pain, love and betrayal, longing and heartbreak.

Kim had been out all day and the post was still on the floor when she pushed open the front door of her flat. A crisp, good quality, white envelope with the name of a firm of London solicitors printed on it was the only proper letter amongst the junk. She needed a vodka anyway but a solicitor's letter made it compulsory.

One drink swallowed and another one poured, she opened the letter. Tara Pentire's lawyers were 'dismayed' to read the article in a recent edition of *Rockissed* and had been in contact with the magazine's legal representatives. Having listened to a tape of a telephone conversation which confirmed…blah… blah…blah… Miss Pentire had instructed them to issue the following demands. Failure to comply with these demands would result in court proceedings.

> *One:*
> *You will engage in a second tape-recorded interview, in person at the* Rockissed *offices, in which you will be asked to clarify the authorship of 'Snowfall'. You will state that this song was entirely composed by our client, Miss Pentire, and that you had no part in writing the lyric or music. You will also confirm when prompted that your reasons for claiming to have written it were entirely related to emotional issues within yourself, and that Miss Pentire has not wronged you in any way, whether deliberately or inadvertently. Any attempt to portray Miss Pentire as partly or wholly to blame for your own emotional condition will result in court proceedings.*

> *Two:*
> *You will consent in writing for this interview to be published in a prominent position within* Rockissed *magazine. The consent will also cover storage of relevant documents and a copy of the tape on our files.*

Three:

Other written or broadcast media organisations may approach Rockissed *magazine for consent to follow up the article. You will sign a written consent that copies of the taped interview may be distributed.*

Four:

You will decline any approaches for further comment or interview on this matter from any person or organisation of any kind.

Five:

An apology has been prepared in the following form of words, which will be included at the end of the interview when you are prompted. A copy is enclosed in double-spaced format. If you wish to make minor amendments in keeping with your personal preference we will consider clearly-inserted changes in block capitals on this copy, to be submitted by return of post. We reserve the right to refuse amendments if they weaken or alter the nature of this apology. If nothing is returned the apology will be published as written.

Demand number five was followed by the apology and Kim held the separate copy alongside, checking they were both the same, realising just before the end that this was an oddly pointless thing to do. It was worded in a depressingly reasonable manner and there was nothing she wanted to amend. The final part of the letter gave her a named person at *Rockissed* to contact by a certain date to set up the interview.

So, Tara just wanted the record put straight. Fair enough. At least now Kim knew where she stood. The uncertainty of the last few weeks had drained her private time of any peace or relaxation. Every time the phone rang she expected it to be some half-forgotten acquaintance wanting to know more about the damn 'Snowfall' thing. In fact, only two people had mentioned it to her face and she had blamed the magazine for getting it wrong. She suspected the band were protecting her a bit and that more was actually in circulation on the grapevine, but the whole thing had descended into a weary fixture on her landscape, like a constant drizzle in the grey sky of her conscience. She regretted what she had done, but more than that, the act of uttering such a lie to a national magazine had proved her to be a person who could do a cheap, squalid, dishonourable thing, and she regretted the entire person she had now become, and from whom she could not escape.

CHAPTER THIRTY

T HE FIRST WARM DAY OF THE summer had been a hard one at school for Roy. He'd not felt hungry at lunchtime and had eaten very little, then they'd had athletics all afternoon. He didn't like athletics. His knee had started to hurt after the fifth lap round the track and they had a gruff supply teacher who'd already informed Darren Grant that the pain in his feet was all in his mind.

By the time he got home Roy was starving and queasy and exhausted. He drank three glasses of water and ate two bags of crisps before he took his shoes off. After refilling the glass with Coke he collapsed in front of the TV and started flicking around the channels. The sport channels were full of golf and tennis, and the comedy channels were not showing his favourite shows. He absently punched in a number, thinking it was one of the music channels he sometimes liked, and ended up looking at a classical concert. The camera was on the conductor at first and he was just about to rectify his mistake when the view changed to the string section. All of the violinists were women. All of them were in formal black dresses.

Roy could sense the chain reaction in his mind and resigned himself to what was happening. Whenever anything reminded him of his dream a sequence of unresolved thoughts churned away in his mind and eventually abandoned him in a desolate place. It was like a strong gust of wind sweeping him up, tumbling him around and dumping him on a mountain ledge in thick fog. Roy always had the feeling he was missing a vital clue that must be hidden somewhere amongst the churning. He'd tried several approaches to it, sometimes letting the thoughts mull around for hours, sometimes a sort of quickfire focus on the key images, sometimes tracking back through his memories.

Very recently, the last few months, he had begun to suspect a connection between his dream and something else he occasionally experienced. The first time it had happened was a few months after he first had the dream. He didn't make any kind of link between the two things at the time, as he was only seven years old and unable to form any articulate views on the matter. His memory had taken a lot of persuading before it began to co-operate and it had been an exhausting effort just to pin down his age for that first time. But now, having gone through all that, he was sure that the dream did come first, in early summer, and the panic attack, or whatever it was, came afterwards during the following winter. He didn't remember suffering any distress at all from the dream and he knew he'd never mentioned it to anyone. He had a lot of dreams when he was small and this one only became significant later when it had repeated.

But that winter afternoon at school, the scene of the first 'attack', was a story of vehement distress. Without warning, he'd become very upset and unresponsive to any form of comfort. Dad was called in to fetch him. When he'd stopped being upset he just remembered being left with a sense of confusion. No one knew, including himself, why he had become upset so suddenly, and it didn't happen again until he was eleven. He'd had the dream four or five times by then so it appeared to be unconnected. However, this time there was a much shorter gap between the dream and the distressed confusion: a few days. And roughly six months later the gap shortened to one day. That was the shortest so far. He'd had the dream twice since then: about a year ago and then very recently just after Easter, with one attack roughly halfway between them, just before Christmas. It was a mistake to call them panic attacks, a phrase he'd heard on TV, because there was no panic involved; it was distress, or perhaps a manifestation of profound powerlessness. Roy could not put any kind of accurate description on it. That was part of the confusion.

He had fleeting memories of seeing his grandmother playing in the orchestra and Dad had told him he was only taken to those concerts between the ages of three and six. So he had the dream for the first time well after those concert visits had stopped.

At the start of the dream, he is floating above the string section of an orchestra, where all of the musicians are women dressed in black. All of their dresses are sleeveless and their long white arms move with perfect synchronisation as they bow their instruments. He has no idea what music they are playing but it is loud and furious. From there the scene jumps to a viewpoint where he is in a sitting position. A position that, in the dream, is quite bizarre, but in reality would be impossible. He is underneath one of the violinists and his eyes are level with her shoes. Her chair is above him and her ankles and shoes straight ahead. Her black dress is resting on the floor in a neat semicircle around the front of her shoes but it must be hitched up behind her feet, or perhaps there is a slit in the back, because the view of her shoes and ankles is clear. Her shoes are black patent leather with a slightly raised narrow heel, a rounded toe, and one strap across the top of the foot. She wears no stockings and her ankles are the same smooth white skin as her arms. Her right foot is slightly forward of her left and there is movement side to side, the sinews in the ankles tensing and relaxing, as she sways on her chair while playing.

There is now an intoxicating fragrance and it's a vivid detail of the dream that Roy knows something about this. Within the world of the dream he has a memory of being told about it by one of the musicians: she has told him, at some point before the concert began, that they would all be wearing the same perfume and he must get close to them while they are playing so he can enjoy it. She had told him the name of the perfume. This was the point at which the dream becomes sinister. He knew she had told him the name of the perfume, and in the dream he knows the name, but after waking up he does not know the name. Repeated replays of the dream in his awake mind produced a crippling sensation that he had a memory of something real that could only be recalled while he was dreaming. And having recalled it he was doomed to consign it back to oblivion before waking.

For his posture below the violinist to be physically possible his jaw would be embedded in the floor and the rest of his body below it; but he knew he was sitting comfortably underneath her. The remainder of the dream plays out in this viewpoint, music and perfume pleasantly wafting around his head, and when the concert ends he sees his overhead violinist stand up and walk off stage among the other black frocks. The audience leaves and the lights go out and he is alone in the concert hall, still underneath a musician's chair. The fragrance fades and the dream ends with waiting. Waiting for the orchestra to return. There is no panic, no anxiety, merely waiting.

Knowing something in a dream that then becomes unknown when you're awake was unsettling and spooky, but Roy also had a deeper worry adding to the confusion. He felt he was subject to a kind of jinx or forfeit that if he ever told anyone about the dream he would lose his right to know the name of the perfume. This conviction was so elusive that Roy often thought he must have made it up and as he could never recall the perfume's name anyway it seemed redundant, but there was a compulsion behind it that always won. He never had told anybody about the dream. The closest he'd ever come to exposing the dream to the world was to write that poem, but even that had unsettled him further. It went off on its own tangent after the first few lines and concluded with a much darker feeling than his dream.

The timing of his urge to write it had convinced him of the connection between the dream and the attacks. His last attack, just before Christmas, had been on a Saturday evening when he was alone in his room. He had coped with it and it had passed. And he'd written the poem immediately afterwards as soon as he felt better. He didn't fully understand the things that had emerged from his mind onto the paper. It felt as if the poem had been buried inside his head somewhere, origin unknown, and had burst out via his hand and his pen like something escaping. Reading it over several times since then, he now felt more of an ownership; he knew it came from some part of him and was not something he'd unconsciously copied.

Memories of his mother's death – certainly the pain surrounding the sudden tragedy – were right there in the poem but the images written down did not particularly mesh with his feelings about that. And he had the dream and the first attack before she died. It was torture trying to make sense of it, and now he had lied about the poem to his dad he was very uncomfortable about that, but if he'd told the truth it would have meant revealing the dream. If he'd tried to make up some other explanation why he'd written the poem there were two big risks attached: his made-up story would make him sound more disturbed than the true facts and provoke some kind of drastic remedy, or his dad would know he was lying outrageously and some drastic remedy would ensue because of that. As it stood, his dad might well have known he was lying about the school thing but at least he hadn't needed to make up a vast amount of false detail.

A rousing finish to the orchestral piece pulled Roy's attention back to the TV and he switched channels. He tried the science channel for anything about space that might be on, and he was lucky. A narrator was in the middle of explaining black holes. Brilliant!

He was becoming quite an expert on the cosmos. He understood the names of everything routinely mentioned in space programmes or books, like quasars and neutron stars and pulsars and black holes, and he was well on the way to grasping the nature of the objects these words described. He had also learned a lot from science fiction novels because the good ones tended to use accepted science as their starting point. He had finished the anthology of short stories by Dylan Zanuck and immediately went on to read two of his novels. The theme of advanced alien beings had gripped him most of all and he'd discovered another writer called Boyd Harman, who seemed to specialise in this area. Roy was on his third novel by this author, whose name sounded American but who actually came from Cardiff.

The current novel was called *Reborn Dimension* and the advanced aliens had just observed the human race destroy itself at the end of chapter three. From browsing in the bookshop Roy had discovered that many science fiction stories predicted we would destroy ourselves before we evolved enough sense not to, and he found this theme very believable. He had started to watch the news and was baffled by most of it. People did the most ridiculous things and got caught, then tried to bluff their way out of it in court with stories only a fool would believe. At school they were constantly told to 'grow out of' behaviour like that. It seemed that people just didn't.

CHAPTER THIRTY-ONE

S HE WAS ABOUT THE SAME AGE as Mona and the family resemblance was unmistakable, but her clothes and hair were entirely un-Mona.

Frank felt himself take a mental step backwards as she moved forwards into the sunlight past the open front door. She looked him up and down and awaited his explanation for being there.

"I've come to visit Mona… Frank McCombie… I was here last Christmas."

This seemed enough for her but there was clearly something wrong. "You'd better come in."

They went through to the back room, which was glistening with freshness: dusted, polished and tidied with extreme attention to detail. All evidence of Mona's cats had vanished and Frank was beginning to fear the worst.

"I'm Dora Stretton, Mona's sister. She's in hospital, I'm afraid."

"Oh dear! Is she all right? I mean is she recovering from whatever…?"

"Blood poisoning." Dora seemed suspicious of Frank but reluctantly ventured a little more information. "We don't know how she contracted it. It was three weeks ago and she has been seriously ill, but, well just the last couple of days really, she's begun to show signs of recovery…are you a close friend?"

Frank felt under pressure to prove his harmlessness. "Well, I travel around a lot but I call in whenever I'm in the area. Mona and I have a sort of bond. We clicked as soon as we met, if you know what I mean. She wouldn't have known I was coming today – it's very…spontaneous."

One of Mona's cats came strolling in from the kitchen and Dora was visibly irritated by it. Frank felt immensely relieved and stooped down to fuss it. The weight of his rucksack threatened to overbalance him and he knew straightening up was going to be tricky.

"You're lucky to have caught me here," Dora continued. "I come round to feed these blessed things and dust a bit, but otherwise the place is usually empty."

"Can Mona have visitors at the moment?" The cat had had enough fuss and slinked away from Frank. Maintaining his stooped position, he started to slide his rucksack off onto the floor.

"Oh yes, by all means. I'll write down the hospital details for you."

Frank successfully stood up minus rucksack and Dora gave him a note in exquisite handwriting listing the hospital address, name of wing, ward number, and visiting hours.

"Can I ask you something, Mr McCombie?"

"Of course."

"Has Mona ever mentioned Pablo?"

Frank was pretty sure that name had never come up but he trawled his memory for a second. "No, can't say she ever talked to me about a Pablo…is he likely to be visiting her or …"

"Oh no no no, it's all in the past but, well, I often wonder and…anyway, family matters, long history. It's what they call 'baggage' nowadays. Well I hope you find her bright and communicative. Could you tell her I'll see her tomorrow?"

"Certainly, no problem." Frank took the cue that it was time to go and lifted his rucksack back into place. Dora showed him out and said a pleasant enough goodbye, perhaps relieved she had survived a visit from one of batty Mona's weird friends. Frank's mind was replaying Dora's revealing mention of Pablo and baggage. It was as if she had become a different woman for the few seconds she talked of it. An unguarded moment, or was she manipulating him? Did Dora want him to ask Mona about Pablo?

Alarm bells were ringing and Frank remembered it was partly because of this kind of relationship 'baggage' that he preferred to keep his distance from most of the human race. He walked towards the hospital, letting it stew in his mind. This was one for the intuition to work on. He would have to mention Dora because Mona would want to know how he knew she was in hospital. Knowing he had met Dora, would it be at the forefront of Mona's mind that Pablo must have been mentioned? Did Dora have an obsession with Pablo to the point of asking all and sundry about him? Unlikely, but not impossible. Hospital visiting started at 2 p.m., which was two hours away – plenty of mental stewing time.

CHAPTER THIRTY-TWO

T HE WARM SPELL HAD NOW LASTED a week and today looked like being another scorcher. Greg felt aware that the summer holiday was coming up fast and Roy seemed to have forgotten he was supposed to be deciding which friend he wanted to take with him for the fortnight at Megaparcs. The holiday company needed details of the third member of the party by the end of July or there wouldn't be time to finalise their insurance arrangements. It was still only the middle of June so there was really plenty of time, but Greg hated leaving things to the last minute and hated that he might forget about it for another couple of weeks if he didn't do something today. He wrote a note for Roy and left it in the usual place on top of the clock in the living room.

The post arrived while he was putting the notepad back in the kitchen. Another postcard from Glenda Gadby was among the bills and junk. Greg looked at the signature first this time and again it was signed only 'Glenda', no John. He turned it back to the picture for a second, It showed a detail from a famous painting by Renoir rather than a photo of a holiday resort – the sort of card a woman sends when she is at home and doesn't want to bother with a full-blown letter.

In two weeks she was coming to a conference in Worcester and suggested it seemed a good opportunity to meet. She offered a time and date and said she had plenty of news to catch Greg up on. She could either come to the house, as Greg's was only half an hour from Worcester, or they could meet somewhere if he fancied an evening out. Her work phone number was at the bottom.

The last time he had seen Glenda and John was over a year ago. The Christmas card had been from both of them but then came the solo communication from Glenda on her skiing holiday. He hoped nothing awful had happened to John. Surely she would have been specific if he had died or something? It looked very much as if they had split up.

He would have to see her, which was not by any means a daunting prospect: he quite liked Glenda. He had known her, as one of Stephanie's friends, for about twenty years, from before she had met and married John, in fact. The date and time she suggested was fine and as it was a Friday night he would stick with her offer to visit him at home. Greg hated going out on Friday nights – everywhere was far too busy with young people blowing off steam from another crap week at work. He wondered whether to try the number now. He doubted very much whether anyone would respond on a Saturday morning but if it was one of those direct-dial numbers straight to Glenda's own desk phone there might be a personal voicemail he could leave a message on. He would call again in the week but at least if his memory failed him he would have left something.

He tried it but it was just the normal switchboard answering service, so he gave it a miss and ordered himself to remember to ring her on Monday. He placed the card on the living room clock next to Roy's note to remind himself.

His morning cup of coffee was still half full so he sat down to finish it and turned on the TV. He put the news channel on and left the remote ready in his hand in case the world looked too depressing. A story about the FBI arresting people was unfolding.

Five Saudi Arabian men had been arrested in various parts

of America, and in related anti-terrorist raids in Europe, another seven men had been detained, again mostly Saudis. Clear evidence had been seized, indicating a detailed plot to hijack passenger airliners and crash them into prestigious American buildings, possibly even the White House. It was suspected that a terrorist group known as Al Qaeda was behind this plot and that they were led by a Saudi named Osama Bin Laden. His whereabouts were not known but the head of the FBI had strongly advised White House staff to make his capture a priority. The studio handed over to their USA correspondent, who seemed a little sceptical about the whole thing but repeated that the FBI insisted the evidence for this plot was very strong. The suggestion that several educated men would deliberately kill themselves in terrorist attacks on American soil was being met with disbelief bordering on ridicule by most commentators. A CIA spokesman had confirmed that the name Bin Laden had emerged once or twice in intelligence they regarded as 'low grade' and they would of course look into the FBI's material, now that they had it. The reporter hinted that in actual fact the CIA were furious that the FBI had kept all of this close to their chest and if it all turned out to be correct there would be some very red faces around Washington.

Greg turned the sound down a little and tried to imagine the mind of someone who would deliberately fly a plane full of passengers into a building full of people. What did the organisation want? Why were they plotting to attack American targets? This had the whiff of a long-running story – perhaps more arrests, trials, disputed evidence, informants being bumped off. Perhaps there would be others not captured who *would* hijack planes and fly them into buildings. The IDC was gathering pace.

CHAPTER THIRTY-THREE

FRANK ARRIVED AT MONA'S BEDSIDE TO find another visitor already stationed there: A very old man with white hair and a white moustache. At first glance he appeared scruffy but Frank noticed his clothes were in fact of high quality. It was hard not to notice his attire: he wore a bow tie of blue spots on a bright yellow background, a light-blue shirt and a Harris tweed jacket showing some wear and tear but still retaining its handmade pride. He was seated on the grey plastic hospital chair, with a hint of formality in his posture, leaning slightly forward with both hands resting atop an ebony walking stick positioned in front of his chest, the other end on the floor between his feet. The blue foldover shirt cuffs jutted the correct distance from the jacket sleeves and were fastened with gold cuff links.

"Frankie boy!" Mona held out her arms. Her other visitor was on the far side of the bed so their embrace was not impeded. Frank kissed her on the cheek and told her she looked well on the way to recovery. The old man was smiling.

"Ooh, Frank, introductions." She gestured a respectful left hand towards the old man. "This is Professor Patrick Wilmington, a very dear old friend… Paddy, this is Frank."

They shook hands over the bed and Frank felt impressed by this man already. Paddy spoke in the refined tone of southern England's middle class, "Mona has spoken of you several times. Good to meet you at last."

"I've told him you're my man of mystery," said Mona theatrically, and they all gave a polite laugh in order to break the ice.

The conversation relaxed into Mona's current progress towards recovery, which was excellent, and when this petered out Mona looked at Frank pointedly and requested the full story of the earthquake. He was certain he had not given any hints to her. How could he? He had only just arrived. But she clearly knew he had been in the thick of it when the earthquake struck. Could she possibly know someone from the museum or Alison's university? He doubted it: both were over fifty miles away.

He knew what the answer was going to be but he asked her anyway. "Who told you about that?"

"Nobody. It's in your chart, Frankie." She smiled and Paddy laughed knowingly.

This was indeed the answer Frank expected. Something about the tone of the professor's laugh sparked an intention to get to the bottom of Mona's astrology one of these days, but for now he played along.

Paddy was extremely interested in the details of the cave art and his knowledgeable questions soon revealed him to be a scientist of some kind. Frank was desperate to find out more about him and tried to manipulate his narrative to trigger more questions, in the hope he could ask a few back. This worked up to a point so that Frank was able to ask, "Is all of this close to your field of expertise?"

The professor was modest. "Oh no no no. I browse the journals and the old grey matter still seems to soak it up, whatever the subject."

Fortunately Mona was very proud of her friend. "Paddy was my physics tutor at Cambridge. Bit of a genius on the quiet."

Paddy said, "Ah, maybe one day." And they both

laughed.

Frank was stunned. Mona had been a Cambridge physics student? That was a bit like Santa Claus announcing he'd once trained as an accountant.

"You studied at Cambridge? You kept that quiet. I think it's your turn to tell me the full story." As soon as he'd said this, Frank was worried he might have waded in too heavily. Perhaps there was a reason she had never mentioned it?

"Ooh, I don't know about that just yet, I like the idea of being a mystery woman for my mystery man. How about that, Frankie boy?" She was her usual batty self but perhaps there was a pang of something best left in the past.

"When you're back home, then. I'll be round there, pestering you. When are they kicking you out anyway?"

"They reckon a couple of days with good behaviour. Hey, you could go round and keep my chair warm if you like. Might as well keep the moggies company."

Frank suddenly remembered Dora and realised Mona had not shown any surprise that Frank had appeared, nor asked him how he knew she was in hospital. Was it also in his chart that Dora would direct him there? He was frightened to ask. "What about Dora? Oh, she said she'll see you tomorrow, by the way."

Mona's face fell at the mention of Dora but recovered immediately. "You met the princess of darkness then, eh? I wondered who told you I was here. Don't worry about that. I'll phone her later and tell her I've given you my key."

Frank was comfortable with Mona's assumption he would be happy to house-sit for her. He *was* happy to do it: he had nothing against comfort in small doses. The house key was in Mona's handbag in the bedside cupboard on the professor's side and she asked him to get the bag out of there for her. He obliged and informed them he would have to be getting along. Goodbyes were said and they embraced affectionately, with promises to be in touch soon. Frank and Paddy shook hands and he told Frank he was looking forward to the TV documentary about the cave art.

By the time Mona had finished giving Frank all of the household instructions and writing some of them down on a pad, visiting time was over and a nurse arrived to do something medical to her. He wanted to give Mona another big hug and kiss, but scaled it down a bit with a crisp nurse standing over them.

Outside the hospital's main doors he found Paddy smoking a large cigar. "Ah, Frank, I hoped I would catch you. Just hold this a second, will you." He handed Frank his cigar.

He rummaged in his inside pocket and pulled out a transparent plastic document wallet with some kind of magazine cutting inside it. "Have a look at this…let's go over there on that bench." Cigar and plastic wallet exchanged hands as they walked over to a seating area in the middle of a circle of landscaped flower beds.

Rucksack off, settled on the bench, and stifling the urge to comment on Paddy's impromptu ambush, Frank pulled the magazine article out of the wallet. There were several pages of it, with a staple in the corner holding them together. It was from some kind of scientific journal and the text was austere and functional – no headline as such, just the title in bold text: 'The Principles of Interdimensional Energy Transmission' by Dr Ramona Alvarez. Frank glanced at the date at the top of the page: 17 October 1961.

He flicked over to the second and third pages. Mathematical equations were dotted liberally throughout the article. He returned to the first page and started to read.

Professor Wilmington interrupted him after barely a minute. "I know the language will be impossible for you, but I wanted to give you a flavour of Mona's professionalism and perhaps some impression of her staggering brain."

Frank was relieved. "Well yes, I'm shocked, and I was hoping you weren't expecting me to understand any of this, except that forty years ago Mona was going strong as a physicist."

"A mathematician actually, and going strong is putting it mildly, but anyway, let me explain why I have accosted you with all of this." Paddy placed his hand lightly over the article Frank was still holding. "The theory Mona puts forward is still far in advance of its time, but enough has been discovered to make me even more certain that her ideas are valid. Back in the 60s there were many who dismissed her mathematics. They used words like 'eccentric' and 'lacking basis' but in fact they simply could not appreciate that she had taken a substantial leap forward. There were only three of us who had some grasp of it. The other two are gone now and I am ninety-one." He paused and repositioned himself to look at Frank more squarely in the eye. "Frank, if I depart this world without … doing something, I will have let Mona down."

"You mean that, after all this time, you are still the only person who understands Mona's theory? Haven't any modern mathematicians caught up yet?"

Paddy gave a resigned chuckle. "Caught up? …Maybe in a sense, but the short answer is 'no', Frank. Mathematics is not how most people imagine. It's not step-by-step progress steadily unravelling an answer everyone can see is correct. Mona had imagination and ingenuity and creativity and she saw something, took a truly inspired shot at what it might mean, and then constructed a breathtaking model of what underpins it. In one of my books I described the others as tramping through a forest, measuring trees, while Mona orbits Earth in a spacecraft mapping the entire planet. A few modern geniuses might be up there with her now but they're still not seeing what she described."

"So what was her big breakthrough? Is that what this article is about?"

"Yes, that was the first one. Years of work led up to that… How are you for time, Frank? It's a long story."

"I've got all day. I'm only going back to Mona's to feed her cats and house-sit. She's given me money to get a few groceries in and something for my supper but that shop near her house stays open until ten, I think."

"How would it be if I gave you a lift and we got the shopping on the way? D'you like whisky?"

"Certainly."

"Right then, I'll treat us to a decent bottle and something to eat. In fact, you keep Mona's cash safe for her and I'll cover everything. Least I can do for her."

The magazine pages were inserted safely back into their wallet and put away into Paddy's pocket, and Frank followed him across the car park.

The professor was quiet while driving, enjoying some Berlioz on his car stereo. Frank sat back and mulled over all of the revelations he had been assailed with today. Mona had been transformed from a dotty old woman with a flair for astrology into a Cambridge mathematician of prodigious intellect. A stab of anxiety ran through him as he realised that in fact the transformation was the other way round. What had happened to her? Why had she ended up alone and unheard of?

The shopping only took twenty minutes, The professor bought *two* bottles of expensive malt whisky, and they were soon settled in Mona's living room with a packet of biscuits to accompany the Scottish nectar.

Frank was relieved that Paddy made no move to get the article out of his pocket again. "This is going to be a bit uphill for you because I don't understand maths and science all that well. You must have thought of a way around that, I expect?"

"Indeed," replied Paddy. He took a large gulp from his tumbler, set it down on the coffee table and leaned back, gazing at Frank in a manner not unlike a judge weighing up a witness. "Do you believe in God, Frank?"

Frank smiled. Paddy's way around the science had begun. "I suppose I believe in something spiritual."

"Good, good. It does not matter what version of God you choose, I'm not concerned with that. It's more to do with the concept of existence. Let's say, for instance, someone might imagine God to exist in a place above and separate from our universe. Would that be fair?"

"Yes. I've pictured something like that, but it's here as well…whatever 'it' is."

"Good, good. So the idea of something being outside our universe but also inside it…and possibly able to move around at will, maybe at one point being totally inside and then later being completely outside…you could be comfortable with that general idea?"

"I don't know about comfortable. It's hard to imagine what it might be like outside our universe. I suppose I've pictured some kind of spiritual realm in different ways, depending on what mood I'm in."

"Alright, perhaps I can make that part easier for you. Instead of a spiritual realm, just picture another universe like our own. How does that look?"

"Like a cosmic bubble floating around next to ours in a kind of grey nothingness."

"Fine, we'll stick with that. Now put a lot more of them in the grey nothingness, all floating around next to each other, quite closely in fact…you can have them bumping into each other if you like."

"Hundreds of bubbles swirling around each other in a kind of infinite emptiness?"

"I know it sounds ridiculous but just indulge me…instead of hundreds, try billions. In fact, as you've already mentioned the word infinite, let's have an infinite number of bubbles stretching as far as you can imagine in every direction."

"Last time I had a conversation like this I was listening to Pink Floyd and smoking some very strong wacky backy."

"The best is yet to come, my friend. I like your cosmic bubbles, it's quite easy to imagine something moving between them. Let's say, for argument's sake, a beam of light. Can you see it, Frank, a beam of light passing through one universe after another and on into the distance?"

"Okay…I'm seeing it, but you need to bring this back to the real world for me soon; I'm a tiny bit freaked out."

"Indeed, you're absolutely correct. We need a correlation within our own real universe." He held up a finger to signal the change. "The energy from the sun travels to us through space and there is not much that can stop it, but if we held up a giant mirror the light would be reflected, yes?"

"Right back out into space, I expect?"

"Without doubt. However, there is more to the sun than just light – there are some bits of energy that go right through the mirror, right through the planet, in fact."

"Cosmic rays?"

"Good. You have heard of particles flying through space at great speed, zipping right through solid matter."

"Bits and pieces of stuff on radio science programmes, I suppose," offered Frank.

"Yes, it's surprising what you soak up without knowing it. Well, to put it as briefly as I possibly can, Mona's mathematical descriptions of the universe predicted that there would be energy capable of travelling not just through solid matter, but back and forth between this universe and others."

"Oh, right, I see where you were going with the beam of light through the bubbles now…but how do you prove something like that?"

"It's only very recently that modern physicists have concluded there's an unknown form of energy in space. It's making the universe expand faster than previous theories suggested, and some think it may be 'leaking' from another universe, but nothing, even in today's technology, can actually observe it or detect it directly. In the 1960s an experiment to confirm Mona's equations could not even be imagined, let alone designed, but that didn't stop her trying something monumentally unorthodox."

"That sounds more like the Mona I know. She didn't write an astrological chart for it, did she?"

The laughter provoked the pouring of more whisky and Paddy continued the story. "It was one of those occasions where two utterly different worlds collided and somehow found a mutual benefit, at least at first. You knew Mona's father was Spanish, didn't you, Frank...no? ...Anyway, he was. Came to England to study at Oxford in the early 30s. Brilliant man, tragically killed towards the very end of the war. But Mona always kept in touch with her grandfather in Spain and around 1965 he wrote to her describing a young man in their village who was undergoing ESP tests by the local doctor. If it had been the UK he would probably have been whisked off to a specialist university department somewhere, but apparently General Franco was suspicious of anything that might give an ordinary person any power or influence, and lips were sealed for miles around. You know about ESP, don't you, Frank?"

"Extrasensory perception, telepathy and all that."

"That's it, and this chap was quite a phenomenon, according to the letter. Mona was sufficiently intrigued to visit and have a look at him and within a year he was installed at Cambridge, being investigated with proper scientific rigour. Mona produced results from him that were far beyond statistical probability and it was all she could do to keep it out of the newspapers. As soon as the documented results were established beyond any doubt, she revealed to me what she really wanted from him. I've got to admit I was worried. It was a bizarre stretch to apply her equations at the human level."

Frank, for an instant, felt like one of those comic-strip characters who has a light bulb over his head. "What was this Spanish lad's name?"

"Ah, yes, a name that lives in infamy...Pablo Montoya... Mona told me she had never mentioned any of this to you but you look as if his name means something?"

"Not really, it's just that her sister asked me if Mona had ever mentioned Pablo and I...well, I gathered there was controversy surrounding him."

"Of course, yes. Dora was here this morning, wasn't she?" Paddy took a sip of whisky and adjusted his position in the armchair. "I'll be honest, Frank, I'd rather Mona told you about all that side of it. A lot went on and I know about some of it but emotional entanglements are not my field, as it were. Having said that, I dare say it was all that stuff that contributed to Mona's difficulties later on."

"I knew there must have been problems arising from all this. I mean, Mona's a charming and sharp lady with an intriguing way of looking at things but I can't imagine her talking to me about equations and things like you are."

"No, it's all gone, Frank – an utter and appalling tragedy. So very, very sad. That's why I feel this urgent need for someone else to take the baton from me. You see, Mona can't do it herself. She has great difficulty revisiting her past. She has ability beyond your imagination, Frank, but she's been through a metamorphosis, and her mind has put up obstacles. She cannot bear to face herself as she once was because it brings so much pain. I've tried to convince her many times but you know how these things go, Frank. Every time I visited she knew what was coming and the barriers went up. I had to make a conscious effort to stop nagging her, and Mona had to feel convinced I had given up. We are alright again now but I still find it desperately hard to talk about trivia when she's made the greatest breakthrough since Einstein."

Frank felt a knot of confusion tightening in his head. Why did he have to be the one who took over this knowledge? Surely there were scientists who could 'take the baton' from Professor Wilmington, and surely it was all written down anyway. Maybe it would all become clear if Paddy finished what he needed to say. Whisky had been topped up and cigars produced, but Frank declined a smoke. He was starting to feel the effects of the firewater and took another biscuit instead. As soon as Paddy's cigar was going well, Frank prompted him to continue. "So how did Pablo's ESP link up with energy going through another universe?"

"The crucial question, Frank! I hope you're ready for the answer. I'd grab your whisky if I were you...it's harder to visualise than my previous examples but I'll just dive in and hope you come with me. The significant part, and it really is a shocker, Frank, is that Mona reversed the accepted ideas about ESP. She attempted to prove that Pablo was not simply reacting to an unseen random choice after the choice had been made, and then showing an extrasensory ability to perceive what that choice was. Her theory was that he was influencing the outcome. He was a primary cause of the end result. He was, in effect, choosing the outcome even though someone else, or a machine, appeared to be controlling the choice. It worked through a process deep in his brain, and his remarkable ability stemmed from his awareness of this process. I'll give you an example. The symbols on those cards they use – you must have seen them – star, square, circle, wavy lines and so on; well, instead of just predicting the next one off the top of the deck was a star, he would actually set in motion a flow of energy that would *make* the next card a star."

"Hold on. How could he make a star card shuffle itself to the top if it wasn't there in the first place?"

"Ah, you've a fine mind, Frank. You don't realise how relieved I am. And you're right, the card does not move to the top in the way you mean. To describe what happens I need to stretch your logical powers to the limit. A little while back I mentioned energy travelling between many universes, yes?"

Frank rolled the images around in his mind again. Was there really more than one universe or was that just to illustrate something? He had a sudden memory of a TV show about space, where lots of spaceships from parallel universes started popping into our universe. He had found it quite funny at the time. "You did mention that, Paddy, but where did they all come from? I mean, are they really there?"

"Are what really there?"

"All these other universes."

"Oh I see. Forgive me. Well, that's a whole story in itself, but the answer is a resounding 'yes'. Even before Mona's equations it was more or less a certainty, and they are unlimited, Frank. There is an infinite number of them – trillions and trillions. Pointless talking in numbers at all, really. Imagine it, Frank: an infinity of other existences. Breathtaking."

"How do you know?"

"The mathematics is the only way to show the evidence and we know you're a bit rusty in that department," Paddy grinned.

"Seized up completely, more like. Go on then, I'll believe you. Amaze me some more."

"The implications of infinity are no small matter. It means that every possible variation of reality must exist somewhere, and that's not just what we understand as 'possible', it's what the maths predicts as possible, which is probably far beyond anything our limited imagination can dream up. There is another universe exactly the same as this one except that it's two minutes past six instead of one minute past six, and there is one where planet Earth has no life on it at all, and another where no energy or matter as we know it can ever exist, and so on and so forth, endless variation. And so to bring it back to Mona's experiments with Pablo, every outcome he could possibly choose was already there, waiting. What he did was to pluck the chosen outcome from the universe in which it existed and transposed it into his own. The energy described in Mona's equations is the scientific basis for this. The energy is channelled by a human brain, so that we are interacting with other universes all the time. Most of us are not aware of it happening because we simply don't have the gift that Pablo had…we may get odd experiences sometimes and wonder what's behind it. Premonitions of future events might well arise from this interaction, but the point about Pablo is that he was aware of it and could control it...up to a point."

Frank was stunned and desperately uncertain about this idea, but knew beyond question that it changed everything. Ben Kirton's dreams bounced into his mind as if shot there by a cannon; they had immediately shifted from the supernatural to the real world of science and infinite possibility. Surely this thing Pablo did must be linked with other psychic mysteries akin to Ben's dreams? Frank could barely contain himself. Paddy's words were snapping about like miniature fireworks: '...we are interacting with other universes all the time'. How on earth did that work?

"Er, Professor, something has just come back to me like a bolt from the blue, I think your...Mona's ideas might explain it."

Frank told the full story of Ben's dreams and was surprised how carefully Paddy listened and questioned small details until his understanding was accurate. Finally he agreed that Ben did appear to have tapped into this same energy but clearly there was an absence of the control mechanism evident in Pablo. Also, since the dreams did not involve his own future actions, it was doubtful he was transposing events in the same way as Pablo. The professor expanded further on the scientific possibilities and Frank listened, knowing he was failing to follow it all, but then Paddy concluded with an idea that was at once obvious and profoundly spooky. "You know, Frank, it will not be a coincidence that you took Ben seriously, that you met Mona, and that you have now met me. You are searching for something, and what you would call your instincts or your intuition may well be more than that. It convinces me even more strongly that you are the man to take this knowledge forward."

CHAPTER THIRTY-FOUR

GREG GREETED GLENDA AS AN OLD friend: a kiss on the cheek, one hand on her upper arm. She put her hands around to his back and pulled him forward slightly in an almost-hug sort of way. Her vanity case was left in the hall and he showed her through to the living room. He offered coffee as it was still only quarter past six but she pulled a mischievous face and asked for gin and tonic. In that case he would have a beer.

While he was in the kitchen pouring the drinks he remembered she had come straight from a conference. He must ask her if she wanted to change and freshen up after a long day of workshops and flipcharts. Actually, at first impression, she looked as if she already had freshened up. Her make-up and hair and clothes had all struck him as immaculate when he greeted her at the door.

But there was something different about her. He could not pin it down. Her hair was a bit shorter than he remembered but it wasn't that; she was wearing glasses as usual, perhaps the frames were more glamorous than her usual style but it wasn't that either. The kitchen was off the back of the living room and he took a quick look through the open doorway. She had flopped in the armchair nearest to him but it was facing away from him so he couldn't see anything besides the top of her head and her left hand on the arm.

He picked up the drinks and walked slowly in, heading towards the left side of her chair. Of course, the wedding ring, absent, as recent communications had led him to expect. No doubt the full story would unfold, but no, it wasn't that – something else was different. She was wearing a lightweight matching skirt and jacket in pale grey, with black shoes and black tights... There it was. A skirt.

Glenda was a woman who, from time immemorial, always wore trousers. This fact had taken several years to dawn on Greg. For all of this time he and Stephanie had socialised with her, and then later with her and John in a variety of ways. They all went on a country cottage holiday together once, so there were plenty of opportunities for him to have noticed it sooner, but it was just one of those banal details that got lost among all the others. He still didn't know what made it finally occur to him but after that it promoted itself out of banality and became a bit of a 'thing' with him. His memory went into a kind of low-level scan of their social history, throwing snippets up for review while he was thinking about something else. The only significant one came to him while he was watching Roy in one of his first primary school concerts: a sudden memory of Glenda and John's wedding. She had worn a traditional wedding dress when she married John. This had elated him for a second but a ridiculous pang of disappointment had followed when he recalled the trouser-suit she had changed into for the ceremonial departure from the reception.

The memory scan did not manage to find a single further non-trouser moment. Other investigations had followed but, bizarrely, there was an obvious avenue of enquiry he found he simply could not pursue. He did not know how to mention it to Stephanie or John. Any form of words he considered to broach the subject just seemed to make him sound as if he had an unnatural need to see Glenda's legs. It did of course occur to him to go direct to Glenda, but this idea lasted milliseconds, far too high risk.

Every visit or social event from that time on contained an extra level of amusement for Greg: would this be the day when Glenda wears a skirt. And she never ever did. He remembered one dinner party at Glenda's when he had found some old photo albums in the bookcase and pretended to be interested out of general curiosity. He made the appropriate noises as old embarrassing snaps were revealed but he was only interested in whether any of them showed Glenda in a skirt. None of them did, and the bizarre thing was that even the shots of beach holidays where she was in a swimming costume were all framed to show her from the waist up.

She had always been a thin person so Greg had eventually concluded that she just had a fear that her legs were too skinny. There was a possibility that she had some kind of unattractive birthmark or blemish but somehow conversations between close friends tend to elicit that kind of detail sooner or later and it never had from Glenda. He remembered Stephanie once telling John about a mole she had removed from under her left breast because it was impossible to find a bra that didn't rub against it. He'd been a bit miffed at the time but it was nothing really.

Eventually, the novelty of Glenda's wardrobe habits faded and when Stephanie was killed it emptied his mind of all that kind of trivial crap. His social relationships were instantly transformed by her death. Some of his friends could not cope with the distraught Greg. To be fair, it was the duration of his distraught state they could not handle. At times Greg thought he was not handling it himself, gravely fearful that he would never emerge from it, but right from the first day Glenda and John had been solid and supportive. He did not appreciate them straight away but as it gradually filtered though his blackness that they were there for him he was very moved and realised he was capable of emotions other than despair. Having Glenda here with him as half of an apparently ex-couple sent a brief shot of pain and guilt through his mind. He had not even given her a call when he got the postcard in February. How could he be so slack towards them after all they went through with him? He knew the answer: he was too immersed in work and single parenting, too attached to his comfort zone. Maybe it was time to get a grip.

So, here was Glenda in a skirt at long last. Greg handed her the gin and tonic and observed that the skirt had come to rest about six inches above her knees. From this viewpoint, above and to the side, looking down on her lap, he could see her feet but did not have good view below the knees. However, first impressions seemed to dispel the 'skinny' theory. Just then her phone beeped. She apologised and bent down to her handbag on the floor, putting her drink down beside it.

While she rummaged for her phone Greg stood still and gave himself strict orders not to stare at her legs. He knew that when he moved over to the sofa and sat down they would be fully on view and if there was anything odd about them it was imperative he behaved correctly. He walked over and put his beer down on the floor by the sofa, then sat down, turning to face Glenda.

"I just need to text a short reply, Greg, then I'll switch it off. Sorry about this." She took a quick sip of her drink, put it back on the floor and began texting.

While she looked down at her phone, Greg felt it was safe to casually survey her legs and he immediately found himself quite shocked by their beauty. They were not skinny or faulty in any way, they were slender and shapely and elegant. When she put her phone down and retrieved her drink, she relaxed a bit more and crossed her legs, giving Greg a more enhanced aspect. The black tights, which were very sheer and high quality, might be hiding something but Greg now discovered he had to stop himself staring for a different reason than he had expected.

"This gin and tonic is heaven." She took another lengthy swig. "I expect you're wondering about me and John?"

"Bit intrigued, yes."

"When was the last time we saw you? ... My birthday thing last September, wasn't it? ...Yes. Well not long after that he came out with a bit of a bombshell; announced he wanted a complete change of lifestyle. Work was getting to him, life was too short, all that kind of stuff, and we needed to work out how we could change things, was it possible to move abroad somewhere and start something new. I was a bit shocked but took it as...well, I thought he was just kicking it around a bit, getting my initial reaction. So he left me with it to have a think and to be honest, Greg, I was very resistant. I've worked my way through a lot of crap in my job and things were just starting to turn round about then, and I've got a strong commitment to the stables. D'you remember that girl Naomi, who won first prize at Moreton a couple of years ago?"

Greg had enjoyed the day out at the horse show but he couldn't remember the names of winners. "I remember it was one of your girls who won."

"Yes, Naomi Winters. She is really exceptional. She could well be in the next Olympic team, so I wasn't about to abandon her to another trainer. Anyway, I tried to tell him as gently as possible, thinking we could plan for something a bit more long term, but he...well he was deeper into it all than he had let on. You know he's always gone abroad a lot for his company – America and Japan mainly – well, things had been happening. It got a bit...complicated and...horrible. Christmas was a write-off. He'd made up his mind, Greg. He was off whether I wanted to go with him or not. America. He'd made contacts there, agreed things, all without telling me. My suspicions went wild, of course. I convinced myself it was more than just a work and lifestyle thing – imagined he must have a woman over there waiting for him and that even if I went he would carry on seeing her. It was his whole personality, Greg. Everything about him was different. I don't know, I still can't believe it all fell apart so quickly. I suppose if I'd just given in and 'believed in him', as he put it, it might have been a different story." She paused for a long drink, emptying the glass.

"So he's gone permanently then, to America?"

"Yep, Miami. He flew out at the end of January and a shipping company came for the rest of his stuff a week later, and that was it."

"No second thoughts, from him or…?"

"No. I went over things endlessly at first, after he'd gone, but the thing was, Greg, he'd never given any ground to me at all, never considered that I had solid reasons for rejecting his big idea. His total selfishness just made me furious every time I thought it through. I couldn't go back to him, even if he came back here."

"Have you had any contact with him at all?"

"Only the divorce documents. Nothing direct."

"Glenda, this is awful, and I feel awful. I'm really sorry I didn't get in touch sooner. I did notice it was only your name on that card from Austria. I really should have called you."

"Oh don't worry. I knew you'd be here when things calmed down. I would have hated turning up and crying all over you in my weepy moments. Just fill that glass up again and then you can tell me what you've been up to."

In the kitchen the food was coming along well. Greg gave the chicken a stir and put a saucepan of water on the hob to heat up ready for the pasta. He returned with another long glass of gin and tonic and told Glenda the food would be about half an hour.

"Ah, right. In that case, do you mind if I have a quick shower and change?"

"Fine. I've put things ready: clean towels and stuff in the bathroom, and the chair in the bedroom is no longer covered in my clothes. I even cleaned the mirror."

"Blimey, I better take my specs off before I look in it then. I'll take this drink up with me. Could you bring that bag I left by the door?"

There was plenty to do in the kitchen while Glenda showered and Greg had just finished preparing the salad when she came back down. She was now wearing a yellow summer dress and cute yellow shoes. Another non-trouser outfit. Greg was intrigued all over again because her legs were now on view in their own lightly-tanned skin. He only caught a glimpse of them as she came in but felt absurdly triumphant that the leg mystery could now be fully solved.

"You can go in to the table if you like. It's just about ready." He gestured at the archway leading through to the dining room.

"Smells gorgeous."

"There's red wine on the table or there's some white in the fridge."

"Red's fine. Shall I pour yours as well?"

"Yeah, thanks."

During their meal Greg told Glenda about Kim and the magazine article and Kim's new stage clothes, Roy's progress at school and his new interest in the universe, and Fatty Tom's funny habit of looking in the cupboard. He did not mention Roy's poem because it was still worrying him and he thought it would dampen the mood, and he wasn't going to mention the irreversible decline of civilisation but Glenda asked him about it. They were into the second bottle of wine and onto their coffee by then so perhaps it was safe.

She asked, "What about the IDC then, Barnsy, are we still doomed?"

"Afraid so. No escape."

"You need to get out more"

"You're probably right"

"Seriously though, do you really think we've gone badly wrong? I mean, there are a lot of good things about life."

Greg had an idea that Glenda felt Stephanie's death was the main cause of his harsh view of civilisation. He had to be careful to talk dispassionately about it. "Oh yes, there's plenty to be happy about in an individual life, and it's not that we don't know how to be civilised. I keep trying to think of it in different ways, trying to get it clear what I actually do think. One way I see it is that too many of us value the wrong things. And it tends to be the people who value the wrong things who get all the power. A love of power is one of the worst wrong things so if a person is driven by that he will probably get power one way or another, and his other values will all be ranked according to how they serve that purpose. All this has been written down by people much cleverer than me."

"But you could say that those people are the natural leaders among us."

"Yes you could but then you need to define exactly what you mean by leadership: strength of conviction, soundness of judgement, dogged single-mindedness. All these things seem good and used in the right balance by the right person they can come out right, but I expect much of Germany in the 1930s thought Hitler had it all about right."

"That's an extreme example but I see what you're getting at: one man's strength is another man's pigheadedness."

"Yes. If you dissect it all intricately there are too many details affected by people's perception, but history can show plenty of examples where the wrong values gained too much support and led to horrendous consequences, and usually there were a small number of people at the top with too much power who didn't give a toss about the ordinary masses."

"So how do we stop the wrong ones getting power."

"We stop being conned by all their clever talk for a start, but the rest of it is what really depresses me. The best people to lead us would have sensitivity and compassion and fairness and wisdom but someone like that might be lacking when it came to defending us from attack, or fighting off the dirty tricks from rivals. We've always been run by the most ruthless warriors among us and I can't see that ever changing. Politics is still a filthy business everywhere you look, so as long as that's going on I don't see how we can call ourselves civilised."

Glenda was frowning and Greg was afraid he had made her miserable, but her expression lifted as she looked him in the face. "You're serious about all this, aren't you? I mean you are making quite an effort to work out what's caused all the mess."

"Suppose I am really but I'd love to be wrong. I'd love something to happen to prove we can overcome all the crap."

"When did you start thinking like this? I mean, it's hard for me to think of my place in the whole direction of human history and where it's going to end up, but something like that seems to have gripped you."

Greg knew this could lead back to Stephanie's death and turn into one of those conversations he had had with Glenda for some time after the tragedy. To be fair, there was some truth in it: Stephanie's death did jolt his mind down some dark byways, and perhaps he never did find his way back to his old self. But he honestly knew that he'd been aware of his quirky ideas a long time before she died. It never came together in a catchphrase until he read that magazine in the police station, but a collection of doubts had been swirling around, probably since his youth. "It's hard to know what triggers you off, isn't it? Something must have made an impression on me when I was young. If you think about the memories you have from school or whatever, they seem a random bunch of images and impressions. Maybe if I was hypnotised or something, it would sort it out, fall into some sort of pattern. But I know it's not just an emotional thing, and it does give me a kind of mental stimulation trying to figure out the pros and cons. I've thought of writing letters to people, maybe get some of it off my chest."

Glenda looked mildly surprised but approving of this. "That could be a great idea – even if you didn't get much back you'd feel that you were making some sort of contribution. Who would you write to? No, hang on." She plucked the after-dinner mints from the centre of the table and made a suggestion. "I think it's time we went back to your comfy armchairs and gobbled a few of these."

"Not without a wee drop of the firewater, we don't. What about you, are you sticking with the wine or…?"

"Another one of those ice-cold gins would go down a treat."

"No problem. You go through… Put some music on if you want."

Greg realised he had not enquired whether she wanted to stay over, or if she had other plans. She was obviously not driving anywhere. First things first: her legs would now be out from under the dining table and opposite him again. There were observations to complete.

When he came in with the drinks she was standing by the stereo reading a CD box. She took her drink in her free hand and he sat down on the sofa. She had made a pleasant choice – a compilation of Nat King Cole's greatest hits, and his voice was filling the room with atmosphere.

She put the box down on top of the stereo and came to join him. The after-dinner mints were now on the coffee table by the sofa and she took two out and handed him one. She flicked off her shoes and sat at the other end of the sofa facing towards Greg. Her dress had receded quite a long way up her thighs and Greg was again shocked. Not because she was revealing so much or that she might be flirting with him – it had not occurred to Greg that Glenda was capable of flirting with him. Their history was all in the zone of friendship and what with her recent break-up and his absence of any female companions since Stephanie died; he was not alert to new possibilities.

He was shocked because her legs were perfect. Her skin was unblemished and the elegant shapeliness continued thighwards. Why on earth had she kept all this covered up for so long?

"Who'd be a good person for you to write to then?" She

asked.

Greg didn't want to speak with a mouthful of minty chocolate. He held up a finger to indicate an answer was coming and Glenda teased him.

"I bet you've agonised over it endlessly, haven't you, Barnsy. Just give me your top three contenders."

"I read a book last year by that anthropologist who was on telly a lot in the 90s, Herman Feldorf. He thinks a whole different system of education is needed. That got me thinking. I agreed with him mostly but there were things he left out that seemed vital to me. I've mentally half written several letters to him."

Glenda looked unimpressed. "Anyone else?"

"The BBC and that minister who resigned over the climate change technology."

"Oh, Clarissa Longman, she's brilliant. She's done wonders for our charity. What did you want to say to her?"

"It just seemed she was the only politician with a scientific background who really understood that carbon dioxide reduction idea, and I wanted to tell her there was at least one ordinary person out here who appreciated her taking a stand over it. I know Friends of the Earth are still making a fuss but she would expect support from them, wouldn't she?"

"Are they? I thought everyone had given up on it when the Americans threw it out."

"Most of the media have gone cold on it but some papers have the odd snippet tucked way at the bottom of page 19."

"That's definitely one you should write."

The conversation stayed just short of heavy duty and strayed all over the place. Two drinks later something prompted Greg to mention the unmentionable. "Can I ask you a personal question, Glen, something that used to intrigue me a lot?"

"Go on then, Barnsy, as long as it's nothing to do with the irreversible decline of my boobs."

This threw Greg for a second. He knew she was joking but

there was nothing wrong with Glenda's boobs and he had to say something light-heartedly positive. He managed something about her being unkind to herself and then built up to his point in a humorously overdramatic way. "In the whole history of our lives I have never known you abandon your love for trouser outfits, and now today I have seen a transformation, and I have seen the exquisite beauty of your legs. So the question is: Why did you hide them for so long?"

Glenda laughed profusely and had to put her drink down. When she replied she continued the mock theatrics. "That, my darling Gregory, is a long and heart-rending story."

CHAPTER THIRTY-FIVE

I T WAS NOW THREE WEEKS SINCE *Rockissed* had published
the interview and apology. They had given it a lot more
prominence than the original article and a couple of the
weekly music papers had picked it up the following week. The
weeklies appeared on a Friday and the following Monday one
of the band's gigs was cancelled. The venue said it was because
of an electrical failure and the weekend of the gig was when
the contractors had to shut the place to repair it. Plausible, but
Kim could not help feeling suspicious and she'd spent the rest
of that week in a panic, braced for a string of bad reactions.
It eased off after a rapturous reaction to their new image
the following Sunday in Bristol, and so far, nothing else had
happened.

The interview contained a lot of stuff that portrayed her
as an obsessive saddo and was much more damaging than
the first piece. For a start, the first piece only damaged her to
people who knew the truth. They were quite a large group of
music business colleagues but spread far and wide since those
early years and it was reasonably possible some of them would
not have read the article, or even heard about it. But the second
piece damaged her to everybody.

This was a waiting time. Her head was telling her that
reaction would spread slowly. People who knew her would
not suddenly grab the phone and inform her how shocked

they were, how she had gone down in their estimation, how reluctant they now were to invite the band to their festival, or how hard it would now be to sell tickets for her gigs. It would all just slowly accumulate like dust in an abandoned house, until a year from now, there would be no shine left on anything.

It was a bad time to be thinking this way. She was about to go on stage at one of the best venues in Newcastle, where the band had a loyal following, and she needed to be up for it. She visualised herself on stage under the lights amid the noise from the audience. She *was* up for it, she was very up for it. It was such a bizarre thing. She felt great in her high heels and tight skirt and knew that nothing would matter as soon as she had the mike in her hand. It was only real life that she had damaged.

CHAPTER THIRTY-SIX

B Y THE TIME THEY GOT ROUND to Frank's interview the TV people seemed to have wasted most of the day. He had been hanging around the earthquake site for hours while they seemed to do everything with their equipment except run the camera. However, it went well once they got started.

The interviewer was a very serious young man named Callum, who positioned him at the spot where he'd regained consciousness, and then walked with him to the cave entrance. They firstly walked through it without the camera and it was too far for a continuous interview, so Callum had a think and pointed out where the cameraman would break off, and where he would resume. There was one more walk though with the addition of the cameraman, so he could decide on his angles, and then they got on with the real thing.

Callum carried his own microphone and sound recorder. During the rehearsals he had deliberately avoided asking Frank too much about the event itself because he wanted the story to unfold with spontaneous freshness. He switched on his recorder, signalled the cameraman, and began the introduction. Then they set off towards the cave entrance, with Frank responding to very simple questions.

The final shot with the entrance in the background was longer than Frank expected. Callum's questions became quite probing and Frank found himself describing his attitude to the cave art, his thoughts on the ancient humans who created it, and some bits and pieces about his own lifestyle and philosophy. He was mildly surprised that Callum was interested in any of that and was sure it would all be cut out of the final programme.

After the sound and the video had all been checked and a couple of short sections reshot, Callum was satisfied and signalled everyone to start packing up. Frank was about to leave when Callum approached him and began asking more questions. He was genuinely interested in why Frank wanted to live on the road. He wrote down the details of the local pub they were staying at and offered Frank some company hospitality if he fancied a good chat about it all that evening.

Frank was surprised and made the right noises but he had no intention of going there. The man was clearly sincere in his curiosity but perhaps the underlying motive was his eye for an opportunity. Did he envisage another documentary along the lines of 'Frank McCombie, King of the Road?' Well, he would have to be satisfied with what he'd already got.

They parted with a handshake and Frank was glad it was all over. Another meeting at the museum was arranged for the end of August, when everyone in the programme could see the rough edit and confirm their approval or express any doubts, but Frank was not excited by it. It was pleasing to be asked and pleasing that the TV people had not wanted to tidy him up or caricature him. His fears in that department had been quashed, but they were still part of a world that he did not want to belong to.

He decided to make his way back to Mona's over the next few days. She had recovered well when she came home from hospital and he knew she'd loved having him around. But for Frank, the mystery of her lost genius and the troubling loose ends of Pablo and Dora had bothered him. Not least because his attempts to steer Mona towards talking about any of it had been met with perplexing non-answers full of Celtic mythology and astrological jargon. Paddy Wilmington had warned him she could not discuss it but he didn't say it was all blocked beyond recall. He wanted another crack at it. He wanted something to justify the task he had been given by the professor – a task he felt increasingly uneasy about.

He was confident he could pass on the knowledge to some as yet unidentified person in the future. Probably someone like Alison at the museum could point him in the right direction. But he was uncomfortable that Paddy was so solidly convinced that Mona's equations were a Good Thing. The whole idea of manipulating events by poaching things from other universes sounded highly dangerous to him. If that kind of power got into the wrong hands, there could be havoc. Maybe Mona could set up another meeting with Paddy and he could find out more.

CHAPTER THIRTY-SEVEN

ROY WAS NOT YET MATURE ENOUGH to be fully aware of his own inner workings – he was still only twelve and feeling that the significant milestone of his thirteenth birthday was being deliberately stretched away from him in some cosmic time trick. There was one more week to go but it seemed, when he thought about it, to be taking forever. Had he been more self-aware he might have realised that, this week, he was not thinking about it that often, and he also might have realised that he could give himself a pat on the back for making the right choice of friend as a summer holiday companion.

Sebastian Paget had a nickname. That in itself raised his credibility profile, although 'Pag' was not strictly a very cool name. He was one of those boys Roy had known since the first day of primary school and their paths had merged and diverged randomly over the years. Pag had an enigmatic bundle of qualities that never allowed him to fit properly into a standard group or gang or clique. He had no interest in football but was good at basketball. He was very clever and geeky but he made people laugh, especially Roy. His main friends were always well towards the nerdish tendency but he was clearly the leader of this bunch and could take them or leave them, and often did drift away from them. His family were well off and had a big house, and Pag had his own observatory in the attic, with a proper telescope, but there was also a full-size skateboarding half-pipe in the garden. His older brother was the skateboard virtuoso but Pag was pretty good himself.

Lately, Pag had been in one of his spells away from the nerds and he and Roy had drifted together again, finding that they had both started reading science fiction at about the same time. So when Dad said Roy could take a friend on holiday with them Pag was the obvious choice. His parents were happy about it, having met Roy many times, and it did not interfere with their own plans, so things fell neatly into place.

They'd been at Megaparcs for a week and the two boys were having a great time. It was an enormous place built around a lake and designed with cycle transport very much in mind. Bike hire was cheap and tracks radiated off into the surrounding forest in all directions. The routes were colour coded for distance and clearly marked, and the entire site was fenced off from the outside world. You could leave through various exits quite easily but Roy and Pag were under strict orders to stay within the site. Out in the forest it felt to them as if they had fully escaped adult supervision, so that was good enough.

Their goal for the last half an hour had been to avoid all the official picnic stops and find a suitable lunch stop in the wild part of the forest. The bumps and the brambles slowed things down a bit but the thrill of conquering new territory made up for it. And they did manage to find a clearing with a fallen tree to sit on.

Pag was speaking with authority. "Suspended animation would be a bit risky: no guarantee your brain would remember anything."

"Maybe all your thoughts and stuff could be downloaded into some kind of organic hard drive and then when you were revived it would be put back in your brain?"

Pag was still dubious. "Maybe, but then you'd still have to keep the organic thing alive, or something like alive, so that means feeding it with something for hundreds of years, maybe thousands. Where would a fully automatic spacecraft get the supplies to keep it going that long?"

"You'd have to take everything with you from the start." As soon as he'd said it Roy imagined an enormous spaceship full to the brim with organic mush for the downloaded brains.

Pag was dismissive. "Yeah, right. Anyway, if they're alive and having thoughts and memories and stuff they'd die of boredom after ten years, or go mad."

"Then all the frozen people would wake up crazy." Roy added a crazy facial expression when he said the word crazy, and Pag responded with a fully animated impression of a crazy interstellar astronaut darting around the spaceship.

Roy laughed unstoppably and Pag kept up the comedy act. He was the only person Roy knew who was clever *and* funny.

Later that day they were in the indoor leisure pool, sliding down the chutes and hurtling round the 'rapids' feature, when Roy felt one of his attacks coming on. His dad was with them, in a more sedate part of the pool, so Roy made an attempt not to panic and tried to ride the feelings as they spilled over him. He found a spot where nobody was flying off the end of a slide or emerging from one of the other aquatic excitements, and he stood still in the chest-high water. Pag immediately asked him what was wrong and to Roy's astonishment he heard himself giving a surprisingly lucid account of what was happening to him.

Pag was not fazed in the slightest. He held Roy's shoulders and reassured him that it was nothing serious, it would pass: it was probably just hormones or something, it was all part of growing up, it was quite natural. And then he suggested Roy pretended it was something inside his mind he could just stand back from and watch from a distance, like watching a movie.

Roy did not have to consciously will this suggestion to be obeyed. As soon as Pag had finished saying it his mind immediately flipped into action and he began mentally watching an abstract display of colours moving right to left across the imaginary movie screen. A noise like a sandstorm accompanied them at first but the colours increased their speed until they were just a blur and this seemed to signal permission for the sound to fade away. There were the usual feelings running alongside this image but the trick was working because Roy felt detached from them. He had become an observer of his own turmoil rather than a participant.

The attack passed much more quickly than previous ones – fast enough for no one to have particularly noticed two boys standing face to face in a swimming pool with serious expressions. Pag wanted them to go straight away to Roy's dad and tell him about it.

"No no, he doesn't know it's still happening."

"How'd you mean?"

"He had to fetch me from school when I was little but I try and keep it to myself now."

"Why?"

"I don't know. Scared of what it means, I suppose. You're the only person I've ever told."

"Your dad would understand though. I mean, he's a good bloke."

"Yeah, course. I don't know. Maybe now this has happened I can explain it better."

"Now what's happened?"

"That movie thing. You said pretend it's like watching a movie inside myself and it worked. I've never got through one so easy. How did you know…?"

Pag interrupted, saying he was getting cold, and asked if Roy was sure he was okay now. Roy nodded and they both agreed that was enough swimming for today, and anyway, it was ages since they'd had any food. They swam to the edge and headed off to tell Greg it was barbecue time.

CHAPTER THIRTY-EIGHT

THE HOLIDAY WAS GOING WELL. THE weather was dry, the boys were finding plenty to do, and Greg was enjoying the relaxed routine. Even the money was diminishing at a reasonable rate.

Today was the first day he had cooked properly and the kitchen of their forest cabin turned out to be surprisingly well equipped. Things were simmering away uneventfully and the timer was set, so Greg wandered into the living room to read another page of the newspaper. The TV was on a news channel with the sound turned down and he noticed the 'Breaking News' logo flash up. He turned up the sound:

> *"Ministry of Defence papers have been leaked which confirm that the SAS did carry out the assassination of Marco Columbari, his wife and her brother. In a remarkably detailed bundle of documents it is also revealed that the operation was directed by the CIA and finance was provided by the American government. One document makes reference to written authority for the mission from the President himself. Our defence correspondent, Martha Kelly, has more."*

The scene shifted to a street somewhere in London. The reporter was in a raised position away from the traffic:

> *"At 8.15 this morning as I arrived at work, a BBC*
> *security officer handed me a brown envelope addressed*
> *to me personally. He said it had been hand delivered to*
> *the duty security chief late last night with instructions*
> *that it was to be given to me as soon as I arrived.*
> *Inside it I found a set of instructions. They were*
> *handwritten on Ministry of Defence notepaper and*
> *signed by Sir Alexander Cannay, a senior ministry*
> *official. The key to a safe deposit box was enclosed with*
> *the instructions and I was directed to attend the bank*
> *building you can see behind me, at 12 noon today.*
> *What I found there contained such astonishing detail*
> *that I immediately suspected a hoax: a leak of this*
> *nature has simply never happened before. However, as*
> *my intense checking progressed through the afternoon*
> *it became clear to me that Whitehall is in meltdown*
> *over this. What we have here is nothing less than a*
> *proven link between the terrorist plot to crash hijacked*
> *aircraft into US government buildings and the murder*
> *of three prominent people by British Special Forces."*

The reporter went on to explain that Marco Columbari and
his wife were not the primary objectives of the SAS mission.
It was her brother, Al Sharim Halib, who was with them
on the boat, who now emerged as the target. Substantial
intelligence indicated that he organised the plot to use
hijacked aircraft as suicide weapons, that he raised finance to
pay for the operation and that he was a high-ranking member
of a terrorist organisation known as Al Qaeda. The leaked
documents referred to difficulties with evidence: none of the
captured would-be hijackers had admitted any knowledge of
Halib; nothing found in their possession or at any of the rented
addresses they had used pointed the finger at Halib; and
gradually the frustration of the security services crystallised

into a reliance on their sensitive intelligence sources, none of whom could ever be used in a court case. When evidence for an arrest and charge was never going to be found, the green light for a 'black op' was given.

Greg had to rush back into the kitchen when an ominous smell diverted his attention away from the television. He was just in time and carried out successful rescue measures before returning to the news broadcast. It was not fully clear how the British came to be involved in the mission to eliminate Halib, and speculation centred on the much-criticised relationship between the Prime Minister and the American President. However, the documentation was unequivocal that the CIA and the SAS had worked together and America had paid for it.

Greg watched with increasing depression as the fate of Sir Alexander Cannay was discussed. He was a widower with no children and no immediate family. His wife had died only eight months ago after a very long and painful illness but previously they had enjoyed a long and stable marriage. Their only child had died at the age of seven when an operation to correct a defective heart valve was unsuccessful. Media researchers had traced his home address and when the cameras arrived there it was already sealed off by plain clothes secret service officers. Within the last half an hour a *Daily Telegraph* journalist with a contact in the ministry had learned that Cannay had left work at lunchtime yesterday without a word to anyone, and his office and desk were subsequently found to be stripped of all his personal items. BBC security videotapes had confirmed that the man who delivered the package at 11.51 p.m. the previous evening was indeed Sir Alexander Cannay.

The news moved on to another item and for the first time in maybe two years a particular memory of Stephanie's death flooded over the dam Greg had built around it. It was the evening report on the regional television news programme showing pictures of the roadside where she was knocked down; a few bricks dislodged from a garden wall and a stain on the ground.

He should never have seen it. He was not at work that day. Stephanie had gone out in the morning to collect a prescription and then on to the chemist to pick up the antibiotics. It was a lengthy walk but the sun was shining and she would have enjoyed the quiet stroll through their leafy neighbourhood. She had only just left the chemist's shop when Arthur Toddingley's van ploughed into her.

When the police came to the house Roy was watching a children's programme on TV. The two female officers did not ask to come into the house and Greg was so glad Roy had never heard those first few crippling words. Getting the husband to the hospital was their priority; the grotesquely humdrum details of transport and getting hold of Greg's mother to come and be with Roy were the grey bones of the remaining conversation.

One of the officers had stayed with Roy initially and he had been picked up within the hour. Grandma had taken him to her house and in the understandable turmoil the TV had been left on.

When Greg arrived back at the house in the early evening he walked straight in to the news of Stephanie's road accident blaring out of the television set. His disbelieving eyes saw the pictures and his ears heard the uncaring voice saying she was dead. And then they handed over to the sports report.

He should never have seen it. He should have come in thirty seconds earlier or thirty seconds later. He had no doubt he would have turned it off as soon as he'd entered the room, whatever was on. The last thing he would have wanted was ordinary banality spilling out all over his wreckage.

But he arrived at the precise moment when he would see those images. For a long time he was tortured by thoughts that he was intended to see the stain on the ground by the damaged wall. He never would have gone there to see it, in fact he never had been to that street ever since. The whole range of possible explanations marched through his mind in the days that followed: superstitious, religious, philosophical, metaphysical; none of them plausible. Endless questions about what it meant. He still found it hard to believe it was just a cruel coincidence.

He avoided watching the news for about a year afterwards but when he finally drifted back to it he found he'd developed a compulsion to understand what the hell was going on. He found he could no longer remain detached from folly and atrocity. He didn't know why he'd become like that and a good part of him did not want to be like that. He'd thought of joining a political party or a campaigning group to channel his feelings into some kind of action, but life had filled his time with 'stuff' and anyway he'd not yet got used to this new version of himself.

In 1999 he had taped every episode of a new documentary on the Watergate scandal and only last month he had watched it again from beginning to end. The miscreants had long since served their sentences and talked on film with new candour. It was still as shocking as it ever was and he couldn't believe that when Nixon had died some commentators talked about him as if he were just a bit of a rogue. But this current president was taking government misconduct to a new level of iniquity and dragging Britain's spineless leader with him.

The lust for power and everything that goes with it are just a fact of life, some would say. But was it compulsory that maintaining power meant descending to the level of the gutter? Even if some of them were glancing at the stars occasionally, the gutter was certainly not civilisation.

The boys came bursting in and food needed rescuing again. He turned off the TV and darted to the oven, Roy said something to him just as he arrived at the sizzling pan but the food was too noisy for him to hear. No doubt it would wait.

It turned out that Pag had banged his knee against a tree and Roy was telling his dad they were going in the bathroom to wash it. When they emerged and sat down for food the knee was fine and the boys talkative. Greg was intrigued by their conversation; he had never heard Roy speak in such a way before. It seemed that all of the stuff he had been reading and watching about science and space was bedding in and giving him a new vocabulary. Pag was obviously on the same wavelength and had possibly been keen on it all for longer than Roy. They were kicking around some ideas on how to feed space travellers over vast distances, lifetimes of travel. It appeared a genius was needed who could invent a way of transforming any random collection of matter into organic nourishment.

Greg had seen a few space movies in his time and at one point he asked whether journeys might become very short with the invention ships that could zap through hyperspace. This was greeted with mature consideration but the consensus was that such advances were at least two hundred years in the future. If we were to launch a ship to the nearest star within the next fifty years we needed an on-board long-term food production system. Greg remembered that, to boys their age, fifty years was much longer than it was to someone of his age. To them, it was about as far into the future as you could realistically imagine; after that it all became guesswork. They seemed convinced that, within that timescale, someone somewhere would make the big leap out of the solar system. He glowed with pride at Roy's problem-solving approach and felt very reassured that he would continue doing really well at school. He also made a mental note to say something complimentary to Pag's parents when they got back. Parental pride apart, the two of them were slightly scary in their youthful confidence and apparent grasp of obscure cosmological details. If it became more than a passing fad, he would soon be left behind.

CHAPTER THIRTY-NINE

FRANK HAD BARELY GOT HIS BOOTS off when Mona told him that Professor Wilmington had died of heart failure. She was particularly intense and lucid and informed Frank they would have coffee and talk.

Five minutes later they were sat in the armchairs with mugs of instant and half a packet of bourbons within easy reach. Mona began by telling Frank the basic details of Paddy's death. He had collapsed while visiting a friend at the university and was dead by the time the ambulance got there. His daughter had arrived from Scotland within hours and she was looking after everything. The funeral was yesterday but Mona had not attended.

Then Mona said, "Paddy knew he hadn't got long and I think I know what he might have done. I'll start from the beginning. I got a letter from an old friend about six years ago, a deathbed letter if you want to be dramatic. He said he would be dead by the time I received it and he wanted to tell me something. He let me know that Paddy had entrusted him with all of my work on interdimensional energy: copies of everything and some notes Paddy had secretly recovered from my desk years ago. Paddy did not want to die as the sole protector of my work... I can tell from your expression you understand what I'm talking about."

Frank was stunned by Mona's direct tone: she hadn't called

him 'Frankie' once. "Yes, Paddy told me all about it as well."

"As soon as you met at the hospital I knew he would. You were his last chance."

"I must say, Mona, I still don't get it. He must have been pretty desperate to give me the job of preserving your legacy, and to expect me to do it against your will. It's a bit much."

"Paddy was a scientist right through to his toenails; he thought knowledge must be put out there and dealt with no matter how dangerous it is. He knew I would never come round on my own; my guess is he was probably hoping you would get talking to me about it and persuade me to reconsider. The other friend I mentioned did actually understand the science, but I'd told Paddy a bit about you before you met him and he probably thought we'd clicked in a different way, if you catch my drift."

Frank thought this was hilarious but managed to stop himself laughing in case it offended Mona. He moved on quickly. "But you said your other friend died six years ago. Surely Paddy has told other people in all that time?"

"It's a reasonable assumption but actually there's not been anyone suitable. You're the only person I've had anything to do with for years apart from Paddy."

Frank was quite disturbed by this. "You mean my visits every few months are your only social… interaction?"

"Yes, except for shopping. Don't look like that, Frankie, I'm not a people person any more than you are, and we've both got Saturn in the same aspect."

"What about Paddy, though. He kept in touch, didn't he?"

"He used to phone me mainly, about once a month. I hadn't seen him for over a year before the hospital."

"Couldn't you have phoned him, you know, if you'd wanted to talk more often?"

"I didn't want to. To be honest, I was a bit miffed with him giving everything to Bill like that. He was the one who died and sent me the letter. Bill was the only other mathematician of our generation who humoured me a tiny bit about my work but Paddy should have known he was never going to come round. His letter confirmed he had never tried to resurrect it, and never would have done."

"So let me get this clear. Paddy was the only other scientist who saw something valid in your work, and he was convinced the others couldn't see it purely because you were so far ahead of your time."

"And because I was a woman kicking all the men's ideas into the long grass."

"Right, yes, so I suppose now things have moved on in that department he expected it was only a matter of time before someone acknowledged your work."

"His faith in it was genuine, I'll give him that."

"What about Dora? She must know about it. Don't you see her now and again?"

Mona became stern. "If you knew where Dora's Mars was in relation to my Mercury, you would not even mention her name."

Frank found this deeply amusing but again held it inside. "Well I gathered there was friction but – "

"And before you ask about Pablo, he got us both pregnant at the same time, made me have an abortion and let Dora keep her baby. They lived together for eighteen months, he went back to Spain, and he was murdered during a poker game in 1977. And that's all I'm going to say about it."

"Okay, no problem. What about this work of yours though, Mona? Is it an earth-shattering breakthrough? Have you got doubts that Paddy never had? What's the truth about it?"

Mona's gaze fell to the floor and her fingers interlocked on her lap. "If I tell you…" She looked up at Frank. "…You've got to understand, Frank, this is dangerous stuff."

She had never called him by his proper first name before. "You already know I'm suspicious of progress and modern values. That's a rich bit of irony: Paddy telling me, of all people.

I'll do, or not do, whatever you want."

"I don't know how much or how little Paddy told you about the science but I know he will have got it right. It's probably sufficient to say that my work is accurate and at some point in the future it will be testable. Technologies will be developed and if my work is known about, they'll prove my equations are correct."

"So this business of energy passing between millions of different universes is true?"

"That's why it's so dangerous. Whoever controls the energy can manipulate reality. Pablo could do it in a rudimentary way without knowing what he was doing, and his existence proved the link with quantum activity in the human brain, but when people understand what they are capable of, ordinary life will be destroyed."

"What had Pablo got in his brain? Why was he the only one connected to this energy?"

"I don't know, and the technology to investigate sub-atomic processes in the brain doesn't exist yet, but he won't have been the only one… Have you ever known anyone who was exceptionally lucky, always seemed to make the right choices again and again without fail?"

"Not really, but I suppose they exist."

"My research threw up eleven examples from the mid-twentieth century. They all had to be fairly old to prove the point of a lifetime of favourable choices, so they are all dead now, but there will be others. They were literally making their own good luck."

"My God! That's horrific. Imagine what they could do if they knew what they were doing? Sorry, you've more than imagined it: you've proved it can happen."

"I don't need to say any more."

"Right, and we are the only two who know about it, so if we keep quiet it might all fade away for a few centuries."

"Maybe, but someone else could work it out tomorrow if

they'd a mind to."

"I don't know about that, Mona. I got the impression Paddy knew you were unique in the way you did your job."

Mona knew this was not a time for false modesty. "I was actually. Mathematics is like a language and I apparently invented one that nobody else could understand at first. It would be a big surprise to me if someone else went at it in the same way, and they wouldn't arrive at my conclusions unless they did."

"So the likelihood of someone else stumbling across interdimensional energy is pretty slim, and even if they find the archives or stuff Paddy may have strategically planted, it will still be a big leap for them to believe it, or even understand it." This was not a question – Frank was confirming the situation to Mona.

"I still wish I could burn every reference to it there ever was."

"We can burn the stuff Paddy gave me if that'll help?"

"Why not? I love a good fire anyway."

Frank went out to the hall and delved into his rucksack. Ten minutes later the papers were burning in the back garden in a metal wastepaper bin. As they watched the flames, Frank had one more question for Mona he was not sure how to ask. "Mona, something is still bothering me. Can I ask you something that any reasonable person might wonder?"

"I've not had much luck with reasonable people, but go on then, Frankie."

"With all this mathematical genius inside you, what on earth attracted you to astrology?"

Her smile was reminiscent of a chess grand master who knows victory is three moves away. "Ah, well, that's just my bit of fun, just my little bit of fun."

Not exactly an answer but that's all she was going to tell him. An hour later, when he was back on the road, her expression came back to him and he had an idea what might lie behind it. Perhaps it was nonsense, but if this multiple universe thing really operated like she said and every possible universe exists somewhere, there must be one where the positions of planets do co-ordinate with events on Earth. Perhaps Mona had decided it was this one.

CHAPTER FORTY

ON WEDNESDAY, SEPTEMBER THE 11TH 2001 the trial began of the terrorists who planned to hijack airliners and crash them into American buildings. This was the date they had planned to carry out their attack. None of them had been captured in Washington, or even anywhere near it, but the President had somehow managed to move their trial there and have it open on this particular date. He was making a big deal out of it all and most of the media found it a little out of place. After all, nobody really believed their plan would have worked. This was America.

It was now Saturday and Greg was watching an interview on the BBC's news channel with a respected American political analyst, Tom Nugent. The issue of the attack was dealt with in about four minutes. The rest of the half-hour was taken up with a discussion on the manipulations of the judicial system. Not only had the President moved the trial to Washington and manipulated the start date, he had also done some very suspicious deals with Germany and Italy to get the other seven suspects extradited from Europe. In fact, technically the extradition had not been completed, and yet the seven men were appearing in a Washington courtroom. What was going on?

Nugent was very worried. He had contacts in Washington who were very worried. Apparently there was a new ideology taking hold in Washington known as neo-conservatism. What did it mean?

Nobody was really sure yet, but there had been a lot of talk about something they referred to as the 'axis of evil', and the decisive steps required to combat it. A number of key advisors were advocating increases in military strength and the need to 'police the world'. It was clear to Nugent that the current administration were taking an aggressive stance on a range of issues including terrorism and nations that opposed western values. It appeared that any opportunity to take a stand would be seized and they didn't seem to mind who they upset in the process, the recent case of Columbari and Halib being a case in point.

The president had claimed that Marco Columbari and Al Sharim Halib were about to carry out a terrorist attack on Israel and they had been sent radio messages warning them to cut the boat's engine; they were only blown up when it was clear these warnings were being ignored. He had authorised that in such circumstances any action to stop them had his go-ahead. A plausible enough justification if it could be proved that they were terrorists, that there were existent plans for an attack, that there were weapons or terrorist equipment on the boat, that radio messages were sent and ignored. Unfortunately for the President, and the British Prime Minister, all of the evidence pointed the other way...this was a covert surprise attack without warning, on the wrong people. So far the President was fronting it out in some style, adopting a ruthlessly unrepentant certainty that he would be proven right in the end. However, Nugent added, the Prime Minister did not seem to be holding up with similar fortitude, and it was lucky for Britain that our nation was not involved in the dodgy extradition deals as well.

Greg recalled the news from a couple of days ago: the documents leaked by Sir Alexander Cannay had been compared with original intelligence reports and significant amendments had been discovered. It appeared that intelligence on Halib had been beefed up in order to persuade the SAS to co-operate, and that the Prime Minister had participated in the process. The opposition parties were demanding a full inquiry into the affair and media observers were convinced this must happen – it was only a matter of time before an inquiry was announced.

The phone started ringing and Greg hit the mute button to silence the TV.

It was Kim, but Greg could barely understand her. "Sorry, Kim, you'll have to say that again. I don't know if it's the phone or what…"

It wasn't the phone. Kim started speaking again and Greg realised she was very drunk. All he could get was something about Tara Pentire. "Try and tell me again, Kim. Is it more legal stuff about the magazine thing?"

"No, no, no, no, no," slurred Kim. "'S'er new CD."

CD sounded like 'siddy' so all Greg could say was "Siddy?"

This made Kim laugh and she repeated 'siddy' several times to make herself laugh a bit more. Eventually, Greg heard her take a gulp of air and say "Ceeeee D, new Ceeeee D. Bloody brilliant!"

Greg got it, but not the immediate significance. "She's got a new CD out and you like it?"

"Ceeeee D brilliant, fuckin' melodies, man, Doin my 'ead in, car'n 'ack it, Greg, car'n 'ack it. Ceeeeeeee fuckin' D too fuckin' brilliant."

Greg finally understood. "Are you at home? I'll come straight round."

"Yeah, come an 'ear it, you'll love it. Hey, man, I'll play it down n' phone, 'ang on."

"Kim! Kim!" He heard the music start after a few seconds and waited patiently for her to pick the phone back up. She started singing along with the music. The singing was not getting any nearer the phone. After almost a minute of distant singing Greg suspected she had forgotten he was on the phone. He decided to go round there – she only lived twenty minutes away and he had a key. It wasn't even lunchtime yet. This was not good.

He had his key ready as he approached Kim's front door but gave the bell a ring anyway. No response. It was very quiet on the other side of her door. He let himself in.

There was an immediate reek of fresh vomit from the bathroom on his left. Most of it was in the toilet. He opened the window and shut the door behind him as he made his way to the living room.

Kim was curled up on the floor asleep, with an empty bottle of vodka behind her head. She was breathing noisily so he decided she was best left alone while he tidied up. Luckily, there was no more vomit anywhere, but he was alarmed by the amount of empty vodka bottles dotted round the flat.

Half an hour later the toilet was clean and the air was an odd mixture of Spring Meadow air freshener and lingering vomit. He made black coffee and woke Kim up. She managed to string a few words together but it was hard to tell where one stopped and the next one started. Patience was going to be required here.

By the end of the afternoon Greg had established that despite the roaring success of the new stage image, and the less-than-expected flak from the magazine article, Kim was still trapped in her obsession with writing a song as good as one of Tara Pentire's. It didn't make sense. Kim had written three original blues songs during her band's recent tour of Europe and signed a new recording deal. The music she loved was blues and she was successful at it. Why couldn't she be satisfied with that?

Greg had to leave at 5.30 because Roy would be getting

back from the football match at 6.00. There was no gig this weekend so he persuaded Kim to come and stay with them for a couple of nights. She knew it meant no more vodka but Greg had a lot more than that in mind for her.

CHAPTER FORTY-ONE

I T HAD BEEN THE WARMEST SEPTEMBER day since records began and the night was still a pleasant fourteen degrees centigrade. Frank was in a remote and dark field, lying on his back. An aircraft had not long flown over and he was waiting for the silence to return… When it came he opened his eyes and fixed them on the stars. There was no moon and no cloud. Every single star seemed to know the sky was perfect; those that were not normally visible were striking a dramatic pose on the infinite stage.

He told himself over and over again that he was looking out into something miraculous. Not that he needed to convince himself: it was more that he wanted to bask in something far beyond his own tiny planet, to wallow in the awesome magnificence of it. He held himself as still as possible and tried to look deep into the universe. He looked but did not search. Realisation came to him that his search could be over.

If Mona's work was correct, it had provided some kind of workable foundation – not exactly the answer to all his questions but maybe a set of possibilities he could live with.

It was possible that we were just one of an infinite number of realities. It was possible that there was interaction between different realities. It was possible that human brains were special in the way they used the energy behind this interaction. Sometimes an intuition could be a fleeting connection to this energy. Sometimes a dream could stray into the flow of energy. Sometimes a certain individual could connect to it at will. Somewhere within the infinity a connection was made and the event was pulled into our own channel of existence. It was a crazy theory. It was a laughable idea. But Mona's mathematics had shown that it was true.

People believed in mathematics. It wasn't like an ancient text showing the true path to enlightenment. It was repeatable. It was checkable. It led from the ordinary to the extraordinary in scientific steps. It was a hell of a thing.

Frank felt privileged to have stumbled into it. He searched and he found the cave art. Was it an accident that he was in that particular place when the earthquake hit? Or was there something in his searching that connected to the parallel where the earthquake hit? How could he ever know? Well, he could not know – none of us could – and perhaps that was for the best.

As a vast picture of eternity, Mona's theory was inspiring and intriguing and utterly beyond comprehension. We could say the words and she could do the maths, but as far as knowing the true nature of it, we were like sea urchins living out our humble lives on the sea bed. Some creature might tell us there was a sky above the surface of the sea, with a sun and a moon and clouds in it, but our limited experience of reality would simply fall short of the capacity to imagine what those things were.

Another aircraft floated into view from the right. It was high and slow amid the stars, its flashing lights and gentle hum the only perceivable evidence of its identity. A month ago Frank would have been irritated by it: yet another symbol of the relentless invasion of man and his dirty machines. But tonight he felt detached from it. More than detached, he felt he had escaped from slavery. This Earth may be infested with wars, crime, poverty, exploitation, consumerism and breathtaking stupidity, but there were billions of others that were different. Some would be much worse, some almost the same, but somewhere there was the one he liked to imagine. The one where human beings had never evolved, where the forests were full of wild unthinking nature. Violent perhaps but none of it founded in a malicious bid for excessive power. None of it motivated by envy, jealousy or greed. None of it manipulated by lies and blackmail.

He knew he was being a bit romantic but he liked to think his principle was sound. He would certainly love to see that world. To visit as the alien anthropologist and observe the ecology find its own level without being jolted this way and that by human meddling. His fantasy could even include a solar system free of rogue lumps of rock: no asteroids or comets threatening to collide and blast the climate into the middle of the next millennium. Frank's human-free world was undisturbed by sudden mass extinctions. The fish and animals and insects would eat each other in blissful uninterrupted innocence for billions of years. Even the volcanoes and earthquakes would be relatively bland.

He laughed to himself. He was fantasising his dream into a fairy tale. A boring utopia was not the idea at all. There had to be risks and hazards and danger, and if Mona was right, in the real Frank's World, there would be.

CHAPTER FORTY-TWO

ROY LIKED BEING THIRTEEN. SOMEHOW IT seemed a lot older than twelve. And even though it was only October and already two others in his class had had their fourteenth birthdays, he wasn't that bothered. He'd been thinking about his dream and his poem and his thoughts about it all were starting to sort themselves out. He felt different from most of the other kids: he felt as if the world might have something special planned for him. It was now his job to be alert and ready for whatever it was. He needed to learn the right things at school. Science obviously, but he was sure other things would show themselves to be important somehow. Teachers often said things like "Your whole life is in front of you" and it hadn't really registered with him until now. But now it seemed to mean something, like being at the start of a long journey. He had to make sure he took the right things with him.

He'd decided to avoid telling his dad the truth about his poem, if at all possible. He didn't really know how to explain it and even if he did think of a way to explain it he wasn't sure it would all come gushing out in the right words. Some things were just not meant for other people.

Glenda and Kim had been taking up a lot of Dad's time as well recently, so Roy felt it was a lot less likely the poem would come up again. He hoped his dad would forget about it completely.

He heard the post arrive downstairs and looked at his clock. It was only 7.30 a.m. but the post always arrived earlier on a Saturday for some reason. He was expecting his new astronomy magazine so he got out of bed and went downstairs in his boxers.

It had not arrived. He plonked down the other post on the hall shelf and decided to get a drink before he went back to bed. He wandered into the living room on his way to the kitchen and discovered Kim asleep on the sofa in one of her stage outfits. Dad had taken him to see her band only last month so he recognised her sparkly dress straight away. She was sprawled in a funny position with one foot on the floor, one leg stretched out along the sofa, and both arms hugging a cushion to her chest. She had her own room upstairs that she'd been using a lot lately so Roy assumed she must have come in and zonked out as soon as she sat down.

He crept past and tried to be quiet in the kitchen, but Fatty Tom woke up and started meowing.

"Who's that fine figure of a man!" said Kim mischievously from the living room.

Roy was embarrassed but he didn't know why really. Kim had seen him hundreds of times in pants or pyjamas or in the bath when he was not much younger. "Why are you down here?" he shouted back.

"Good question…must have been cream crackered when I got in. It was only about three hours ago. Just never made it upstairs… While you're in there, d'you remember I taught you how to put the kettle on?"

Roy was already feeding Fatty Tom and started to wish he'd stayed in bed. "Kettle? …Nah, completely forgot how that works."

"Aaah, go on, Roysey-boysey, a nice strong coffee would keep me busy and stop me giving you a big sloppy kiss."

Roy knew that she would give him a *very* sloppy kiss and hug him round his bare chest, which somehow made him feel funny. "You stay right where you are Kimmy-Whimmy. Coffee coming up."

He put the kettle on and had an idea there might be one of his tee shirts in the tumble dryer. Yes, excellent. He slipped it on and felt much better, and warmer. The Indian summer seemed to be over.

Kim was sitting up when he brought her coffee in. She called him an angel, which he didn't like but now she was almost famous he forgave her. He offered her a biscuit from the packet he'd brought back with him but she declined. He sat down opposite her and took a biscuit for himself.

"How's the guitar playing going?" she asked.

"Bit slow. Back at school, y'know, and I'm trying to learn astronomy now. Takes a lot of time."

"Astronomy, right, loads of stars to learn. I only know that one with the belt in the middle…?"

"Orion."

"That's it. Always seems much more obvious than the other patterns. What started you on that, then?"

"Dunno really. Kind of followed on from reading science fiction stories and I saw a few programmes on telly about black holes and things…"

"You've always been curious about how things work and why things are like they are…you asked me once why the snow doesn't melt when it's sunny at the top of a mountain. You were only about six. I still don't know the answer."

"It's because the air is so thin it never warms up." Roy munched another mouthful of biscuit.

"Aaah, now I know! And there was another one when you were a bit older… How do trees stay alive for hundreds of years? You'd been on a school trip somewhere and there was a three-hundred-year-old tree."

Roy stopped munching for a couple of seconds. "Yeah, I remember that tree. The teacher didn't know the answer. I asked loads of people and nobody knew… I still don't know how they do it. Dad tried to find out for me but then we forgot about it, I suppose."

"Now you're at high school there must be someone who knows. It's one of the best schools around here, y'know. People go to Oxford and Cambridge from your school."

"Yeah, they were on about it in assembly the other day... A woman called Laura Benningford came from Cambridge to give us a talk about it. Her little sister's in my year."

"What did you think? Did she show you photos and everything?"

"Yeah, there was a great one of their telescope. If we go on a visit I'm definitely having a look through that."

Kim smiled warmly at Roy's enthusiasm. "Is that what you want to be when you're older: an astronomer?"

Roy was not yet decided. "Maybe...but a few other things are just as interesting...seems like I come across something new every week."

"Oh yes, plenty of time to discover what really fires you up. Tell you what though, Roy...and this was said to me when I was at school... When you find what you really want to do you should go as strongly for it as you possibly can. 'Be single-minded', this person said to me. 'Don't let anything distract you, and even if it takes a long time, you will be successful'."

Roy had never seen such a serious look on Kim's face. She was leaning towards him with her elbows on her knees. "D'y'know, Roy, that person saying that to me, in the way that she did, was probably the thing that's kept me slogging away at the music business all these years. Every time I felt like giving up I would hear the determination in her voice and I knew she was right. I know I'm having a few problems at the moment but your dad's found me a good therapist and I know I'll get through them. Thing is, singing is what I love and what I manage to make a living from, so I've proved it works, haven't I? When you find what you want to do you'll feel something inside telling you it's really right. When you get that feeling,

Roy, be single minded. Make up your mind that you're going to be successful no matter what, and you will be."

"Who was she? ...The woman who said it to you?"

Kim gave a brief laugh. "Believe or not, she was a politician, a government minister actually. She came to our school because of the election campaign but she did give us a really good talk about how she'd become one of the first female ministers. Then we could ask questions, and I asked her if there was one particular thing that was the secret of her success."

"Dad's not keen on politicians."

"I know, so it also proves that sometimes the truth is found in the most unexpected place... Remember that as you climb the ladder of success, my boy!" Kim thrust her hands up towards some imaginary ladder, then she slinked towards him, hands clasping his shoulders, and lips planting a big kiss on his cheek.

CHAPTER FORTY-THREE

G REG AND GLENDA'S AUTUMN MINIBREAK IN Cornwall began with a spectacular sunset. Their hotel, the Kings Head at Pentallock, was on the north coast, a few miles short of Land's End, and their room faced south-west along the jagged coastline. The day had been crisp and bright, with lingerings of late summer rather than threats of coming winter, and the red globe of the sun was just on the sea horizon as they unpacked before dinner. The sky was full of purple and orange, wisping and streaking from the waifs of cloud. They paused from filling drawers and opened their complimentary bottle of wine. Standing by the window with full glasses and an impossibly dramatic sky seemed to be all that was needed for that moment to seduce them. Greg knew that it would be dangerous to say something, but putting his arm round Glenda's waist seemed free of risk. As he slid it around she leaned against him, and almost in the same movement she put down her wine on the windowsill and embraced him. Her head settled on his jaw and the scent from her hair took a piece of territory in his memory that nothing would ever reclaim.

At dinner, the evening sailed along with no nasty shocks: the waitress was friendly, the service was quick, the food was good, the background music was tasteful and the Cornish beer was close to nectar. Greg began to suspect that civilisation had stopped declining for the weekend.

"Everything still going well with Kim?" asked Glenda in a making-conversation sort of way.

"Yes, seems to be. She gets on really well with the therapist, which is the main thing I think; she's told me more than once that he completely understands her."

"Do you understand her?"

"Can't make up my mind on that one. Sometimes I think I do, but Kim's got stuff going on in her that ...I don't know, sometimes when she's drinking it's like watching her trying to be an imaginary version of herself. I can understand when she explains it later but not when I witness how she gets."

"I think everyone with real talent has a kind of pain. They can imagine perfection in whatever they do – art, music, whatever – and their talent persuades them perfection is achievable. So they try to create what their imagination can almost touch... and, well...they're always going to be disappointed. Reality can never be as good as a powerful imagination."

"You'd think with Kim that if she can imagine the kind of tune she wants to write then it would just be a case of playing it, or singing it out loud...given that she has the talent. D'you really think she's highly talented?"

"Oh yes, certainly. When we used to go and see her a lot – seven or eight years ago – I was convinced it was only a matter of time before she was a household name. Her voice is remarkable and even when she used to wear those dingy denims she just glowed on the stage."

"Blues is a bit specialist though, isn't it?"

"That's true, I suppose that is the reason she hasn't burst through a bit more, and what you just said about singing out loud from what she can imagine...I think it's a bit more complex than that. I mean, you wouldn't expect her to come up with a Celtic folk song...just because she wanted to. She can probably conjure up the sound of them in her head but her thing is blues – that's what she's tuned into in some deep and mysterious way, so anything different she tries to create would have to fight its way clear of that."

"Yeah, I said something similar to her a few months ago, and the gist of what she thinks is that her classical training and understanding of musical theory means that she should be able to direct her ability away from blues patterns, enough to at least write a decent melody."

"Have you heard any of the non-blues tunes that she's attempted?"

Greg made a you-must-be-joking kind of noise, and said, "That would be like hearing the discussions for a new pope before the white smoke has been released."

"I just had a crazy idea. It wouldn't surprise me if she had actually written a few good tunes but, entirely because she is so obsessed with it, she can't …kind of mentally step back from them to hear that they are in fact as good as whatshername's."

"Tara Pentire."

"Even better, probably."

"That would be tragic."

The waitress came over to ask if coffee was wanted and offered to serve it to them in the lounge, where comfortable armchairs were available. Her kind offer was accepted and they moved from the restaurant through to a cosy corner of the lounge.

The small table between the chairs was quite low, enabling Greg to resume his admiration of Glenda's legs. She had worn skirts or dresses fairly often since they had been seeing each other and tonight's had a slit in one side, which revealed an exciting amount of thigh as she crossed them.

Converting their long-standing friendship into a sexual relationship had not been easy for Greg. He remembered the slight panic he had felt that first time she had come to the house for dinner back in August, the moment when it became obvious she needed to stay over. He still couldn't believe how half-baked he'd been, to let her just arrive without clarifying whether she had checked out of her hotel; whether she was going on later to stay with a friend; whether she was driving home. He was the sort of person who liked to think things through and on that occasion his thoughts had barely left 'go'. He remembered mulling over the change to Glenda visiting as a person on her own rather than as one half of a couple, and how she might find it odd. But he was sure he had no inkling of his own changed role, he had no prior notion that when she arrived they would be 'on a date' as a couple. He had not expected to find her attractive.

So when it finally came up that she would appreciate the use of the spare room if it was at all possible Greg had, at first, treated the situation like any other friend staying over. He made welcoming noises and assurances it was no trouble, and lied that he had been expecting her to, and casually wandered upstairs to freshen up the spare bed. Then it hit him. When he'd said he'd been expecting her to stay over did it come out with more implications than he intended? Did she think he was expecting sex right from the moment she arrived? Was she horrified and at that moment collecting her things together and secretly phoning for a taxi, suddenly remembering the friend who'd already got a spare bed ready?

Greg felt himself getting hot from just the memory of that moment. He made some excuse that it was a lot warmer here in the lounge and stood up to take his jacket off, taking his time to arrange it on the back of the armchair. He recalled how he'd gone over and over the exact tone of the incriminating 'expected you to stay' phrase. The problem was compounded by the amount of alcohol he had imbibed that evening, making it difficult to have clear thoughts about anything. Had he said anything else revealing him as a blatant leg-over merchant? Who knows? He knew he'd been looking at her legs a lot but he was certain he'd rationed himself within acceptable limits.

In the middle of his panic Glenda had come trudging up the stairs with her bag asking if he needed any help. He'd replied that he was fine and just at that moment she turned the corner into the open doorway and plonked her bag down on the floor. As she bent down her hair fell across her cheek and neck and that was when he'd realised all his panic was caused by his profound attraction to her.

If she was just an old friend who'd got the wrong end of the stick they would have a good laugh and forget about it, but suddenly she was more than that and he didn't want to ruin it. A gentlemanly dignity had kicked in and he had overcompensated by bidding her goodnight and backing out to the landing in the manner of a Victorian butler. Ten minutes later he was in his own bed, wondering if she might have *wanted* him to make advances. He was not equipped for this kind of agony. Fortunately, the high quantity of alcohol in his body was more than a match for his emotional turbulence and he'd fallen asleep within the minute.

He was still undecided whether she would have welcomed any sexual advances on that first night. He felt content that things did not get that far. She had stayed in the spare room after a long working day and a late night and she was probably glad to get to sleep. He would probably ask her about it one day. The next morning she was enthusiastic to get together again 'very soon' and apparently could not have been happier with the way things had gone. As soon as she'd left, Greg slid into a whirl of shifting ideas over possible next steps, medium term options, risks and pitfalls, where it might go long-term, and what did he actually want?

Their second date was a visit to the theatre and Greg had found it reassuring and a tiny bit unsettling. Reassuring because Glenda seemed to want things to develop into something meaningful; a bit unsettling because she seemed to have an uncanny awareness of his hesitant feelings. They had not had sex that night either but their parting embrace left Greg in no doubt that the physical attraction was mutual.

Their third date was dinner at her apartment on a Saturday night and as she lived fifty miles away it was all very up-front that he would have to stay over, and they could do something the next day if he wanted. If Greg had been a bit more switched on in the sexual signals department he would have realised with one-hundred per cent certainty that this was the green light for a night of unbridled physical passion. As it was, he had a vague hope that something sexual might happen before he trudged off to her spare room.

Something sexual did happen, several times. The spare room was not used, and now they were sharing four days in Cornwall together. Greg took a sip of his coffee and decided he was no longer unsettled by Glenda's uncanny insight.

The waitress came to clear the table opposite and temporarily delayed the progress of a middle-aged couple who were making their way towards the door from the back of the room. They could have backtracked and taken a different route around the furniture but instead they paused patiently and continued their conversation:

The woman said, "I think we're about to pass the point of no return."

Greg and Glenda looked at each other and similar thoughts caused mischievous expressions to be exchanged. It sounded as if they were about to go upstairs and consummate an illicit affair.

The man said, "If we acted quickly, the Arctic sea ice could recover, but I know what you're saying."

She replied, "It's not just the depletion rate, it's the link with Greenland's land ice. My latest results show the entire northern hemisphere is locked into a cycle that will affect Greenland."

Greg and Glenda's expressions were now devoid of mischief but still responsive to the hint of drama in the woman's voice.

The man said, "So what's your projection?"

She replied, "It's a bit early for anything public. I need another couple of years data at least, but Greenland could be 30 per cent down by 2050."

The waitress had finished her task and gone but the man had turned towards the woman and not noticed their way was now clear. He was apparently somewhat alarmed and said, "Have you got those results with you? I need to take a look before the meeting with Wadhams tomorrow."

"Of course, I thought you might want to. You'd better buy a couple of large ones first." She smiled and gestured that the way to the bar was now clear.

When they'd gone Glenda said, "They were talking about global warming, weren't they?"

Greg was reeling a little. Unlike some people, he didn't enjoy spooky coincidences. Only that morning he had read an article about climate change in the newspaper. A scientist called Wadhams had been quoted in it. He'd had a teacher at school called Wadhams so it was a name he tended to remember. The Greenland ice sheet problem was set out very succinctly in the article and Greg knew exactly what the woman was talking about, but he decided to resist his darker side and keep the mood light. "Yes, I think so. Sounds like there'll be vineyards in Inverness before long."

CHAPTER FORTY-FOUR

FRANK STEPPED OUT OF THE MUSEUM and decided the meeting he'd just had with Alison and Angus would be his last one. The meeting had gone well and he understood a lot more about the significance of his discovery but he felt the whole business was edging too far into his life. His imagination struggled with an accurate image of his own boundaries and he'd been through a few versions to help his quiet reflection. A sphere worked quite well. Various things could land on it and spread over its surface, but when something started digging through the surface and burrowing down inside the sphere, that's when he resisted. That's when it was intruding into his inner life. He had allowed Mona and her history to penetrate his sphere quite deeply and he was still comfortable with that, but the museum people now had the television people in some kind of long-term deal and he felt the sphere's crust hardening against them.

He no longer wanted these people. He had discovered some cave art that turned out to be hugely significant and his name would forever be associated with it and that was fine, but he could feel the publicity animal digging its claws into the surface. If he let it penetrate the sphere he could see himself becoming a museum freak show, a celebrity cave art discoverer. They'd offered him involvement in the future plans but it was not at all clear what would be expected of him and he was not prepared to 'see how it goes'. Basing such an offer on one TV documentary seemed ridiculous to Frank, no matter how 'powerful' his 'delivery' was. It had not even been broadcast yet: they'd provisionally been promised one of the prime BBC2 'culture slots' over Christmas.

Most of the meeting had ended up being about follow-up TV work, but that's not what Frank had attended for. The publication of Alison's academic paper in her profession's most respected journal had taken place a month previously. The agenda concerned reaction to it and a review of opportunities arising from professional interest. The most interesting part for Frank was the summary of why Dallag Stead was a major discovery.

Apparently, the art represented a dream state induced by ritual. More of it had been found in the nooks and crannies of the cavern, plus a few artefacts, and the dig would progress for at least another year. But there was more than sufficient to support Alison's conclusion that Dallag Stead was once a place of profound spiritual significance. In addition to the quality of the art, its age rewrote the textbook on the development of prehistoric psychology, shifting back the thresholds of complexity by thousands of years.

It all confirmed for Frank that human beings were a threat right from the start. Perhaps there was a period of simplicity when all we cared about was survival, but we quickly developed an awareness that our existence might mean something. From then on, our insanity deepened. We tried everything to unearth the meaning, or impose the meaning, or force the meaning to submit to our rapidly growing lust for power.

We killed enemies or friends or family who didn't see the meaning in the same way. We found better ways to kill and more reasons to kill, and for some, the killing became the meaning. The power gave them meaning and so the meaning was more and more power. And nothing had really changed. Those who are best at accumulating power were still keeping the rest of the world crushed under their boots, and now they were destroying the planet with the same underlying insanity that has always been the human hallmark.

Frank looked up at the November sky and made another decision. It was a long time since he'd been to Scotland and now was the time to return there. He could have solitude anywhere he wanted really, but the solitude in Scotland had a special quality. He needed the mountains and the lochs and the biting rawness of the air. Perhaps he would stay there for a while.

PART TWO

Submarine Vessel Courage

Science Log: Professor Roy Barnes

YEAR 17: 21 May 2071.

Up to this point, this log has been a dull, scientific record of the submarine's performance with an emphasis on the advanced features we were forced to initiate before completion of the testing programme. After seventeen years at sea and the last twelve almost permanently submerged, it is safe to conclude that the vessel has proved itself. The reactor is running at an efficiency even more frugal with fuel than we dared hope and the chief engineer's figures show we could remain at sea for another fifty-eight years if necessary. My process for extracting hydroponics nutrient from seawater has been equally successful and analysis of the past year's figures show that the tri-stage process has maintained optimum production: seawater yield of fresh water, breathable oxygen, and hydroponics nutrient is running at 98 per cent efficiency. Within all projected maintenance scenarios, there is an above average probability we can maintain our survival indefinitely.

Of course, things could take a turn for the worse and I will record details as and when the need arises, but I intend to broaden this log out into more general areas. I am eighty-two years old and it occurs to me that I may not have much more time to set down a few reflections.

Memory organises life into moments. A significant one ran through my mind again today and I've never written about it before so it seems right to put something down. I have to believe we will survive in some form, and that one day our epic voyage will provide abundant material for the historians of the future.

Why is it that certain moments of our lives give us prods and jolts towards the future that we rarely perceive at the time? Are there times in our lives when a heightened state of awareness kicks in and things that are done or said take on mystical significance, as if we are, for short periods, in perfect harmony with destiny's navigation system?

It was Christmas 2001. I was thirteen years old. My future stepmother, Glenda, had come to spend the holiday with us and I think it was during that week that Dad decided he wanted to marry her. He was the happiest I'd ever seen him.

Dad told me much later he was very worried and hopeful that I would click with Glenda when she came that week. I'd met her of course, but that was the first time she'd ever stayed at our house as Dad's new long-term partner. He needn't have worried; I thought she was great right from the start. She loved science. She had an anthropology degree, although she never worked professionally in the field, and it was Glenda who insisted we watch a certain television programme on Christmas Eve.

The man's name was Frank McCombie. He discovered the famous cave art at Dallag Stead and the otherwise stodgy documentary that first conveyed its significance was given a shot of trenchant insight from his eccentric mind. He pointed out that although the art was thousands of years old we should ask ourselves if we had progressed too quickly for our own good. We should reflect on the millions of years of evolution before humans and ask ourselves if we had developed with steady improvement or frantic chaos. He said that the childlike simplicity of the cave art reminded him that we are still a childish species ruled by emotion and motivations that are essentially primitive. We had infested the planet (I'll never forget the way he said the word 'infested') with disregard for its ecology, like children who leave toys and half-eaten sandwiches all over the house and garden.

I would have remembered Frank even if his views had been the first time I had encountered those ideas. He had a gritty appearance and a confident way of speaking that grabbed my attention. He was quirky but full of authority and I know I'm not the only one who picked up on it. There was a brief run of stories in the media for a few weeks after that Christmas broadly along the lines of 'What's become of Frank?' or 'Let's find Frank'. Apparently he had disappeared after making the programme and, as far as I know, he was never seen again.

As it was, I perked up when I saw Frank on TV because he was expressing the same ideas I'd already seen portrayed in a story. That story was the first time I'd encountered those ideas and I wish I could remember the title of it, or even the author's name. How silly that it means so much. Anyway, a few other things I saw, or read about, seemed to keep reminding me that our place in the universe did not yet amount to all that much, and so when Frank McCombie came on the TV talking about how immature we were as a species, it began to seem too much of a coincidence. Was something trying to tell me something?

At that impressionable age I probably let the idea take too much of a grip on me but the choices of those formative years have now become the facts of my personal history. At the time it was not so much a conscious choice, more a change of direction. Frank triggered something that started me down one road and excluded others I could have taken.

In those days the internet had only just got started and it was easy, and still free of charge, to do research on it. I fed in all kinds of searches and gradually built up a picture of our evolutionary journey and our progress through pre-history.

It was a very sketchy picture and the realisation was slowly coming to me that I needed to get more answers from recorded history. This linked up neatly with Frank's question: was it steady progress or frantic chaos? Had we shown some signs of maturity or blundered into most discoveries, as Orson Welles once suggested, in an attempt to impress our girlfriends?

The thought of studying history with serious enthusiasm did not come easily to me. I wanted to be a scientist of some sort and I was too young to realise that science had a history of its own, interwoven with all the other histories. Luckily, my history teacher at the time was one of the friendly and helpful sort who had time for genuine curiosity. His name was Gordon Tranter. I appeared at his staff room door so often after school that eventually he gave in and we organised our own miniature history club. I told him about Frank McCombie and he'd seen the programme and knew exactly what I was driving at.

I stuck with it right through school. Even when another history teacher took over my class, there was no suggestion the 'club' would stop. I think I'd become a bit of a protégé to the history department. The thing was, Mr Tranter understood that my future was in science and he told me that he'd never put scientific discovery into historical context before. Several historians had done so, of course, but he said it had become his thing to now do it in his own way. He was enjoying it more that I was, but not by much. We couldn't go to the depth of detail I later achieved at Cambridge but by the time I left school I felt I'd done justice to Frank's question. Human progress was certainly not steady. Frantic was probably not the right description either, although I conceded there had been periods of frenzy. But chaotic probably was accurate for most of it. However, beyond meaningless general descriptions the conclusion I came to was that Frank was fully justified in expressing his concern.

By then of course (I left school in the summer of 2006) the climate change problem was well established – I'd studied it as part of my physics A Level. It soon fell into place for me as a concrete example of Frank's words: our progress had been too quick for our own good. At least, it had been too rapid in the wrong directions, and not rapid enough in areas that were now obviously of vital importance. And so, with the climate crisis looming, it was obvious my view of scientific history was tending to sympathise with Frank's note of caution. That combination...hindsight plus an understanding of global warming, probably gave even more meaning to that moment when I watched Frank on TV.

Whatever the exact psychology of it, the moment lodged in my mind and stayed with me.

I can't go much further without mentioning my father. When I told him I wanted extra history sessions to help me understand scientific progress he was extremely encouraging. I didn't know it at the time but he had a secret agenda behind his delight. When he revealed it, just after my fourteenth birthday, he said he didn't want to tell me straight away because it might have tainted my own view of science. I think he might have waited longer if he could have contained himself. When Glenda knew we'd finally discussed it she said he'd been bursting to talk with me about it right from the start. In fact, he was surprised I didn't know about it already – it was his main 'soap box'. He apparently slipped a little test out one day to see if I would react, and I didn't. So then he knew he'd never actually talked about it in front of me.

My Dad didn't believe in progress. He had grave doubts about western civilisation and thought it was doomed. Not because of climate change, not then at any rate, although obviously the impending catastrophe soon overtook his less dramatic vision of a slow and painful decline. I'm thankful he and Glenda both died of natural causes before the carnage began.

He believed civilisation was fundamentally unbalanced. He thought many things contributed to the imbalance and it was very complex but perhaps the easiest way to view it was to contrast the extremes of human behaviour. We had a long talk, comparing all sorts of behaviour, and he told me to watch for the influence of power and money throughout history. I think he did taint my view but perhaps I needed that extra bit of caution when I interpreted the possible reasons behind events.

It crossed my mind that my dad and Frank McCombie must have had a lot in common and I found that a bit spooky at the time: it added more weight to the feeling something was trying to tell me something. But in fact I think they were both fairly typical of a mood that set in at the time, perhaps just a bit more analytical when it came to reasons, causes, effects and risks. As it turned out, they both had good reason to be disillusioned with our troubled species.

> ### YEAR 17: 28 May 2071.

Some of the moments in my memory will always trouble me. Most of the confusing or unresolved episodes have faded into the background but one in particular pushes through to the foreground every so often; it still intrigues me.

From early childhood until late into my post-graduate years at Cambridge I experienced a recurring dream where I was in a concert hall with an orchestra playing. At first I was floating above the orchestra but for most of the dream I was in an impossible position below one of the musician's chairs. I was not curled up on the floor like a cat and I was not a miniature version of myself. I was in a comfortable sitting position with my eyes just above the floor. From the chin down my entire body was under the floor, but the floor itself did not impede me and might as well have been non-existent. I could move my head and look this way and that as though the wooden boards were nothing more than air. At the end of the dream I was alone in the building, still in that bizarre position.

Alongside the dream ran a curious form of psychological seizure. I was a very young child when it started and I remember being distressed by it but as I got older and became more self-aware it seemed to feel less threatening. I learned a technique for dealing with it and eventually managed to prevent any evidence of it becoming apparent to people who were with me.

When two things seem to be linked it's natural for a scientist to analyse the factors that appear to conjoin them. I have to admit that, objectively, there was nothing to link them conclusively. But as I am describing personal experiences that took place inside my mind the concept of objectivity is all but redundant.

I had an awareness that they were linked. I was conscious during the dream of an emotion, a tension, an atmosphere, and the same subtle feeling ran through my mind during the seizure. Over the years I visited two therapists and offered them this notion, plus many more little details, but despite hours of fascinating discussion on the mysteries of the human mind an explanation never did emerge.

Only one repeatable piece of evidence came forth to support the link. As I became older, from about eighteen onwards, the pair of events became less frequent but when they happened they were closer together. I kept a record of every occurrence and they were never more than three days apart. Sometimes the seizure would be on the first day and the dream on the night of the third day, sometimes the dream would be first and the seizure would come within three subsequent days. They could be closer together and very occasionally the seizure and the dream would be within twenty four hours. I trained myself to wake up when I'd had the dream to check for time correlation. This was only a partial success and I didn't always wake up but when I did the time never did show any significance. However, this did enable me to note that the shortest ever recorded time between seizure and dream was fourteen hours.

It always infuriated me, and it still does, that the order of the two events was interchangeable. I would have preferred the dream to be consistently first, giving me a signal that a seizure would follow within three days. This would have been more comfortable than the reverse order, at least giving me some opportunity to prepare myself. Conversely, the sudden onset of a seizure at some inconvenient moment during my waking hours, leaving me with the knowledge that the dream was on its way, was not very helpful. As I would be asleep anyway, the foreknowledge in this order had no practical use.

Apart from those minor practicalities, the inconsistency was infuriating in a scientific way because it was less logical. It was much harder to theorise about the mental processes when things happened in reverse order, with differing time lapses. There was never even a pattern to the reversals. If it was always the opposite of the previous episode then I might have drawn some comfort, but the records I kept for over six years showed no pattern or sequence.

And then it stopped. The last time was between the 4th and 6th of March 2012: dream first (did not wake up), and seizure at 2125hrs on the 6th lasting seven minutes. It took me about seven months to believe it might be finished, and a much longer period to finally conclude I was rid of it for good. I think I was in the second year of my work on marine ecology. I have a memory of being on a boat just off the Azores and having a conversation about it with someone, probably Charlie Tolskov. One of the crew had a rare form of epilepsy and had to use a supplement to his medication while at sea. One of my therapists had once thought my seizures were a form of epilepsy so I was reminded of it, and when I worked out how long I'd been free of them it came to over two years.

As soon as I was sure they had stopped I began asking why they had stopped, and I'm still asking it. I'll never know the answer unless it was purely the sheer amount of change I went through at that time. It's not satisfactory to blame a whole series of changes. Very unscientific. But I have always been nagged by the feeling that the dream and the seizures where trying to tell me something, perhaps trying to nudge me to do something, and maybe I finally did it.

I did a lot of things in those two years. In 2012 I finished a research project on solar radiation and decided to look for a means to apply my findings, which were startling in certain aspects. My fellow physicists thought I was mad, of course, and they were correct in pointing out that I was jumping to an entirely different discipline. But that's what I wanted to do. I set myself a challenge and made a shortlist. In a very short time my shortlist was reduced to one item: Greenland. As it turned out, I had picked the one challenge that no one was ready for.

Those were early days but even then there were climatologists predicting disaster. They were not taken seriously by most colleagues as their timescales varied between ninety and three hundred years for a total meltdown, so most of us thought that even if they were right we had time to sort it out. I went there hoping I could prove the pessimists wrong and it would have been profoundly satisfying to come up with proof that actually the land ice was good for another few thousand years. Unfortunately, it was mainly my work that proved the opposite.

I arrived there in the autumn of 2012 and everything about my life began to change. Project Neptune was fundamentally a Danish set-up and most of the staff were Scandinavian, so the supplies tended to lean towards their national preferences. My diet adjusted accordingly and although there was alcohol if you wanted it I found the days so full and satisfying that my intake reduced dramatically: a couple of whiskies on somebody's birthday was about it. The outdoor life was also a big change: darting around in a helicopter, which I learned to fly; tramping around on glaciers; pootling around the bay in our tiny boat dangerously overloaded with instruments; and then the football matches when the summer arrived. I'd given up football when I went to Cambridge and it was wonderful to start playing again.

That was the infamous summer of 2013, when the sunspot activity broke all the records and injected the solar wind with…well…the arguments never did get settled. I know what my research found, of course, and I still cannot understand the resistance I encountered. They were my closest colleagues and they simply refused to believe the evidence.

I'm getting very old and crabby about it now. But I think it's safe to say, at long last, and in great sadness, that Greenland's ice was triggered into an accelerated thaw by the bizarre cocktail of solar particles I discovered that summer. I still take out my paper on it and make the occasional revision. Without the necessary instruments I have never been able to do further research but over the years my original findings have continued to perplex me. Lately, I have tended to feel that the solar radiation had a much broader range of effects on the greenhouse gasses in the atmosphere, rather than just the limited damage to hydrogen molecules in water and ice.

That, really, was a much bigger change for me than all the others. I was plunged into a maelstrom of groundbreaking research that, if correct, had serious implications for the planet. I had to think fast and marine ecology seemed to offer the most solid prospect of proving the radiation's effects. It was a roundabout route but I knew I could demonstrate the effects within seawater and to then explain how it was amplified within ice appeared an easy step.

And so began my jaunt around the world's most prestigious marine research establishments: Monterey, Hawaii, Osaka and Lisbon. I learned much more from them about the marine environment than I taught them about physics but that was the general idea really. By the middle of 2015 I felt I'd gathered enough evidence and worked out a cast iron technique for repeating my findings. I went back to Greenland and flew over the ice sheet with some new instruments I'd developed. The results were encouraging and all I needed were a few ice cores to back up what I'd found.

I suppose that was the moment the shit hit the fan. Neptune had a new boss: an American named Mason. He'd been quite welcoming when I first arrived but I found out later that, at that juncture, he had no idea about the implications of my work. While I was out all day in the helicopter somebody must have explained it to him.

He came up with some bogus nonsense that they were about to start high security research for the US Government and as I had no security clearance I would have to leave immediately. The whole atmosphere of the place had changed and if I'd been a bit more streetwise I would have realised sooner what had happened. My dad always warned me to be careful of governments, especially the Americans. When they invaded Iraq in 2003 I was too young to believe that world leaders could be so devious, but my dad used to go on and on about it. He tried to explain all about the Alexander Cannay thing, when the SAS killed some innocent people for the Americans and it all came out. Apparently, the British would have joined forces with the Americans and got mired in the Iraq fiasco for thirty years if it wasn't for Cannay's leak forcing the Prime Minister to resign.

I learned fast later on. The USA became increasingly isolated while I was at Cambridge. During my second year, their entire justification for attacking Iraq was once and for all discredited when all the documentation linking the hijackers to Iraq was proven false. The media soon dug up their real history and found that, contrary to initial information, the men were mostly from Algeria. Their terrorist organisation was international and they had strong links with Saudi Arabia but there was in fact a private feud in progress between its leaders and Saddam Hussain. They had rudimentary plans in place to attack Basra and make it look like a CIA operation.

Their plot to attack New York and Washington was authentic, apparently, but no one at the time really believed that when it came to it, they could have crashed commercial airliners into the Pentagon and other prestigious targets. After the guilty verdict at their trial the Defense Secretary buried that notion single-handedly. In a torrent of reassurance after the horrific details of their plot had dominated the news broadcasts, he announced that the USA's defences were so advanced that any deviation from commercial flight patterns would have been picked up immediately and air force fighters could have 'dealt with' the threat instantly. All questions about how, precisely, this could have been done were of course met with the answer that this information was classified. The American nation slept soundly again. However, a serious threat had been identified, and it was just what the President needed to concoct all that nonsense about terrorist links to Iraq.

Against that background it didn't take me long to work out what America was doing in 2015. I did manage to tell Mason that the situation was more urgent than he thought but he didn't believe me. Their own scientists were telling them things were getting serious and I think America had decided it had a hundred years to protect itself from both the climate and the rest of the world. The fortress mentality kicked in; they were going to stick to their plan no matter what.

I was so angry. And determined. I could be a determined person when my research needed it but this was determination of an irrational kind. I was going to find a way for others besides the Americans to survive, and I had no idea how it would happen, just that it would.

My seizures probably stopped because I'd been seized in a different way. I was the stereotype of that old cliché, a man possessed. And my dreams, from then on, have always been about my work.

When my Aunt Kim committed suicide in 2020 it was much more of a jolt than it should have been. That seems harsh in a way, as though we always thought she was doomed but the truth was closer to the opposite: I think we all had an impression of her as a fighter who would claw her way through somehow. Hindsight is not so kind.

The blues revival that started while I was at Cambridge swept Kim to the best times of her life. She was already well established as the most respected female blues singer in the business and suddenly the world was 'discovering' her. At the age of forty-something this amused her immensely. She was in demand for pronouncements on the significance of blues music and all manner of appearances extra to her singing. I think she genuinely enjoyed it all for three or four years. For a time it looked as if something with a culture and a history was going to be appreciated in the right way. But then the idiots got hold of it. The media idiots with money and power.

Kim spoke out, of course. Whatever else was flawed in her, she genuinely loved blues music and the defiant spirit it originally sprang from. The loyal following she'd always had stuck with her, and a few newcomers saw the light, but the distortions of 'Soft Blues', as it came to be known, had spread a sickly treacle over the road to Memphis.

When Tara Pentire entered the market it was a sickly dollop too far. She had all but retired and Kim must have been feeling some kind of satisfaction that blues had outlasted Tara's pretty tunes. But now Tara was invading Kim's territory...no, I must be accurate, she was invading the territory that Soft Blues had created, and giving it the kind of credibility that contradicted everything Kim stood for. Unfortunately, as had always been the problem, Tara Pentire was very talented, and her new success ripped into Kim.

I was all over the world by this time, but I always spoke to my dad regularly, and he thought Kim was fighting soundly. He thought she was handling it really well. She'd had a lot of therapy and Dad thought it had worked and given her strength to deal with Tara's invasion. I caught her on the net a couple of times, being interviewed after Pentire's second tour, and she did seem strong to me, arguing the case for real blues, and still looking great.

Anyway, the revival fizzled out and tastes moved on. I suppose it's fair to say that, superficially, things returned to their previous state. In fact, I think Kim had an even stronger following because of her outspoken support for the few purist bands like her own. But it's always very hard after a pinnacle of achievement to carry on as before, and at a deeper level Kim must have been fatally wounded by the ease with which Miss Pentire just sailed in and made a mockery of traditional blues.

I went home for Christmas in 2019 and my dad was beside himself with worry about Kim. Her drinking was out of control and all she could talk about was hitting back at Pentire on her own ground. She'd been in rehab since the autumn and spent all her time trying to write songs like Pentire's early stuff. All the progress she'd made in twenty years was wiped out. Her old obsession was back and nothing would shift it. We went to fetch her on Christmas morning and I'll never forget the darkness I felt when I looked at her.

Her beauty was gone and her eyes were bleak. She managed a few smiles that day, but the fight was ended. We took her back on Boxing Day and on the way back home my dad told me the rehab place couldn't keep her much longer. He and Glenda had agreed to have her permanently at home and to do as much as possible to get her through. They expected her to be living with them by February.

I went back to work and Dad phoned me on 28 January to tell me Kim was dead. Cut her wrists in the bath.

It was while we were going through her belongings

that the true nature of her life hit me with some force. Social history has never been my field but I couldn't help making certain observations. It appeared to me that the times in which Kim grew up, the late twentieth century, were no better than any other period of human history in terms of greed and ruthlessness. The rapid onset of catastrophe in the first half of the twenty-first century has tended to overshadow, in my mind at least, how problematic the twentieth century was.

It sounds trite to say it was no better than any other time if measured against a scale of brutality and selfishness. It's a sweeping generalisation of obscene proportions and the scientist in me is nauseated by it. There were clearly many people of heroic kindness grinding out a brave rescue attempt. But their efforts really were engulfed by a vicious tide of declining values. It's as if we gave up trying to understand how we should live, and decided that shallow affluence for an elite was the best form of civilisation we could manage.

Kim was born into a time when it was encouraged that you should always want more. A dictatorship of consumerism undermined all attempts to turn our attention to more important matters. The tragedy of Kim's life was the infiltration of consumerist envy into her creative process.

The tragedy created by consumerism was that it distracted us from one important matter too many: the destruction of our civilisation.

> **YEAR 17: 12 June 2071.**

I'm thinking of Jane today. I think of her every day, of course, but today would have been our forty-fifth wedding anniversary. I met Jane in 2022 at Cape Fergusson, Northern Australia and four years later we were married. This morning I tried to recall every detail of our wedding. I tried to start at the moment she arrived at the church, and relive every moment of the day in the correct sequence. Memory is a very non-linear process and it's hard to discipline it. I found my thoughts jumping back and forth to the best moments, but I persevered and eventually forced it to remember things step by step.

It's awkward to write about it. I'm conscious of not knowing the precise purpose of this journal. It gives me pleasure to let my thoughts unfold onto the page but it seems irresponsible to ramble in the manner of a purely personal diary. The seventy-eight people in this submarine might be the only human beings left alive on Earth and if we, or our children, do make it through to some kind of new start on the surface, there will be a need for useful information, not pages of nostalgia.

On balance, I'm probably being too hard on myself. I've provided seventeen years' worth of scientific data, and there is still the odd useful update in between these personal entries, so perhaps I can trust myself to impart a bit of reflection that may or may not be useful in other ways. I'll press on and let the future decide.

It wasn't the most spectacular wedding but everything went well. Everyone managed to get there, they all got on well, the food was superb, the weather was great, nobody got so drunk they were an embarrassment. Some would say it was boring because of all that, but for me it was a really pleasant day. And it has to be mentioned that I first met Henri at my wedding.

He'd been a friend of Jane's since university and was working for the Australian Defence Department at the time. The day before the wedding Jane told me not to ask him about his work and she was quite worried he'd get irritated fending everyone else off. It's just one of those questions that's always asked, isn't it: What do you do? When Jane introduced us he asked me an enormous amount about my work. At the time I thought it was just a tactic to control the conversation but I remember being surprised that he did seem genuinely interested. In view of our later collaboration and his current status as chief advisor on this vessel there is now no doubt that he *was* genuinely interested.

Henri was very kind when the launch of *Courage* attracted some attention from the scientific community, saying he'd got the basic design idea from some of my work. But it needs to be stated in the strongest terms that without the drive and genius of Henri de Nerval, *Courage* would never have become a reality.

It's possible our paths would have crossed without that early introduction by Jane, but then again they may not. I might have struggled for years to find the right person to work with and none of us had years to waste. There might have been other wrong turns with a different designer. For instance, I envisaged a surface vessel as the ideal option and the figures are clear it would have been more energy efficient. Most designers would have gone along with that, but Henri's defence department background told him how vulnerable to attack we would become once the world went crazy.

I must check the official archive on that last point. It would be easy for future historians to assume we built a submarine because of the storms and that would be incorrect. It must be made clear that we decided on a submarine for reasons of security from attack. It is still not recorded in the official spec but I can't see the point in being secretive any more: *Courage* is packed with advanced military defences to block detection by other craft, not to mention some awesome firepower. That decision was taken in 2035 and the storms, in their present form, didn't get going until 2056, at which time we'd been at sea for two years.

More to the point, I suppose, is that no one predicted the storms. We could not have built a submarine to be safe from the storms because there was not a single climatologist anywhere who put them into any scenario. They were a complete surprise to the entire human race.

They put paid to any scheme for survival on the surface,

unless anyone came up with a last-minute breakthrough in suspended animation, inside a mountain, with unlimited power. Unlikely in my view.

However well protected a community might be from the elements, the disruption to food supplies would be insurmountable. The only exception might be the base at Antarctica, which had its own systems for sustaining its few staff from marine-based food supplies, but too many people knew about it. It was probably overrun years ago by waves of desperate refugees, when there were still gaps between the storms. No one would get there now. Twelve years ago the storms merged into a single continuous global tempest, which is still raging above us right now. When we hooked up to the satellite network a few days ago the winds were close to three hundred miles an hour over the entire planet.

When Jane died in 2049 I cursed this overgrown cigar tube. She insisted on checking the hydroponics inlets herself while we were fine-tuning the biofilters. She was an experienced diver, but she had an undetected heart defect. At fifty-four years of age I suppose diving might have been considered a bit of a risk even for a healthy woman, but she'd been diving every week for most of her life and she was enjoying the work so much. I still miss her every day.

YEAR 17: 21 June 2071.

The years between 2022 and 2033 were pandemonium; a wild and productive chaos that stretched every member of the team beyond reason. Two did not survive it. Blistering disagreements caused their abrupt departure and when I found out later that I had been wrong on both occasions it damaged me. Two exceptional scientists who are now certainly dead could have been with us today on this vessel.

By the time I met Jane I'd confirmed that the Greenland ice

sheet was breaking up in accordance with my calculations. A range of preposterous theories emerged, in an atmosphere of growing desperation, all purporting to offer ingenious ways of slowing down the thaw. Most governments believed one or more of these ideas in preference to my own submission that the process was unstoppable. I found this self-deception incomprehensible for a while, but the facts of history didn't take long to disabuse me. We love to deceive ourselves. The few that don't have always been the misfits.

In 2022 I accepted this situation and gave up trying to be some kind of figurehead for the rest of the world against the USA. Instead, I set about inventing a survival strategy for an as yet unknown group of misfits who accepted the truth. Eleven years later the group of misfits had an identity, a workable idea, and money to make it happen. The struggle continued, of course, but those years pulled everything together. Jane was a crucial part of it and her love kept me sane. Her scientific ingenuity must also be acknowledged: she probably nudged me in the correct direction much more often than I realised at the time.

And then we were blessed with Stephanie. Born in 2032, she became a daughter to the whole team. By then all of us needed something to transport us away from government bureaucracy and financial wrangling. Thankfully, the project seemed to mirror Stephanie's development from then on. Steady growth, meaningful landmarks, joyful breakthroughs, unforeseen setbacks but nothing critical. Stephanie was exactly the daughter we had dreamed of: beautiful and bright. More than bright – her brain showed its promise from about the age of twenty-two months if I remember correctly, and she understood every detail of the hydroponics process by the time she was twelve. She told me a few weeks ago that a childhood memory suddenly came to her of Henri rushing in through our back door at the Dobson Bay house with a large rolled-up drawing in his hand, saying something about a fool. He opened up the drawing onto our kitchen table and it was a diagram that meant nothing to her at the time, but the flash of memory still retained the feeling of quizzical confusion she felt. She is convinced that she knew, at the time, that a fool had to be a person and this drawing was definitely not a person.

She teased me a bit because I couldn't remember the incident at first, but what she witnessed was Henri breaking the news to us that the new design of reactor would be at least ten times more efficient with fuel than any previous one. The drawing was a detail of the reactor. We worked out that Stephanie could only have been about twenty months old. We moved from that house just after her second birthday and Henri had already been in Canberra for three months when we moved.

Once the project actually got started on the construction of *Courage*, it went remarkably well. It's hard and painful to drag up all the memories from the world scene throughout those years. By 2040 the sea level rise and the changes in the climate were already causing many deaths. The descent into chaos continued, with countless examples of violent backlash and horrific attacks on 'safe' regions. None of them were safe of course, but a deluded belief persisted that some parts of the world would remain inhabitable even through the worst of the crisis.

Courage was completed in 2054 and we had intended to conduct extensive trials for two or three years. The nuclear attack on Moscow put paid to that and, amid rumours that our project had been targeted by the same terrorist group, we launched on February the 10th. The early launch had quite an effect on the mix of people we have ended up with. No, I'll qualify that: it was really the fact that we never returned to port which ultimately decided matters.

When we launched we fully expected to return at some point, when a window of safety presented itself, and collect our official contingent from the Australian Government. A handful of Defence Department top brass had managed the last-minute scramble and there were many from various scientific departments who took the opportunity in place of their masters, fully expecting to be replaced when we returned to dock. But it never happened.

I'm still not fully convinced by the reasons given. I'm suspicious that many of the government officials simply had no faith in *Courage* and preferred to gamble on the luxurious underground bunker they'd been preparing for decades. Most of their colleagues had been allocated places there and I imagine the 'groupthink' prevailing portrayed it as a much better option than being cooped up in some experimental submarine. And of course, at that juncture, there was still the erroneous belief that Australia would be one of the regions that would come through it all. A bit roughed up maybe but inhabitable and fertile within a foreseeable future.

Even when the storms began, two years later, we maintained regular contact for a while and they still didn't want us back. The last message we got in 2059 confirmed that the bunker was now fully staffed and sealed, with food for eight years. They confirmed that any option of *Courage* returning to port was now cancelled and that they would cease communication for security reasons. They obviously didn't think much of our chances; it was thank you and goodnight in more ways than one.

I suppose their climate experts had some theory that the storm would blow itself out within a set time and they could all emerge into the calm new dawn. When the food began to run low there must have been discipline and gritty resolve at first. A small group probably went outside to survey the devastation, desperate for some opportunity to come, their last grains of strength driving a hopeless belief that survival might somehow be possible. Maybe they never went back, unable to admit to the others that there was no escape from death. More likely, they were killed within minutes of stepping outside – how could anything survive an entire atmosphere in ferocious transition?

Transition to what? As far as we can tell from the limited meteorological instrumentation on board, the composition of the atmosphere is only changing in two ways: the water vapour content is much higher and the 'burn' from continuous lightning is producing a new layer of charged particles. The altitude of this layer has not settled down yet: it will depend of how long the storm lasts. The effects of this new layer are complete guesswork. It might make the planet uninhabitable for centuries, or it might form a kind of damper that eventually blocks the storm's energy. Or something else might develop. It would only take a massive volcano eruption to add more ingredients to the tumultuous recipe. We have a small team constantly feeding the computer with an ever-changing mix of exotic combinations. But I get the feeling that the world is making a point and telling us to take note: all knowledge of what will happen is now beyond our capacity to predict and we should submit to its authority.

YEAR 17: 1 July 2071.

About six months before my dad died we had a special conversation. I've always wanted to tell Stephanie about it and never known how to launch into it. I've had an idea that if I try to write it down it might show me a way in that will get round the barriers, not that there are any barriers really, it's just me.

It was a perfect day in some ways. Dad was already ill but his painkillers were working and I was just spending time with him one afternoon at the house in Adelaide. Glenda was out at her book club. We caught up with all the family and neighbourhood news and I made some more tea. When I came back from the kitchen with it Dad just came to life. "D'you remember when you were sixteen your school did that drug education project, the one the parents were involved in? ...

We went to the school in the evenings for three weeks...on a Wednesday."

I was taken aback by the sudden journey to my youth, but I did remember the project. We had visiting speakers during the health education lessons and the parents had the same speakers in the evenings. We did all sorts of follow-up stuff for the rest of the term. I probably looked at Dad a bit oddly and told him I did remember it.

Dad continued, "The last one of the three was a woman from Dublin, Fionnuala Blackwell. She told us about her work with heroin addicts and from the moment she opened her mouth the room was gripped. It wasn't just empty charisma like a politician, her work was important and successful and she knew if she told people about it in a straightforward way the story would speak for itself. She knew how to put it across, she knew how to phrase it for a group like us and she had an easy voice to listen to. I might even have been suspicious of her for the first twenty minutes...people who are good at public speaking can make any old crap sound good sometimes...but she had been dealing with real people for many years and it was all solid stuff."

"Yeah, I remember her... Can't drag up much of what she told us though, Dad. I always felt a bit distant from the drug thing...never felt it would tempt me. It was always science or football with me at that age."

"Sure, you never troubled us over drugs. It wasn't a personal thing at all that made me listen to her so intensely; not a family thing anyway. As she spoke I knew she was heading somewhere deeper than her drug treatment work... She started off by telling us it was easy to get people off heroin. There were substitute substances that worked perfectly well and you could have addicts cured from the physical addiction within a fortnight. That stopped everyone in their tracks, but then of course she went on to explain that the real problem was to stop people wanting it. She took her time and made us understand that wanting it is different from being addicted to it.

"She told us about the soldiers in the Vietnam War. A massive amount of heroin use had gone on out there and the American health experts back home were bracing themselves for a grim battle with widespread addiction when all the soldiers finally came home... I can't remember the exact figures she quoted. I know she kept stressing the final figure was on the side of caution, but even allowing for that, only about 5 per cent of the long-term users remained addicted when they came home.

"Well, experts were baffled the length and breadth of the USA. It eventually dawned on someone that something more was going on than just a chemical dependence. The ones who wanted to stop could stop...they were glad to be home...family support...new start, new job and all that... Whatever form it took, the important stuff was happening in their hearts and minds.

"So then she ran through everything that had been tried with addicts. Not just the American soldiers, but everyone and everywhere up to that time. Gradually she made it clear that whatever a drug worker does can usually work quite well in the short term but ultimately, to stop wanting the drug, a person needs to feel some kind of connection with their immediate world, their community if you want an old fashioned word, and she summed it up in a way I've always found very moving. She said, 'You can talk endlessly about what works but *humanity* is what works.' ...Humanity is what works."

My dad fixed his gaze on me as he repeated the powerful phrase. He might even have repeated it twice. He continued, "It might sound a bit touchy-feely if you detached it from everything else she said. You have to remember this woman and her team would spend months, years in some cases, providing a kind of substitute family for people who would certainly have destroyed themselves without her. And they had to be better than a real family: most real families are diabolical with each other."

He paused for a moment and changed gear. "Don't worry, you'll see where I'm going... I went to see her, you know...in Dublin."

I had genuinely never had an inkling of that. "Really? ... Because of what she'd said at the school?"

"Yes, pretty much. Somehow it connected... Well, you know I always had that thing about civilisation disintegrating?"

"The IDC," I chanted, probably mockingly. Although by then it was clear that civilisation as we had lived it was indeed doomed, albeit for different reasons than my dad had wrestled with. Perhaps I was not so mocking any more.

"I had a kind of 'that's it!' moment when she came out with that phrase. Humanity is what works and the lack of it is what is making us fail. Not just with drug treatment, obviously, but everywhere, going right back to the beginning. The amount of people who have what she had has never been large enough. The balance has never been right. The recipe for the human race has always been too much power, not enough humanity."

"Power?"

"Yes. Lusted after and clawed at. People who need power are like those unstoppable weeds that choke your garden. You can hack them back a bit for a while, but they don't care about balance and what's best for the whole garden. They don't feel good unless they are dominating everything and it means nothing to them that it will all die sooner because of their ugly presence."

"Right."

"It is right, Roy. Too much power is dysfunctional. Too much humanity is a phrase you would never hear. It's not possible for there to be too much humanity."

"History would have been very different." I had to admit he had set me thinking again, as he often used to when I was younger. Not believing in progress had never been a serious option to me when I was younger, but now, with the world in such a mess, the old order was in pieces.

"You're capable of being different, Roy. I know its technology that may save your future but if you do get through to some kind of future, don't forget what works…" He held out his arms like an orchestra conductor about to begin a concert.

I smiled. "Humanity is what works, Dad."

He told me a bit more about when he'd been to visit Fionnuala in Dublin and he gave me a notebook with everything set out along the lines of the conversation we'd just had, plus details of his visits to Fionnuala, with loving descriptions of the way her work had turned people round. Some of them had given permission for her to name them and he had met them and jotted down their personal stories.

I learned that he had told me all this once before. He said he had tried to impart it to me when I first started at Cambridge. He remembered the conversation clearly and hoped the excitement of the day would also make his words memorable. We had just arrived in Cambridge and were having a coffee, he said. I remembered that, of course, but the excitement had the effect of wiping all memory of what we talked about – the exact opposite of his expectation.

He realised a few years later, just from things I said, that I had no recollection of it and since then had deliberately delayed mentioning it again until it would have most significance. He'd written it all down in case he'd suddenly died before the moment came. I am holding the notebook now as I dictate to my computer. It already has an envelope addressed to Stephanie clipped inside the front cover, but I will talk to her; soon.

YEAR 17: 15 July 2071.

Today I came across a poem I wrote when I was twelve. Reading it again is not a happy experience. It's an extremely dark poem for a twelve-year-old and I can still recall the confusing knot of pain that squeezed it out of me. I didn't know where the pain came from then and I still don't know. I knew it was connected with my dream but I also knew it signified more than a mere need to understand the dream. I was very upset by it and hated it when Dad found it by accident and tried to have a talk with me about it. I hid it away for many months after that.

When you progress through early teenage years, every birthday is meaningful and seems like a giant step towards knowledge and maturity. I think it was the day after my fourteenth birthday when I next read the poem again. I probably believed that my intelligence would now be sufficient to make sense of it. I was wrong, of course. The pain returned but understanding still eluded me. I remember thinking that when I wrote the poem I was not myself. The state of mind and mood I was in at the time did not resemble the real me, before or since. I was like one of those superheroes in a comic who is exposed to some freak radiation in a laboratory accident and develops an extraordinary power of some sort. But in my case, it had only lasted a few hours, and if it was provoked by something that had happened to me it was certainly nothing memorable.

I put the poem away, still thankful that at least Dad had never asked me about it again. Also thankful that it had only happened once, unlike the dream and the seizures, which kept on coming. If I had suffered a recurring compulsion to write incomprehensible and distressing poems for the foreseeable future I think I might have turned out less than sane before long.

I must have believed that understanding would eventually dawn because I kept the poem safely hidden and read it again and again after long intervals. The last time I remember looking at it was when I showed it to Jane not long before our wedding. She was as mystified as I was, and suggested I might have unconsciously regurgitated it after reading it somewhere. Perhaps she didn't believe I could have written such a thing at the age of twelve. The part about the ocean seemed strangely prophetic of course, but then again, as Jane commented, images of wide or deep oceans are a common symbol in many poems.

Looking at it now, the old frustration still nags me but actually I do have a new feeling about it. By the time you reach old age, nothing is more certain than the inexplicable weirdness of human beings. We ought to be just a more complex level of animal life, a more highly evolved species but still positioned within the natural science of the planet. We should be able to observe ourselves and arrive at conclusions that fit into the larger scheme, the global ecology, and I've read countless books and papers that purport to do this. Somehow none of them is satisfactory: there is always something that doesn't quite slot in. My poem comes, I think, from that part of me that doesn't quite slot in.

Maybe that part of me fits into something else: something, perhaps, that the species lost in the distant past? Or maybe it's something we haven't developed yet, the first intimation of a new potential?

It would be comforting to think we can be more than we have been, but to be honest, I think the weirdness of humanity is very much the same as the weirdness of the universe. A snake living out its life in a desert can only perceive the hot, dry world around it. It has no concept of a vast cold ocean; how far up the sky is; or outer space. We might be desert snakes in relation to the rest of the universe; perhaps our weirdness arises from knowing there might be some truth in that thought.

YEAR 17: 2 August 2071.

We tried to surface today. The weather boffins thought they'd detected a lull in the storm but it had only reduced in wind speed and electrical activity. We paused at a depth of seventy-five metres and sent up a probe but I could feel *Courage* being buffeted; it was obvious there was still a good wind blowing. The probe confirmed it was still raining and the wind speed was 120 miles per hour. Four hours later it was back up to full speed and crackling with ferocious lighting again.

I went down to see Paul Spinetti and have a chat with him about the seawater samples I knew he would have taken. We stay at around 150 metres most of the time, which is the optimum depth for the various water inlets to work efficiently, so whenever that varies I know Paul likes to monitor the changes to a range of marine organisms. He is actually a mathematician but one of those types that is interested in everything; he was a big help to me a few years ago when we improved the nutrient formula and he stayed interested in the organic content of seawater. He likes to do something practical and as options are a bit limited down here I suppose that messing about with jars of briny is as good as anything.

He had his Bob Dylan music on as usual, the one predicting hard rains were 'gonna' fall was playing when I arrived, so I remarked that Bob was damn right for the foreseeable future.

The 75-metre sample was very revealing. We are in the North Atlantic at present but the higher average temperature of the oceans has given results you would normally find close to the equator. We had some trouble comparing it with results from previous samples as none of them were at the same latitude or depth. The best comparison was a sample taken 800 miles south of here in 2060 at 55 metres. There was too much guesswork really but it does seem that the warmer sea is provoking a healthy spurt of organic development. Temperature is not the only factor, of course: others to consider include the levels of man-made pollutants: it was striking that already in 2060 we noted a significant decline in these levels compared with data I had on file from 2035. The levels from today's sample are so low it would be fair to describe them as barely detectable. The planet is starting to clean itself up.

I stayed chatting to Paul for most of the evening. He's been working on some old chestnuts in the maths department – just puzzles to keep himself amused really, but also one or two new things. He got quite excited about one of his new things; said the seeds of it have been around for over a hundred years, just waiting for someone to join up the dots. He wanted to show me this particular piece of work and got me settled in front of his computer.

The conversation became quite technical and he kept producing yet another screenful of equations. I did keep up with it all, just about, although I have to say there is a very unorthodox departure from convention right at the heart of it. If we still had a mathematics 'establishment' I imagine a lot of them would have had a problem with Paul.

I was sceptical of his thinking at first, but he expected my doubts and had a detailed explanation for everything. Reflecting on it now, at the midnight hour, I must say I am very impressed and prepared to go along with him. He has a lot more to do on it, of course, but I think he might well be onto something important.

His work re-establishes the eleven-dimensional model of reality requiring an infinity of cosmological membranes, or parallel universes as they were more often called. I was quite sad when Hindali Bhant debunked this model in 2039 and replaced it with his famous One Universe Theory of Everything. That, in its way, also used a rather daring mathematical…no, I won't call it a trick – Bhant deserves more respect than that – but it was certainly, shall we say, an imaginative leap.

Paul has told me before of the epic rivalry between his mentor, the legendary Teresa O'Brien, and Bhant. She was never convinced by Bhant's work, and the full and frank exchanges between them were notorious. He must feel very pleased to be in sight of something that vindicates O'Brien at last and extends her work to a new level. The main thing that Paul's work predicts is a form of energy that can pass between the various universes. How it would manifest itself is yet to be envisaged and it may be so insubstantial as to be of theoretical interest only. But, who knows, it may be significant. The principle is certainly significant: if parallel worlds exist, their security relies on being safely shut off from each other. If Paul is right, that security may have been breached. Imagine if we could propel *Courage* into a parallel Earth where the climate had never been disrupted? A fine way out for us, perhaps, but what about the versions of ourselves that already live there? And if we could go there, so could beings from an advanced and barbaric version of Earth, bent on exploiting its resources or taking over completely. I'll choose to believe it cannot work like that. After all, if it did work like that, it probably would have happened already.

I must have a pleasant thought to go to bed on…that Bob Dylan song Paul was playing had a tranquil image among all the gruesome ones. It made me think of paradise… *'I saw a highway of diamonds with nobody on it.'* Yes, an empty highway with unlimited beauty stretching far into the distance. There are probably quite a few of those up on the surface right now.

YEAR 18: 25 February 2072.

Stephanie Barnes, Team Leader, Hydroponics Section, is making this entry. I have recorded my father's death in the official archives and the vessel's main log but it never occurred to me that he would have kept such a personal record in the science log. I have just read through the last few entries and the emotional effect on me has been profound. It would not be right for his reflections to end abruptly and, I must say, it gives me some comfort to be able to say something about his life and death in a more personal way than the two official records.

The day after his last entry, back in August, my father suffered a major stroke and immediate surgery to his brain was carried out. It was not really successful but we were able to keep him in a medically-induced coma for several months while options were considered. It was hoped he would show signs of recovery, even as the end of the year approached, but a review was carried out on January the 4th and it was clear that there had been no progress. Also, it had to be faced that the likelihood of any change in the future was now zero.

I gave permission for his life support to be withdrawn and on January the 5th a few of us gathered around his bed to... well, just to be there at the end of a remarkable life.

The funeral was two days later at 14.00 on January the 7th and not only did every single person on board attend, they all managed to find smart clothes from somewhere. Apart from the commander and his naval officers, who mostly dress in civvies anyway, I had never seen anyone in remotely smart clothing before. We did have someone die of natural causes about ten years ago but his funeral was a very personal affair between the few people who knew him before he came on board. It's an indication of how things have moved on I suppose, plus, of course, a confirmation from everyone of the fact that Dad was a very special person. Quite literally, none of us would be here at all if it wasn't for Dad.

The ceremony was held in the mini-sub deck so that Dad's body could lowered down through the sea hatch we use to launch the mini-sub. He was wrapped in two or three weighted survival blankets with our newly-designed 'Flag of *Courage*' providing the final layer. It was the first time the flag had ever been hand-painted onto fabric and they'd made a fine job of it. Everything had to be improvised and I don't know where the straps came from that held him just above the water, but I was pleased the effort had been made to do it that way: it would not have been the same if he'd been manhandled into the water from the side of the hatch.

I am his daughter and it would be expected that I place him among the heroes of history, so rather than me go on about it, I have decided just to reproduce here the eulogy given by Henri. He gave me his notes after the funeral and the first part is written out in full. As the chief designer and honorary First Officer of *Courage* I think it carries some weight:

> *We owe our lives to Professor Roy Curtis Barnes. 'We owe our lives.' There have not been many funerals in the whole of history where those words could be said by everyone present. And it fills me with a sense of privilege and gratitude, not only that I am standing here as the one chosen to share this thought, but also that I was the one, all those years ago, who Roy chose to work with on his most important project. I am profoundly grateful to Roy for diverting me and convincing me, not to mention cajoling and manipulating me, because, like so many things in life, it could easily have been very different. You have all heard the stories many times. Indeed, many of you were part of them, so I won't rehash all the details, but I do want to mention three things: food, water and air.*
>
> *I know Roy was not much of a nuclear engineer, and that part of it was my responsibility, but all I did really was provide the power to fire up his genius. It was Roy who specified that three entire decks of Courage would need to be dedicated to hydroponics, and this vessel is 270 metres long, don't forget. It was Roy who invented and developed the process for extracting nutrient from seawater, and finely tuned the range of foods we grow so that surplus organic matter is fed continuously back into the cycle. It was Roy who enhanced the fresh water process so that desalination required no extra catalyst other than his own organically-produced compound. And it was a similar enhancement of Roy's that gives us a highly*

efficient and reliable oxygen production process. In short, it is entirely down to Roy that this vessel is a self-sufficient miracle; as long as the reactor keeps plodding on, his systems will keep us alive.

On a more personal note, I want to say something about Roy's qualities as a friend. Many of you will recall his fondness for telling stories about his father, usually along the lines of how pessimistic he was about the human race but how warm and uplifting he could be with people who knew him personally or even with some who only met him briefly. Well, I did only meet Gregory Barnes very briefly, at Roy and Jane's wedding, and everyone was having a wonderful time that day so it was not a time to satisfy idle curiosity. But what I really meant to say was that everything Roy said about his father always struck me as so descriptive of Roy himself. Whether he was consciously trying to emulate his father's best qualities, or whether he was just a chip off the old block, we will never know, but either way Roy was filled with qualities and talents that made you feel secure. He had the knack of defining what was valuable about a situation or a team of people or, of course, an individual person. You might be his closest friend or the newest member of his latest research team – whatever the context, Roy was tuned in to you with uncanny insight. He knew what irritated you and he knew how to encourage the best out of you. I remember one occasion…

Henri's notes then become very brief and I cannot recall in detail the story he told about Dad – I was a bit emotional by this point – but I think the first part of his speech says it all really.

One or two other people then said a few words, including myself of course. Commander Moxon was last, leading us in prayers after making his personal farewell remarks. He then gave the order for the body to be lowered and the music I had chosen was faded in very sensitively by my good friend, Charlotte Tamuru, from the medical team. I threw some penstemon petals just as Dad touched the water and they floated off as he sank below the surface. Penstemon was the first ornamental plant he grew in a rotational cycle, making sure there would always be a bed of them in flower.

I am so pleased I discovered the music in time for his funeral, if a little sad that he never heard it himself. I started moving my stuff into his cabin, which is plenty big enough for two, when it became clear that even if he survived he would need constant care. Most of the cupboards and closets are built into the walls so space inside them was becoming a bit cramped and I needed to move the locker from my cabin. It's my only piece of portable storage, about waist high, but good and deep with three shelves inside; it grips the floor magnetically. When we came to move it I found four envelopes behind it, which had clearly been squashed against the wall for some time. I squealed like a schoolgirl when I realised what they were.

My mind raced back to the last-minute panic of *Courage's* launch. The decision to launch early was taken about three weeks before we finally steamed out. It was a tumultuous three weeks to say the least. I was at university in Canberra and saying goodbye to everyone without being at liberty to say where I was going was awful. I paid off the final rent and service charges on my apartment and just about got everything I needed moved to the sub in time. The final day came and just as I was about to leave for ever, the mail arrived. I picked up the four envelopes and stared at them. No, I thought, if there is anything in those envelopes that needs dealing with, it's too late. I stuffed them into my handbag, took one last look at my home, and headed for the taxi rank without looking back.

When I got to my cabin on board *Courage* I cannot recall my exact movements. I know I was not in it very long before

I was off helping people with last-minute jobs. I probably needed something from my handbag as soon as I landed in the cabin; in all likelihood I just pulled the envelopes out of the top, set them down on top of the locker, and then thought no more about them.

About six hours later the launch went ahead as planned and I remember being in the forward mess room with Dad, looking out of the small observation window. I think I've worked out what must have happened. After a long think, I recalled that the sea was a bit choppy when we set off; at some point the movement must have caused the envelopes to slide to the rear of the locker and fall down the back. I went to bed exhausted that night, straight from cabin door to bunk with no thought about the mess I was stepping over. I finished getting myself settled in the next morning, adjusting the position of chairs and lamps and so forth. I do have a memory that the locker was positioned a few inches out from the wall and I slid it back as far as it would go. There is a lateral joist, or whatever they are called on sea vessels, riveted to the wall just behind the top edge of the locker and it pushed right up against that. But of course there was an inch of space below the joist, down to the floor, where the envelopes were snugly tucked, and by this time the excitement of the launch and a certain amount of terror at setting off on a completely unpredictable phase of my life, had wiped their existence from my mind.

So there they were, forgotten for eighteen years. Charlotte and the lads helping me move the locker found it hilarious. Three of them were nothing important but the fourth one was a bulky padded envelope with American stamps on and a Chicago return address handwritten on the back. It was probably the thickness of this one that had kept them all trapped in position.

When I opened it, the story that unfolded was touching and remarkable. Inside there was a letter, a necklace in a very upmarket jewellers case, and a plastic thing in a case the size of my hand. The letter was from a woman called Carla Hayes. She explained that the plastic thing was an early form of high-quality digital memory stick used in professional recording studios before 2020. In the case with it were connectors for modern computers or sound systems. Recorded on it were five songs by Kim Barnes of the famous KB Blues Band.

I nearly fell over when I read that name. I have every song the KBs ever produced. The Great Aunt who died before I was born is my all time favourite singer. I suppose I'm a bit biased, being related to her and knowing lots of stuff my dad told me that no one else knows about her. But anyway, I could not have been more thrilled, and it got better. Carla Hayes? Carla Hayes? ...It couldn't be Carla Trenton, the band's lead guitarist? Married and now Hayes?

It was indeed. I'm forty years old in a couple of months and you would think I was seventeen as I stood there reading Carla's letter. She explained that the songs she had sent me had never been released, that Kim had recorded them privately, just her and a piano, and sent them to her towards the end of 2019. They were not blues songs. There was a long explanation about Kim's lifelong struggle to write a melody with something special about it but I already knew about this from my dad so I sped through that part, eager to finish the letter so I could figure out how to connect the memory stick and actually listen to them. Carla concluded that these five songs represented Kim's final triumph over her obsession with writing a good melody. Sadly, from the way things turned out, it seemed it was still not enough to placate her inner demons.

There was a lot more about Kim's suicide, which was only a few weeks after Carla had received the songs. The death was painful enough for Carla but carried the added heartbreak that she had not even found the time to listen to the songs before news of the tragedy reached her. She was deeply guilty about that and felt some prompt encouragement sent to Kim from her may have sparked a last effort to soldier on.

Next, a lot of stuff about Carla's attempts to get the songs recorded in a more commercial way by musicians who cared about Kim; the problematic world situation affecting the economy of the music business and so on; and exasperation that she could never make it happen. She was now a very old woman and strongly felt the songs really should belong to Kim's family. Dad had been quite famous for a while when a few journalists took his climate warnings seriously and Carla had managed to find an email address for him. He had replied saying his postal address was now classified information but instead she could mail the items to me. Of course, Dad being Dad, he didn't mention any of this at the time; or at any time since, come to that. I suppose he assumed the parcel had never arrived in time so there was little point in mentioning it.

The story of the necklace then followed. I took a look at it before reading on, and to be frank, it did not really do justice to its ostentatious jewel case. It had style and charm in its own way but it was never going to make my fortune from its intrinsic value. The neck chain was titanium and there were three pear-shaped pendants hanging from it, the middle one larger than its companions. All three had a blue stone set in titanium mounts. It was one of the necklaces worn by Kim on stage from about 2001 onwards, after the KBs had revamped their image a bit; by far her favourite piece of jewellery.

Carla said she'd really enjoyed that part of the band's career. The new emphasis on stylish stage costumes gave her and Kim an excuse to be girly together but also, because they both felt a bit naughty about it, they tried much harder with the music – the more feminine the clothes, the dirtier the blues.

When the band finally called it a day, Kim had given Carla the necklace and she'd treasured it for many years, but when she got the email and found out Roy Barnes had a daughter she knew it was right to send it, along with Kim's music.

I listened to the five songs over and over again for the rest of that day. Three were very sad love songs; one was about childhood; and the fifth was an instrumental, just Kim playing the piano. The piano piece was the only one with no title. I listened hard for the pain Kim had gone through to create these tunes. Two of the melodies were immediately fresh and very clever; the other three took a bit of patience: 'growers', I think music people would call them. I went back to them the next day and my mind had done some readjusting while I'd been asleep. Strange how music gets into your soul like that, while you're not even awake to play it in your head.

The piano piece tore into me like a dagger. It was unbearably poignant; it filled me with longing but then promised to give me everything I longed for. As soon as it ended I had to hear it again. I lost count of how many times I played it. When Dad died a few days later, I knew this piece would say my farewell.

We could see Dad's body for two minutes or more as it slowly descended, still supported by the straps until they reached their full length.

The untitled piano song continued for another two or three minutes after the straps were released and when it ended people were still reluctant to move. Commander Moxon said a final prayer and people embraced before drifting off to the small buffet we had arranged in the main recreation room.

I stayed behind after everyone had gone and collected the penstemon petals from the water. I couldn't reach all of them but a handful was enough.

THE END

MELROSE BOOKS

If you enjoyed this book you may also like:

Mind Bomb
Luke Mitchell

It is said that when death draws near you your entire life flashes before your eyes.

With perhaps only seconds to live, that's what happens to Hamish Macleod, except the life he sees is not his own but that of his rebellious twin brother.

The moon was rising. Hamish strolled along the beach. He came upon a solitary coconut palm and decided to sit underneath it. Click! The sound heralded the arrival of a ten-second eternity. Red light flashed in his brain. A torrent of adrenaline screamed through his bloodstream and in those ten flesh-creeping seconds he recognized who he was; Hamish Macleod, the man who had just sat on an unexploded landmine. His mind spun into fast rewind.

Size: 234 mm x 156 mm   Pages: 320
Binding: Royal Octavo Paperback   ISBN: 978-1-906561-93-2
£8.99

Lucifer Rising
Nigel Hogge

Max Krueger's girlfriend has disappeared, and the tough ex-mercenary is angry. Very angry.

What Max and Manaha's crafty Chief of Police, Colonel "Diablo" Fernandez, don't know is that the beautiful woman has fallen into the hands of a fiendish religious sex cult and the dreaded grip of the Yakuza, the centuries-old Japanese mafia, who have come to the turbulent south-east Asian island nation of Verubia to expand their empire and feed their insatiable appetite for helpless, delectable young women.

But the Yakuza and the strange, charismatic leader of the cult have made one mistake: they've pissed off Krueger - big time!

Heart stopping excitement, weird and wonderful characters and lovely yet vulnerable women, Lucifer Rising takes a wild ride down the violent paths of Asia.

Size: 234 mm x 156 mm   Pages: 224
Binding: Royal Octavo Paperback   ISBN: 978-1-906561-43-7
£9.99

St Thomas' Place, Ely, Cambridgeshire CB7 4GG, UK

www.melrosebooks.com sales@melrosebooks.com